Carry Me Home

ELIZABETH BRIGHT

INTRODUCTION

Dear Reader,

It is my honor and privilege to welcome you back for one final ride at Lodestar Ranch.

For those who have been here since the beginning, words could never express how deeply grateful I am for your support—and I should know, because I've tried.

For those joining us for the first time, saddle up! It's a fun ride. I'm so glad you're here.

Reviews are incredibly important to authors. We rely on word of mouth to get our books in readers' hands. Thank you so much for all you do. I appreciate each of you more than you know.

Elizabeth

PROLOGUE
JANIE

Twenty Years Ago

I stretched my arms as wide as they could go and stared at the sky until it became my whole world. The breeze lifted my hair from my neck and tickled my fingertips. *Feathers*. I was made of feathers. I was a bird. A bird couldn't be bad because it was just a bird doing bird things.

"You shouldn't be here," a boy's voice rudely intruded.

It stole the wind from my wings. I wasn't a bird who belonged in the sky. I was a girl, and I shouldn't be here.

I lowered my arms and turned. The boy was taller than me and older than me. He stood there with his arms folded across his chest, his legs wide to take up space, his lips turned down in a frown.

I didn't like boys.

"Good," I said. "I'm supposed to be bad."

His scowl shifted to curiosity. He considered me in that irritating way boys had like I was a bug he wanted to poke with a stick just to see what I would do about it.

"I'm Jack Price," he said. "Who are you?"

Oh, he was one of the Price twins. They lived in one of the small houses on the other side of Aspen Springs, but I knew of them on account of how my mom liked to whisper with her friends at church. *Twins before she graduated high school! That's the price you pay for having relations before marriage.* And then they would all giggle, like they were happy about something bad happening to her.

"I'm Janie Belmont," I said.

He nodded and I knew he recognized my name like I had his. Everyone knew the Belmonts, for a different reason than everyone knew the Prices. We had the biggest cattle ranch in this part of Colorado.

"Well, Janie Belmont, why are you supposed to be bad?" Jack asked.

"Mom said I needed to go get all my bad out before the party tonight," I explained. "So I don't ruin everything."

Jack eyed me. "You can't have that much bad in you. You're too little."

I sighed with my whole chest. "Maybe that's the problem. My body is too small to hold all this bad inside me. It comes exploding out." I circled my arms to show what I meant. "Like, boom!" I shouted.

He didn't look impressed. "Oh, your mom means you're loud. That's different from bad."

"I wasn't loud when I dropped a dead lizard down Mrs.

O'Keefe's neck at church. I was as quiet as…" I scrunched my nose, thinking.

"A mouse?" he suggested.

"As a dead lizard." I grinned.

He laughed. There was no blue on this earth quite like the blue of Jack's eyes when he laughed. I still didn't like boys, but I liked his laugh.

"Why'd you drop a dead lizard on her neck?" he asked.

"Well, I couldn't use a live one, could I? It might have gotten hurt."

"No, I mean—" He rolled his lips together, like he was holding back another laugh. I wished he'd let it out. "Why Mrs. O'Keefe? What did she do to you?"

My cheeks felt hot. I turned away to hide my red face and kicked a rock, sending it flying with a cloud of dust. "I just don't like her, that's all," I muttered.

He didn't say anything, but when I peeked at him over my shoulder, he was looking at me like he knew. But he didn't know. No one had been in the supply closet but me and Mrs. O'Keefe when she had given my hair a sharp tug and said, *Only hussies have red hair. Be mindful that you don't let your red hair cause problems for a nice boy.*

I didn't know what she meant, but I knew I didn't like it.

"Jack," I said, "do you know what a hussy is?"

It was something bad. I could tell by the look on his face. Now I wasn't even a little sorry about the lizard. Between here and moseying river were several rocks where snakes liked to hide. I bet I could find a skin. Mrs. O'Keefe would hate that more than the lizard.

"She call you that?" Jack asked. "Don't you pay her no mind. It's better to be a hussy than a mean old bitch who's jealous of anyone who isn't as miserable as she is. Anyway, you're too young to be a hussy."

I set my chin. "I'll be a hussy when I'm older. Just to spite her."

Jack's mouth didn't laugh, but his eyes did and that was even better. He sat down on the biggest boulder and linked his arms around his bent knees. "I didn't think anyone would be here, but I guess I don't mind that it's you."

"I guess I don't mind that you're here, either, even though you're a boy," I said.

"Oh, you think boys have cooties?" he asked.

"No. They're just annoying."

"Well," he allowed, "that's fair."

He watched the river and I watched him, sneaking peeks while I looked for the prettiest pebbles. I couldn't say what drew my attention to him time and time again. I just liked looking at him.

"My dad said he's going to visit today." Jack kept his gaze on the river as he talked. "He won't, though. He never shows up when he says he will. He'll surprise us in a week or two when we're not expecting it. Try to pull us out of school or something."

I nibbled my lip. I would love someone to surprise me by getting me out of school. Jack didn't look like he felt the same way.

"Essie's gonna cry about it." He heaved a beleaguered sigh. "I hate it when Essie cries."

"Yeah," I said. "Crying is for babies."

He shook his head. "It's not that. She's my twin, you know? When she cries, I have to make it better somehow. I have to fix it. But our dad...I don't know how to fix that."

I nudged a rock with my toe and chewed my lip again. I wasn't great at solving problems. I was better at making them. Anyway, this seemed like a grownup problem and I was just a kid. So was Jack, though. But fourteen was almost a grownup, right? Maybe that was why he had to fix adult problems.

The crinkle of a plastic wrapper in my pocket reminded me that I had swiped a snack from the secret stash I shared with our housekeeper, Maria. I reached into my pocket and pulled out the packet of M&Ms. "Here. You can give it to Essie. Maybe it will make her feel better."

He looked from me to the candy and back to my face. "Okay. Thank you."

I nodded. "I have to go now. My parents will worry."

"Wait." He tilted his head. "Did you get your bad out?"

"I did my best." I wrinkled my nose. It wasn't like I ever *tried* to ruin everything. It just...happened.

"Goodbye, Janie. Thanks for the candy."

"Bye, Jack."

Shortly after that, Mrs. O'Keefe had a string of unfortunate incidents. It wasn't me that slid a dead fish through her car window while she was in the grocery store. I didn't leave a clump of horse manure on her front porch for her to step in, either.

Jack Price didn't do things like that. He was the kid everyone pointed to and said, *that's a good one. He's going places.* He would never prank someone.

But still...I wondered if maybe Jack sometimes had to get his bad out, too.

1

JACK

"Welcome home," the robot voice said as warmly as a robot could.

I had crossed an ocean to hear those words. Let doctors poke and prod me overseas and then again at Walter Reed just for them to tell me I was *fine* but somehow not good enough for anything but a medical discharge, which in my opinion wasn't fucking fine at all. Four airplanes just to get me to the United States, followed by a 1700-mile drive from Virginia to Colorado born of some sentimental desire to see something of this country I had sacrificed for. To prove it had all been worth it.

It hadn't proved shit.

Now here I was in the driveway of my childhood home with the gearshift in park but my foot still ghosting the gas pedal. I leaned my elbows on the steering wheel and peered through the bug-splattered windshield at the place where I had spent the first eighteen years of my life and precious little of the sixteen years since. A cute craftsman bungalow trimmed in dark green, nestled between a blue spruce to the left and a trio of aspens to the right, their branches bare except for a random golden leaf hanging on for dear life like it could hold back the winter through sheer force of will.

The map was unnecessary once I turned off I-70. I knew the two-lane highways and dirt roads that spider-webbed across the Colorado Rocky Mountains to Aspen Springs like the back of my hand. But I had left the map app running anyway, just to hear those two words.

Welcome home.

They didn't sound right, coming from a robot. And they didn't feel right.

My mom was in that house. My best friend's truck was in the driveway, which meant my twin sister, Essie—who had gone and married Brax without even telling me—was there, too. Probably they had all just sat down to dinner, Brax and Essie on one side of the old pine table that still had crayon marks from the days when we did our homework there, Mom divvying up whatever savory pie she had made extra of at Sweetie Pies, my usual chair next to her empty. I could picture it. Hell, I could even smell it. The pie and the vanilla extract that Essie had spilled in the pantry when we were thirteen and that undefinable scent of *us*. A family.

If I walked in there now, unexpected as I was, there would be a ruckus. Whoops and hollering and tears. A cold bead of sweat slid down my spine. I threw the stick in reverse and backed out of the driveway like I was fleeing enemy territory.

One drink. Two, tops.

Then I would come home.

THE PAINTED Cat was the only bar in a ranching town where cows outnumbered people, and it took that seriously. Did you see the bank loan officer swaying unsteadily by the ancient jukebox that didn't play a single song past 1989? No, you didn't. Was that the high school guidance counselor doing shots with a transient cowboy? Mind your business. Everyone knew each other at church on Sunday, but every Friday night at the Painted Cat, they pretended they didn't.

"The sun just hit the ridgeline. You know what that means, right? It's quittin' time."

"You ain't the boss of me, Janie," the older man scoffed at the bartender as I pulled up a stool several down from him, the only seat that put my back to a wall.

I shifted, angling myself so I could see the door. She nodded to me and held up a finger to indicate she'd be with me in a minute, then turned back to the man.

"Now, Saul, you know that's not true." Janie patted his gnarled hand. "So long as you're in my place of work, I am absolutely the boss of you. Settle up, okay? You have just enough light to walk home."

"I could drive," he said, his words slurring together in a way that suggested it was a bad idea.

"Hard to do that when I have your keys," Janie said cheerfully. She spun away, her red ponytail whipping behind her, pulled open the washing machine behind the bar, and started unloading the clean glasses. "You can pick up your truck tomorrow morning. The keys will be in the usual spot."

"You're too pretty, that's what it is," Saul grumbled. He flattened his palms on the bar and pushed unsteadily to his feet. I watched, ready but not particularly willing. "Pretty girls always think they can boss a man around. Trouble is, they're right."

Her laugh was light and musical, and Saul was right: the woman was pretty. She looked like a fairy tale princess that should be frolicking in a wooded glen with chipmunks and unicorns or some shit. But when she turned around again, her big brown eyes had a mischievous gleam.

She leaned across the bar until her pretty face was inches from Saul's ugly mug. The man didn't have a stitch of hair on his shiny head, but great white tufts of it sprouted from his ears and eyebrows. "That's a lie, Saul. Tell me the truth. Why am I the boss of you?"

"Becussh yurr mean," he slurred honestly.

Her grin widened, her teeth flashing under the dim

light of the bar. "That's right. I'm mean. Do you want me to be mean to you, Saul?"

He looked like he was considering it. I didn't blame him. Hell, I was half tempted to change my name to Saul and let her be mean to *me*.

"No," he said resignedly. He pulled his threadbare wallet out and handed it to her. She flipped it open, counted out a handful of bills, then handed it back to him. "Have a good night, Janie."

"Have a good night, Saul."

She watched him shuffle out, her forehead knit in a thoughtful frown. When he pushed through the doors and disappeared into the dusky evening, I cleared my throat. She jerked and her gaze snapped to mine, dark eyes widening like she had forgotten I was there.

"Shit, sorry," she said, hustling over. "What can I get you?"

I had expected a flash of recognition—Aspen Springs damn near threw me a parade every time I came home on leave—but found nothing in her expression that said she knew who I was. Not even a sliver of curiosity. I hated that kind of attention, but I didn't much care for the distracted way she looked past me, either.

"Got anything local?" I asked.

She nodded. "On tap we have Fat Tire. I also have Yeti Stout bottled."

"I'll take the Yeti."

"Good choice." With another nod, she pivoted to the fridge behind her, where rows of brown bottles with bright, graffiti-style labels glistened behind the glass door. She grabbed a bottle from the middle shelf, popped the top off, and set it in front of me. "Here you go."

"Thanks." I took a sip, let the rich, dark flavor coat my tongue and settle something tight in me. I refused to call it nerves. "Not too busy tonight," I said, noting the way her gaze slipped over my shoulder to gauge whether the handful of people milling around needed something from her.

"Not tonight," she agreed. "The weather will keep people home."

She looked toward the door again. It had grown darker in the last two minutes. She ran her tongue over her bottom lip. "Snow is coming." She said it softly, more to herself than me.

In this part of Colorado, snow was always coming. The early snow tended to melt quickly under the sunshine, but higher in the mountains, some patches of snow stayed year-round. "Saul will make it home before it gets bad."

"Oh." She blinked. "I wasn't worried about him. Saul can survive anything. Like a cockroach, except he's not nasty. I was just..." Her voice trailed off as she looked wistfully toward the door.

"Some place you would rather be?" I asked, lifting the beer to my lips.

Suddenly I had the full attention of those dark eyes, and the force of it made me freeze with the bottle at my mouth.

"Oh, no," she cooed sweetly. She bent over the bar and

propped her chin on her palm and batted her long, thick eyelashes at me. "There is nowhere I would rather be than right here with you. So handsome. So smart. Such a good tipper."

And then she chuckled because we both knew that was a lie.

Well, not the part about me being handsome, smart, and a good tipper. That was all true. But that wasn't enough for Janie to want to be here with me. Her mind was clearly occupied with something else, and I wanted to know what it was. That had always been my problem. I was too curious about people. Too interested in understanding.

All the understanding in the world didn't make a lick of difference in the outcome. I still had to pull the trigger.

I finally remembered to swallow my beer. I set the bottle down again and delivered a quick, sharp flick to the knot of muscle between my index finger and thumb. It jolted me back to the present. This bar. This woman. No dirt road. And not a turtle to be seen.

"What would you be doing now, if you could do anything you wanted?" I asked. No harm in indulging a little curiosity, was there? I was a civilian now.

She lifted a shoulder. "What would anyone want to do on a snowy night? Make a cup of hot cocoa, snuggle up in bed, and read books."

"Books...plural? You expecting to get snowed in for a week?"

Her mouth crooked up. "Maybe they're short. I'm a big fan of *The Bear Snores On*."

I read a lot of books, but that title didn't ring a bell. It sounded like a children's book. A comfort read from her childhood, maybe? Before I could ask, a glass shattered to my left. Janie jumped a little, but I didn't move. Loud noises didn't startle me or let the dark places in my mind swallow me up. The psychiatrist at Walter Reed had taken that as a good sign. I was *fine*.

"Excuse me." Janie stepped away from the bar and pushed through the door to the kitchen.

A moment later she returned with a broom. I rolled the beer bottle between my palms, studying her distorted reflection in the brown glass as she swept up the mess. She dumped it in a trashcan before rounding the bar counter again.

"Ready for another one?" she asked.

My hesitation was brief. Mom and Essie could wait a little longer. "Please." I nudged the empty bottle toward her. She swapped it for a new one, popping the top off before she handed it to me. "Thanks, hussy."

Her eyes narrowed and her head tilted. I jerked my chin at her torso. "Your shirt."

Janie looked down at herself, where the word hussy was emblazoned in bold, hot pink sequins against her black t-shirt. "Oh. Right." She laughed. "I like to let people know who they're dealing with up front. Just so there's no misunderstanding."

"Noted," I said.

The door swung open and a man I didn't recognize prowled into the bar, looking all kinds of aggravated as he claimed the stool two up from me. Janie stiffened, which sent me to high alert.

"You shouldn't be here, Steven." Janie braced her palms on the scarred pine bar top and glowered at the man.

I glanced sideways to gauge his reaction. Ready, and suddenly a whole lot more willing. This one at least might make it worth the effort.

Steven huffed an annoyed sigh. "Janie. The one who likes sunflowers," he muttered.

Janie's head tilted, her shiny copper ponytail falling over her shoulder. "How did you know I like sunflowers?"

"Chloe's shoes. James likes columbine, Essie likes red roses," he said, and my hand flexed at the sound of my twin sister's name. "Hannah likes violets, you like sunflowers. Chloe likes peonies." The last one came out wistful.

Janie narrowed her eyes. "That's right." She studied him for a moment, then shook her head. "No. You still shouldn't be here."

Steven glanced around warily, like he might be expecting trouble. "Any of the Hale brothers here tonight?"

Since the Hales had been my second family practically from birth, and now that my best friend was my brother-in-law they were family on paper too, I made their conversation my business.

"You got a problem with the Hale brothers?" I asked.

Steven grunted. "No. The Hale brothers have a problem with me."

"Why is that?" I asked. I turned on my barstool to look him squarely in the face. That curiosity again. I liked to know who I was about to flatten.

Steven looked at me, quickly understood the way of things, and turned his gaze forward. "A misunderstanding," he muttered. Janie guffawed loudly. "On my part," he clarified.

"The Hale brothers are pretty good at judging character," I noted. They were more than capable of fighting their own battles, but hell. I had nothing better to do except go home, and truthfully, I didn't want to.

Like she sensed a sudden change in the wind, Janie's head whipped toward me. "Just drink your beer, Jack. I'll handle this."

My eyebrows shot to my hairline. Most people didn't surprise me, but Janie had managed to pull it off.

She rolled her eyes at my stunned expression. "I knew who you were the moment you sat down. Essie has a photo of you on her fireplace mantle."

Shit.

"Did you tell her I'm here?" I asked. Because if she knew, I had maybe ninety seconds before she stormed in here looking for me.

Janie's brow furrowed. "She doesn't know?"

"I wanted to surprise her," I lied.

"Then it's a good thing I didn't tell her, I guess." Janie

turned back to Steven. "I haven't decided what to do about you yet, so don't get too comfortable on that barstool." She sank a hand on her hip. "Maybe I should follow Chloe's lead and tell you to get the hell out. That's what she always did."

"And now she lives with me, so…" Steven spread his arms wide, smirking. "Seems like a risk on your part. You might actually end up liking me."

"Doubtful." Janie pursed her lips. "Still not sure she wasn't under duress."

Steven huffed and rubbed his palms over a crack in the wood. "Chloe could tell me to get the hell out of my own home, and I'd go," he grumbled. "I'm not forcing her to share space with me."

Damn. Steven had it bad for this Chloe chick, whoever she was. I couldn't help but feel a little sorry for him. Clearly her friends didn't like him, and that would be tough to overcome.

Janie took pity on him. "One beer," she said. "That's it." She didn't ask him what he wanted, just grabbed a bottle of IPA from the fridge, popped the top, and handed it to him.

"Thanks," he said.

I sipped my own beer and pretended not to notice as he kept sending curious glances my way. He'd talk when he was ready, and I wasn't much in the mood for a conversation. Not with him, anyway. I looked at Janie, who was rubbing water spots from the clean glasses she had taken out of the dishwasher. The Painted Cat's clientele wasn't the sort to notice or care about water spots at a dive bar, but she did it anyway.

That shouldn't surprise me. Brax would notice, and he was an owner of the bar, so of course he would hire someone who also paid attention to the details. Now that I thought about it, I could see that he'd made improvements. It was still a dive, but one where you were a lot less likely to pick up a staph infection. Some of the wood beams dated back to when the Painted Cat was a brothel under ownership of Brax's great-great-great-great grandfather, and those remained sacred. He'd sooner chop his hand off than tear them down. But the lighting had been updated and the booths had been recovered in gleaming burgundy leather.

"You got a favorite flower, Jack?" Steven asked, pulling my thoughts.

I paused, the brown beer bottle dangling from my hand. "Why do you want to know?"

"The flowers they embroidered on Chloe's shoes. Apparently that's the kind of thing friends know about each other." He jerked his head in Janie's direction. "I don't think that's normal. Hell, I'm not sure I even have a favorite flower."

I eyed him. "We're not friends," I said.

"No, we're fucking not," he agreed and for a moment I wondered if he had a death wish because he seemed to be squaring up for a fight. Janie shot him a warning look as she swiped by with a towel. He shrugged and swigged his beer. "What are those colorful flowers that look like balls?" he asked her.

Janie scrunched her face like she was thinking. "Dahlias?" She tugged her phone out of her back pocket and tapped the screen a couple times, then turned it to face him so he could see the picture. "Is this what you mean?"

"Yeah." He studied the image for a moment. "I like those."

I moved to the barstool next to him because, again, I had nothing better to do and I was too curious for my own good. I leaned toward Janie's phone. "Those are nice. My mom grows dahlias."

A woman down the bar lifted her hand to get Janie's attention. Janie stuck her phone in her pocket and pushed away from the bar. "Holler if you need something."

I watched her leave, then turned to Steven. "Why are you at a bar, talking to strangers about fucking flowers, when you want to be home with her?"

He rolled the bottle between his hands. "It's complicated."

It was funny how often I'd heard that phrase when nothing in this world had ever struck me as complicated. Not even killing people. "Nah, that's lazy." I shook my head. "It's pretty simple. If you want to be with her, hooking up with a random woman at a bar is self-sabotage."

He glanced around the bar, seeming to weigh his options. From the way his mouth tightened, I could guess that not a single person in the room held his attention like the girl waiting at home for him. "You got a better option?" he asked.

"My advice?" I tipped my beer to my lips, appraising him over the rim, and took a swallow. "Go home. Take a cold shower."

"Unless you want to get snowed in with us," Janie offered.

Steven's cheek ticked. Then he swigged his beer with long, deep swallows, draining the bottle. He slapped a handful of cash on the counter, nodded to me, and he was gone.

The remaining stragglers took that as their cue to leave, too. They followed him out, one by one, until the only people left were me and Janie.

We looked at each other.

"The snow is coming down hard now," she said. There was a question in her eyes.

"That it is," I agreed.

But I didn't move.

2

____

JANIE

He didn't remember me. Why would he? It was one day twenty years ago, and we hadn't spoken a single word since. I hadn't even seen him again until my first day at Aspen Springs High School, when I'd been a freshman and he was a senior.

By the end of the first week of school, I'd had his schedule memorized. I knew he saw me standing there against the lockers that lined the halls, pretending I had some reason to be in his vicinity because Jack Price saw everything, but he never acknowledged me. He'd already forgotten me, even then.

But I remembered him. I remembered the way he moved through the high school, so sure that every step he took was the right one. He never got in trouble, never clowned around, and somehow he was still invited to every party. Every teacher wanted him in their classroom. Every guy wanted to be him. Every girl wanted to date him.

Including me.

Not that he cared about some gawky freshman stalking him. And at fourteen, I was definitely gawky. I blossomed my junior year and never wanted for dates after that, but by then Jack had graduated. He left Colorado and joined the military.

Whereas I stayed put and got in trouble.

Probably a good thing he didn't remember me, actually.

I grabbed a rag and a spray bottle of cleaner and started wiping down the tables. No one else would be walking through that door tonight. Not with the snow coming down like this. If Jack weren't here, I'd call up Brax and ask him for permission to close the bar early. Brax wasn't a jerk, so he'd let me.

But Jack *was* here.

And I wanted him to stay.

I glanced over my shoulder at him and found him staring straight at me. He had turned around on his stool so his back was to the bar top. My cheeks heated and I wiped harder at the wood table. Jack didn't have to know it was already so clean you could lick it.

"You play cards, Jack?" I asked.

"Sure," he said. "You got a deck?"

"Behind the bar," I said.

His gaze tracked my movements as I finished cleaning up. I could feel it on my skin, hot and teasing, like a physical touch. Awareness shimmered through my body, a heady rush that made my hands vibrate and my stomach swoop. I would call it a premonition if I believed in all that woo-woo stuff, which I didn't. What I did believe in was chemistry and straight-up horniness and right now the pheromones coming off both of us were enough to choke an elephant.

I squatted behind the bar by the old pine cabinet where we kept odds and ends, angling my backside away from Jack's all-seeing gaze. These jeans tended to give me plumber's crack and that wasn't a good look on anyone. I pushed aside the notebook and colored pencils I kept for doodling when things were slow and located the deck of cards that were floppy from years of use. They were faded but each card was a work of art, if you considered paintings of pinup girls to be art, which I did.

"What are we playing?" I asked, setting the deck on the bar top between us.

Jack's blue eyes dropped to the bare-breasted Marilyn Monroe card on top. The tiniest twitch of his eyebrow was the only sign that he saw it at all. "Poker?" he suggested.

I shook my head. "I'm too gullible for poker. Can't lie and can't read people to save my life," I confessed. "A man could run out of a bank with cash spilling from his pockets and a bandana over his face, alarm bells ringing, but if he told me it wasn't what it looked like, I'd hear him out."

He laughed and *whoosh* went my stomach. There was nothing as blue as Jack's eyes when he laughed. "Rummy, then. Although, for the record, I think you're selling yourself short, Janie. Unless you're just bluffing."

"What do you mean?" I asked. I pulled the jacks out

since we wouldn't be using them and split the deck in half, then shuffled the only way I knew how, pushing the cards against my thumbs so they alternated falling together, bits of tits and ass flashing as they went.

"I mean you're reading me just fine."

He kept his gaze on my hands like he knew eye contact would be too much for us to handle right then. Too honest. That frisson of awareness danced down my spine again, but I pretended it didn't. Pretended I didn't know what he was talking about or where this was going. I wanted to wrap all that delicious tension around me like a cloak and burrow into it. It had been so long since I had felt anything like this.

"Nine card draw, aces high," I said, laying down the rules.

"Aces are low if they're paired with a number card," he countered.

"No, aces are always high. Fifteen points for aces, ten for face cards, five for number cards."

His head tilted as he thought that through. "Why?"

"Because they're pretty."

"As good a reason as any, I suppose." His eyes drifted over my face, and I felt warm all over. "Hard to resist something pretty."

I rolled my eyes. "Was that a line, soldier?"

"Not a line. A confession." His lips quirked. "And I'm not a soldier."

He drained the last of his beer on a long swallow, his head tipped back to expose his throat. My mouth went dry.

Goddamn. How was everything this man did so damn sexy? Just...*how*?

"Hm." I gave him a stern *don't try it, mister* look despite the fact that I absolutely wanted him to try it and butterflies were swooping dizzily in my belly because *ahhhh! Jack Price thinks I'm pretty!* The gawky teenage girl inside me was about to embarrass us both.

He gave me an impish smile and I melted further. With an exasperated huff, I pushed the deck at him. He rapped his knuckles once on the top card, a show of trust, and I dealt the cards, alternating between us until we had nine each.

"Another beer before we get into it?" I asked.

"It's what, seven-thirty? I'll take one more."

I glanced at my watch before pivoting to the fridge. "Seven thirty-three," I said over my shoulder as a confirmation, not a correction. "Lucky guess."

He smirked. "I was rounding."

I laughed as I set the bottle down in front of him. "Is that your special talent? You never lose track of time?"

His blue eyes locked on mine as he wrapped his long, thick fingers around the base of the beer bottle. His thumb absently stroked up and down the neck, condensation forming in its wake. My own neck broke out in goosebumps like I could feel his touch on my nape. "I never lose track of anything."

Me. You lost track of me. I bit the words back. They weren't even true. You couldn't lose track of something you never knew existed, and I hadn't existed for Jack. I couldn't expect him to remember a half-hour spent with a little kid twenty years ago. That sting I felt was wounded pride. Because maybe back in high school I had suspected he didn't think of me the way I thought of him, but now I knew for sure.

But tonight...tonight I could give him something worth remembering.

"How long are you home for?" I asked, studying my cards to cover my flushed cheeks.

I fanned the cards out in my hand and quickly reorganized them to my liking, from useless to promising, with high cards I wasn't ready to part with to the far right. Three of hearts, six of clubs, a pair of tens, the queen and jack of spades, and the ace of diamonds that I couldn't do anything with, but I wasn't going to hand over fifteen points unless I had to. It was a decent hand. I liked my odds.

"I'm not home yet," he said. It sounded like a dodge.

I glanced at him. His cards were still in an untouched heap in front of him. Catching my gaze, he scooped up the pile, considered them without changing their order, and set them down again.

"So tonight doesn't count?" I teased. I flipped over the top card on the deck and my stomach dropped. Ace of hearts. Goddammit. Well, at least he knew I hadn't stacked the deck in my favor.

"It counts, Janie," he said simply. Firmly.

My mouth went dry.

He didn't look at me as he ignored the ace and slipped

the top card from the stack, added it to his pile, and put down the seven of diamonds, lining it up neatly with the ace.

I blinked. Had the seven been in his hand, or was it the card he had just picked up? He had moved so fast I couldn't be sure.

Suddenly I had the feeling I was going to lose. Badly.

"So, really. How long are you home for?" I asked. We moved through our first few turns quickly, neither of us keeping anything. The line of unwanted cards grew longer. "A week? Two weeks?"

"For good."

That surprised me. My gaze shot to his face, but he kept his eyes on his cards. "You're out? Essie didn't mention that." This was different than just surprising her with a visit. Essie worried about him all the time. She would have shouted the news from the rooftops, if she had known.

"She doesn't know," he said, confirming my suspicions.

I cocked my head. "Why doesn't she know, Jack?"

He rolled a shoulder.

I figured that meant he wasn't going to talk about it. Fine. I wouldn't push. I picked up the king of clubs. On his turn, he picked a card from the deck and used it to form a set with a ten, jack, queen, and king, all diamonds. Dammit. I chewed my lip. I could put down my ace of diamonds and play it off his set, but I wasn't going to. Not with the ace of hearts still sitting there, calling my name. *You know you want me, Janie. Ignore all those cards between us. I'm worth it.*

"Four months ago, I took a bullet to my shoulder. It made me medically unfit to perform with my unit. I could have stayed in uniform, but shit. I'm thirty-four. I figured enough was enough, so I resigned my commission."

"You were shot?" I whispered. I stared at his shoulder like I could see through the fabric of his shirt to the injury underneath.

His eyebrows went up in amusement as he made his next play. "More than once. But it was the last one that went septic and left me with nerve damage."

"Essie doesn't know." It wasn't a question. If Essie had known her twin brother's life was in danger, nothing could have kept her from his side. "Your mom doesn't know."

Jack rubbed his fingers along his jaw line. "I figured it was better to tell them I was in danger after the danger had passed."

My mouth dropped open. "But what if the danger didn't pass? What if you had…" I swallowed the sudden thickness in my throat. It was hard to say the word aloud. "Died?"

"I wasn't going to let that happen."

I shook my head. "You can't control everything, Jack. Especially not death."

"I've done a good job of it so far." His cheek twitched under his eye. He put down another set and discarded the ace of clubs. "Your turn."

I stared at the ace. "There are two aces down. Kind of risky, don't you think?"

"No."

I looked at him. He held up his card—his *last* card. His sets were better than mine and worth more points, and he could go out at any second. If I picked up that line of cards to get the aces, I would lose for sure. There was no way I could turn all those cards into sets before he went out, and anything left in my hand would count against me.

I couldn't resist.

I scooped up the cards with a flourish.

"Kind of risky, don't you think?" he teased, using my words against me.

I laughed. "I'm holding all the aces. I can't lose," I joked, quoting a line from one of my favorite country songs.

He watched me put down the set: ace of hearts, ace of diamonds, ace of clubs. "Not all of them," he noted, taking me literally.

The ace of spades had to be in that stack somewhere, and we were down to maybe ten cards more. There was a fifty-fifty chance it wouldn't be me, but I wasn't worried. I already knew how it would end.

I was *definitely* going to lose.

After I had played everything I could—number cards that I could play off his sets or mine—I was still left holding ten cards, and a few of them had faces. There was no coming back from this.

Jack arched an eyebrow at me. I grinned unrepentantly. "Aren't they pretty?" I murmured, tracing the calligraphy lovingly with my index finger.

The game went fast after that, each of us moving

rapidly through our turns, Jack still holding that same single card, me playing what I could, until I was down to two cards in my hand. The deck had one card left and the ace of spades still hadn't made an appearance. On his turn, Jack picked up the card with his right hand. He didn't even glance at it, just put the card in his left down with the rest of his sets.

The ace of spades.

He'd had it the whole fucking time.

I narrowed my eyes at him. "You could have gone out ten minutes ago."

"I could have." He discarded the four of hearts and stretched, lifting his arms up and out.

I tried not to stare. He was just so *big*. His hands, his wingspan, the breadth of his chest. He took up so much space and, judging from the way my breaths turned shallow, all of the oxygen. "Why didn't you? Were you letting me win?"

"You didn't win. I wasn't done playing, that's all." His blue eyes met mine. "It stopped snowing ten minutes ago."

Oh. My skin prickled. He could have gone home ten minutes ago, but instead he had dragged out our game to stay here with me.

He hadn't touched his third beer, I noticed. He was definitely sober enough to drive home. I glanced to the window. "The roads might be slippery, though. Essie would never forgive me if I let her twin brother die in a horrible crash." It would be so easy for him to take the hint and blame the weather.

He didn't take it. "My truck can handle it."

Dammit.

"Janie." He said my name like he was holding back a laugh. His large, warm hand covered mine and his thumb stroked over my knuckles. "If I'm staying, it's not because of the snow."

Butterflies erupted in my stomach. "What would Essie say about that?" I asked, even though I already knew the answer. "She's my best friend."

"Well, your best friend happened to marry my best friend, so I'm thinking there's not a hell of a lot she can say about it without looking like a hypocrite."

I bit my lip and looked out the window again. I felt… restless. *Reckless.* Maybe it was the fact that I'd harbored a crush on Jack Price since I was ten years old. Or maybe I just needed to get my bad out, like my mama always said. Either way, I was doing this. I squared my shoulders.

"I have a room upstairs," I said.

3

JACK

I didn't have time to process the fact that I had just told my twin sister's best friend something private that my own family wasn't aware of yet. Janie could easily spill it to Essie, out of loyalty or accidentally. But I knew she wouldn't. It didn't matter that the woman was virtually a stranger to me, and I hadn't even asked her to keep her mouth shut. I knew I could trust her. People played cards the way they lived life, and Janie? She didn't have a dishonest bone in her body.

I didn't open up easily, but I had opened up her—something else I couldn't process right now.

Because right now, I was too busy trying to process the fact that Janie was my twin sister's best friend and I was about to fuck her within an inch of her life.

We were already kissing when we crashed through the door of her apartment upstairs, our hands roaming each other's bodies in search of whatever bare skin we could find. Her wrist, her neck, the inch of stomach above the waistband of her jeans—I wasn't picky. I wanted all of it.

I cupped her round ass and pulled her flush against me as I swept my tongue into her mouth. God, she was sweet. She tasted like the limes she had squeezed into her water while we played cards. I couldn't hold back my groan and that seemed to drive her wild. Her fingers dug into my shoulders as she leaned into the kiss, making eager, greedy little sounds that nearly had me bursting out of my jeans. I was so fucking hard for her and I thought I might die if I couldn't find out how wet she was for me.

Fuck. *Fuck*.

I didn't *do* this. I didn't have spur-of-the-moment sex. I had carefully planned encounters with women who had clean background checks and valid STI paperwork. The stakes were too high. Few things in this world had the potential to ruin your life like sex. I'd seen too many men I'd respected face the consequences for a night of fun. Disease, kids they mostly abandoned, espionage. And for what? Getting their dick wet with a woman whose name they couldn't even remember. Hell no. Could not be me. I didn't fuck around with fucking.

But with this woman? I didn't care that she was virtually a stranger. I didn't care that she knew my secret. I didn't care that I didn't know a damn thing about her outside her name and that she was my sister's best friend.

She made me reckless.

The crazy thing was, I was actually enjoying it. For a man who liked his control nice and tight, it was a revelation. Having her in my arms, it didn't feel like I was teetering on the brink of disaster. It felt like winning.

I caught her by the backs of her thighs, just under the ample curve of her ass, hefted her off her feet, and pinned her back to the closed door with my body. Her long legs locked around my waist, her ankles crossed at the base of my spine. When she pushed her pussy against by cock, I groaned into her mouth.

"Do you have any idea what you're doing to me?" I panted, pulling back to see her damp, puffy lips smirk back at me.

Her eyes lowered to our crotches smashed together. "I have a pretty good idea, yes. But I think…I could do more."

Using the door as leverage, she pushed harder against me. She stared at me, doe eyes half lidded, as she gave another purposeful roll of her hips. A slow smile bloomed across her lips at the desperate moan that tore from my throat. I was coming undone and she loved every second of it. And I didn't even care. I didn't care that she knew the power she had over me. That triumphant smile was the sexiest fucking thing I had ever seen.

"I hope you don't think I'm going to let you come like that," I murmured.

Her head jerked back, her eyes narrowed. "*Let* me?" she said testily.

Damn, I loved that flash of spirit. But watching her surrender? I was going to love that even more. "As much as I enjoy the way you're grinding that sweet pussy on me, I need you to hold off a little longer. We're not taking the easy way out tonight, Ace. You're going to make me work for it."

She considered, all that shiny copper hair spilling over her shoulder with a tilt of her head. "I can do that."

I grinned. "Fuck yeah, you can."

I kissed her languidly, just to prove I could. For the first time in my life, I wasn't rushing toward the next thing. No one knew where I was. There was nowhere I had to be. I could just...*exist*.

But that was another thing I couldn't process right now because not knowing what came next scared the ever-loving shit out of me. I preferred confined spaces and known variables. What the hell I was going to do with the rest of my life, that was too nebulous to contemplate. Too many wrong answers.

This room, this woman, this moment. I could handle that.

More than handle.

I could *excel*.

Exceling was where I was comfortable. And by god, Janie would reap the benefits of that tonight.

"You're wearing too many clothes, beautiful," I murmured, pressing a kiss just below her jaw where her pulse beat wildly.

I felt her throat bob against my cheek as she swallowed. Then she slowly unwrapped her legs and I eased her down until her feet met the ancient pine floor with a soft thump. She stretched her arms toward the ceiling, a small grin on her lips and a challenge in her dark eyes.

Fuck me, that was an invitation I couldn't pass up.

With the hem of her shirt fisted in my hands, I dragged my knuckles up her torso. It was like unwrapping a sweet treat. Soft skin so pale that I found myself thinking of moonlight and stars, followed by a nude, lacy push-up bra that served her spectacular tits up on a platter. Golden freckles dusted the curve of her breasts, making my mouth water. I tossed her shirt aside and skimmed my tongue along the lace edge before delving straight into her cleavage as I unclasped her bra behind her back.

I stepped back to admire her. Her ponytail was mussed from my hands and lower than it was fifteen minutes ago, sliding over one shoulder and curving around her breast. My gaze slid lower. Apricot-hued nipples adorned with little metal studs that I was dying to play with. Silver stretch marks that flanked her navel and peaked over the waistband of her jeans on her hips, barely noticeable against her pale skin, zigzagging like ski tracks on fresh snow.

"You're beautiful, Janie." My eyes ate her up, landing again on her nipple piercings. I bit my fist. "Perfect."

Her cheeks flushed. She didn't like me staring at her. I could tell by the way her gaze shifted down and sideways. But she liked the compliment. She bit her lip and, still not meeting my eyes, flicked open the fly of her jeans and shimmied them down her legs.

I groaned because she was red there, too. She looked like a sunrise, all pink and gold and peach. If I had known all this beauty was waiting for me in Aspen Springs, I might have been tempted to earn that medical discharge a lot sooner.

I could have stared at her for another hour, but Janie was done with having all the attention focused on her.

"Your turn," she ordered. She tugged at my belt.

I laughed. "Eager, are you?" I meant it appreciatively, but she dropped my belt like she'd been scalded.

I frowned. This wasn't the time for a heartfelt conversation, but I wasn't going to pretend I didn't see her, either. I took her hands and put them right back where they belonged: reaching for my dick.

"Don't pretend you don't want me, Janie. It hurts my feelings." I whipped my shirt off over my head. "Now put your hands on my dick and tell me you think I'm pretty."

Her eyes shot to mine and her flush deepened. But then she quirked an eyebrow at me and tossed her hair like she was accepting a dare. Her gaze swept over me, over the muscles women liked and the scars they sometimes didn't. I knew people felt some kind of way about my scars. They were too thick, too ugly, and far too close to vital organs.

She took her time about it, and I could feel a blush climb my cheeks in spite of myself. I wasn't soft like Janie. I wasn't made of moonbeams and sunsets. People looked at Janie and saw beauty. They looked at me and saw death.

But when she slowly dragged her gaze back up to mine, her eyes were dark with hunger. "I think you're pretty, Jack. But I think you would be even prettier on your knees." She placed her hands on my shoulders and gave a firm push.

Hell, yes.

A shocked chuckle escaped me. It was the second time tonight Janie had surprised me. Whatever baggage she carried, she wasn't going to let that stop her from asking for what she wanted.

And right now, what she wanted was exactly what I wanted to give her. I dropped to my knees so fast I made a breeze.

God, it had been too long since I'd done this. With my fingers on her thick thighs, I used my thumbs to spread her open. My mouth watered at the sight of her. Pink and copper everywhere.

"So fucking pretty, honey," I murmured.

And then I couldn't wait another second to have her taste on my tongue, her scent in my face. I licked her from her entrance to her clit, swirled my tongue right *there*, and licked her again.

"Oh, *wow*." Her head lolled back and hit the door with a thunk. "Do that again."

I did it again. Again and again until we were both groaning. I licked and sucked and nipped. One of her hands went to cup her own breast, and when she rolled her nipple between her thumb and finger, I nearly went out of my mind with jealousy. I wanted to play there, too, but not until I made her come on my tongue.

She was close. So damn close.

With one hand toying with her nipple piercings, her other hand clutching the back of my head, she rocked her hips against my mouth, taking her pleasure as much as I gave it. The taste of her...those fucking sounds she made...I was so hard it was painful. When I finally got my dick in her, I wasn't going to last long.

That was fine. I was already planning for round two.

She ground her hips against my face as I found the rhythm that drove her crazy. Her grip tightened in my hair.

"I—"

She didn't get another syllable out before she broke against me, her body quaking. I slipped my tongue inside her and lapped up every drop. She bowed over me as the pleasure ebbed, and I took the opportunity to haul her over my shoulder in a firemen's hold.

Two steps to the bed and I tossed her on it, then crawled up her body, caging her in.

She stared at me with half-lidded, sated eyes. "Hey."

"Hey," I replied, and then kissed her. My heart beat hard in my chest. Fuck, I wanted her. But—"I don't have a condom."

"I do." She fumbled open the drawer of the nightstand, felt around a bit, and produced a foil square.

I took it from her and tore it open. "Were you a Girl Scout, by any chance?"

"For a few years." Her eyes narrowed and she tilted her head. "Why?"

"I was a Boy Scout." I rolled the rubber down my dick, pinching the tip to make sure I had space because *fuck*. When I blew, I was going to blow *hard*. I squeezed the base of my dick and tried to pull myself together. "We used to go camping. One time, we couldn't get a fire started. It was the stupidest fucking thing. The wood was wet and we weren't prepared for it. But the Girl Scout troop at the campsite over from ours, they were prepared. They saved our asses that night. I can always spot a Girl Scout. You know how?"

"How?" she asked.

"They're always good in the clutch."

I pushed into her. My eyes crossed as her slick, wet heat welcomed me in. I pushed further. And further. And then a little more.

"Jack," she sputtered. Her nails dug into my bicep while her other hand went between us. Her fingers grazed the two inches of my shaft that hadn't made it inside her yet and her eyes widened. "You're not all the way in yet?"

"Almost," I muttered.

She made a frantic squeaking sound. "This isn't going to work. It's not going to fit."

My chin dropped to my chest and I got us another half inch. "It will fit," I gritted out. "Those muscles are flexible. They're made for this. Breathe, honey."

She glared up at me. "Do not mansplain my vagina to me, Jack. I will—" She gasped as I sank deeper. "*God.*"

"Good?" I asked, my voice thick and drugged.

"*So* good."

I caught her nipple in my teeth, flicked my tongue over the cool metal stud. She arched and I bottomed out with a groan. I paused as long as I could take it, ten seconds, fifteen, then pulled out halfway and drove right back in.

She stared up at me with wide eyes and shiny damp lips that made me nearly spill right then and there, and then she tucked her chin and craned her neck like she was trying to get a better view.

"You want to see?" I roughed out.

"Yeah." She tugged her bottom lip between her teeth. "I want to see."

I straightened my arms and lifted my torso so she could watch me thrust into her. She stared down at where her pussy stretched tight around my pumping cock.

"Look how well you take me," I murmured. "Fuck, look at you."

She looked. Her eyes glazed over and her breaths turned short and hollow. I watched her watch me fuck her and—

"Christ," I bit off. I needed her to get there right fucking now. "Touch your clit, honey."

She didn't even hesitate. Her hand delved between us, found her spot, and rubbed. I pumped harder as her whimpers turned to moans, and then I needed to feel her for myself. Leaving one arm to hold my weight, I covered her hand with mine, learning the way she liked to be touched.

It sent us both over the fucking edge. Her pussy pulsed around my shaft, her orgasm deepening my own, and I spilled everything I had inside her.

I braced my arms on either side of her as I slowly lowered my body, not wanting to crush her. But she wrapped her arms around me and pulled me down against all that warm, silky skin. I sank in with a grateful groan.

Fuck, I was tired. I had been tired for a week now. A month. A fucking year.

My whole lifetime.

I shouldn't stay the night, but my eyelids felt like rocks were holding them closed.

"Just a nap," Janie mumbled in my ear.

"An hour," I agreed, rolling to my side and curling around her body.

I waited for the regret to hit, now that my dick had gotten what it wanted and my brain was fully operational again. But it never came. I didn't regret a damn thing.

In fact, I wanted more.

4

———

JANIE

I wrenched awake, clawing desperately at my throat. The hand wrapped around it didn't budge except to squeeze tighter. Jack's taut face hovered inches above my own, his mouth a grim slash, his eyes closed, his brows pushed together, looking like he had every intention of ending my life. But the sounds he made—agony. Like *he* was the one in pain.

Shit, shit! I tried to wiggle, but his big body crushed me to the bed, and not in a good way. That self-defense class I took in college for a P.E. credit was a joke. I couldn't even get a knee to his balls. What was I supposed to do? *Never wake a sleepwalker.* Was that real, or just untested internet advice? What about sleep stranglers? Did the same rule apply? If Chloe Adams, one of my best friends and a fantastic social worker, was here, she'd know what to do. She'd be gentle and calm and—

I wheezed. Oh, god, I was going to die. I was going to die and everyone would know it was because I had a one-night stand and Maya—

Hell, no. I was not going out like this.

I flicked his forehead.

"Jack." *Flick.* "Wake." *Flick.* "The fuck." *Flick.* "Up."

"Turtle—" His blue eyes popped open, boring into mine right as I gave one final, hard flick between his eyebrows. He blinked rapidly. "Janie?"

"Can't—breathe—" I gasped.

In an instant, his hand was off my neck and his weight lifted from my body as he rolled to his back. I gulped in air. My lungs burned. My throat felt like I had swallowed a sword. And Jack—I twisted my neck to squint at him in the dim light.

Jack looked as shocked as I felt.

I rolled onto my side to face him. "Are you okay?" I asked softly.

He barked out a short, angry laugh. "No." He scrubbed a hand over his face. "Are you okay?"

I breathed again. My lungs felt fine. My heartrate was still elevated, but it was slowing down. I swallowed. My throat still hurt, but even that had lessened. "I'm okay. I think you might have left bruises, though."

He jackknifed into a sitting position. "Let's get you to a doctor."

"A doctor? Where do you think we are, Denver? The closest hospital is forty minutes from here." I grabbed his bicep—my *god*, it was a *boulder*—and tugged him back down. After a brief hesitation, he allowed it. "I'm *fine*," I insisted.

"People keep using that word," he muttered. "I don't think it means what they think it means."

I laughed. It only hurt a little. "You're fine, too. Things can't be that bad if you can still quote *The Princess Bride*."

He scoffed. "Janie, I am *not* fine."

I looked at him. At the purple shadows under his eyes and the deep groove between his eyebrows. I wanted to press my thumb there and smooth his worry away. "I know," I said softly.

I wiggled across the bed until there was only an inch or two of space between us. His gaze flicked down to me, his eyes dark as they studied me. With a sigh, he lifted one arm, curled it around me, and dragged me the rest of the way. "Come here," he said gruffly.

I curved my body against his, resting my cheek on his chest. "You said something about a turtle. Was that…a code name or something? A person? Was that how you got this?" My hand drifted to the scar at his shoulder. The one that ended his career and sent him home.

"Not a code name. Not anything to do with my shoulder." He twitched under my fingers. "My shoulder…that was a rescue mission that didn't go as planned. My team made it out alive with the hostage, though, and that's what matters."

"I'm sorry." He'd dodged the actual question. Whatever the turtle meant to him, he wasn't going to talk about it. I didn't push. Given his line of work, maybe he wasn't *allowed* to talk about it. "And I'm sorry for flicking you."

A low laugh rumbled near my ear. "I'd say that was the least I deserved."

"It wasn't your fault." I meant that.

"It wasn't my fault," he conceded. "But that doesn't mean it's not my responsibility."

I craned my neck to look up at him. His lips were pressed in a grim line, the muscle in his cheek popping like he was grinding his molars. I had a feeling that responsibility wasn't something this man took lightly. Jack Price wore responsibility and duty like a teenage boy trying cologne for the first time, dousing his body with more because he couldn't smell it on himself.

"So, what are you going to do about it?" I asked, my voice wary because Jack struck me as the sort that believed responsibility came with action, and I really didn't want to leave this bed.

"Get you a glass of water."

There was barely a second between the words leaving his lips and Jack leaving my bed, his large palm gently guiding my cheek off his chest to soften the landing. He padded across the room to the kitchenette: a sink, a small fridge, a microwave, and three cabinets hanging above the countertop. If he noticed the bare-bones layout of the place, he kept it to himself.

I propped myself up on my elbows and enjoyed the view while he located a glass from the cabinet and turned on the tap. God, that ass. I wanted to bite it like an apple.

Scars peppered his skin, but that only added to the appeal.

Then he turned around and that was even better. He wasn't even hard and it just...looked like *that*. Long and thick and so pretty that my fingertips itched with the need to sketch him.

"Thank you," I said as I took the glass from him. He watched while I took three grateful gulps in a row, his forehead knitted in a frown. The cool water soothed the rough, scratchy feeling.

"How is your throat?" he asked. "Any trouble swallowing?"

I shook my head. "The water helped. I'm okay, really and truly. I don't need a doctor. I wouldn't sacrifice my own health just to make you feel better about choking me, I promise."

He snorted a laugh. "That actually *does* make me feel better. I don't want you to hide something like that from me. Then I can't fix it."

A memory flashed. *I have to fix it*. That was what he had said about Essie crying all those years ago. I eyed him over the rim of my glass as I took another swallow. "You've been an old man since the day you were born, haven't you."

"I'll take that as a compliment." He snagged his underwear from the floor.

"You don't have to go," I said, setting the glass on the table. "It's barely morning. The sun's not even up yet."

"Staying isn't a good idea."

He buttoned his jeans, then leaned down to cup my face in his hand. When he tilted my head, I realized he was looking for bruises. I arched an eyebrow at him. "Anything?"

"Not yet."

He tugged his shirt on over his head. I sighed. That was that, I guess. The end of the best fuck of my life.

He moved to the back door, which exited to a fire escape behind the bar, and paused with his hand on the knob. "You know where to find me."

He didn't even pretend he wanted my phone number. I tried not to let that sting. It wasn't like I didn't know this was a one-time hookup. Hell, I *wanted* this to be a one-time thing. Sure, for my ego's sake, it would have been nice if he had at least been interested in something more. But I didn't have time to date.

I smiled. "I'll call you," I said glibly.

His eyes searched my face, but I couldn't make out his expression in the dim light. I hoped that meant he couldn't read mine, either.

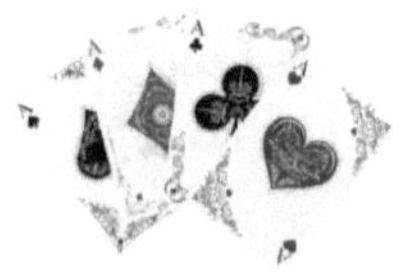

THE HOUSE WAS dark and still as I slipped off my shoes and shrugged out of my coat, wincing at every crinkle of fabric. I padded silently across the marble floor of the mudroom —the bane of their housekeeper, Maria's, existence—and zigzagged up the stairs. Muscle memory guided my feet between the creaky spots. Dad wouldn't be awake yet, but Mom was putting on her face right about now and she'd expect me to do the same before we all convened in the breakfast room at the appropriate time—which, according to my mother, was 8 a.m., 8:04 at the absolute latest.

Maya and I had our own place in Aspen Springs, but we spent almost as much time at my parents' ranch because free child care was not something I could afford to pass up as a single mom, even if that generosity came with strings. I had already showered and washed off my makeup at the one-room apartment above the bar, where Brax let me crash on nights I closed, but I knew my face needed a solid fifteen minutes of effort to meet Mom's standards. Still, I bypassed my old bedroom in favor of the room next to it with butterfly stickers all over the door.

"Hey, ladybug," I whispered as I slipped inside.

Maya was awake, sitting cross-legged on her bed, still wearing her frog pajamas, her red curls ratted from sleep. If I had been home last night instead of getting railed by my best friend's brother, I would have braided her hair before putting her to bed. Maya wouldn't let anyone but me touch her hair. My throat burned, but it had nothing to do with Jack's hand. It was straight up mom guilt. I always crashed in the upstairs apartment on nights I closed the bar, but normally that meant going straight to sleep, not getting my brains fucked out.

The guilt always hit especially hard when I had actually enjoyed myself. *Ah, motherhood.*

Maya turned her serious eyes to me, her gaze landing just past my cheek. "Mother," she said as gravely as a six-year-old with a missing front tooth could, "I don't wish to alarm you, but there are over eight thousand species of amphibians, and none of them start with X."

I bit back a grin. *I don't wish to alarm you.* Where the heck had she picked that one up? The radio, maybe, or a TV show. Or maybe she'd overheard it in a random conversation somewhere. It had been her phrase of choice for about three weeks now, and I figured we had another month at least before she moved on to something else. She didn't always use it correctly. The last time she didn't wish to alarm me, it was to inform me that it had started to rain.

But this time, she had it right. Eight *thousand* amphibians, and not a single one that started with X? Fuck my life, and fuck scientists for not predicting that one day there would be a child whose sole ambition in life was to write the *Ultimate Guide to Amphibians A to Z*, and would therefore need an amphibian that started with X. That seemed like the sort of thing a bunch of dorks should have at least *considered*. I was absolutely alarmed.

I sighed, pulled my phone out of my pocket, and immediately consulted the internet, even though I knew Maya wouldn't be wrong. A short list popped up. I skipped the top two I had no chance in hell of pronouncing correctly. "Xenopus coptodon," I said. "It's a type of frog."

"That's the Latin name. Our book uses common names. X won't be the same as the other letters if we use the Latin name," Maya said.

"Then it will just have to be different," I said.

I tossed my phone aside, grabbed the detangler and hairbrush from the vanity that Maya had never once sat at, and handed her the squeeze toy filled with colored oils. She hated having her hair brushed—it was the sound of it more than the feeling—but we had a routine that made it more bearable for both of us.

"Different is good," I encouraged. "I like different."

Her lower lip trembled, a sign of an impending meltdown. For someone who didn't easily recognize emotions in others, she sure did have some big feelings of her own. "I don't like surprises. I don't like different."

My chest tightened. Maya didn't like different, but Maya *was* different. Watching her attempt to categorize herself into a neat and tidy box like she was a new species of amphibian broke my heart a little. Honestly, her autism diagnosis six months ago was a relief because at least now we had a label. Maya fucking *loved* a label.

"We have three options, ladybug. There is not a magical fourth option where you discover a new amphibian and name him Xylophone. Okay?" I liberally sprayed her head with detangler and then tackled the knots, starting with the ends. "One, you can decide *not* to do *Amphibians A to Z*. You could do butterflies or bugs or not do a book at all. Two, you can use all Latin names, if there are Latin names for all the letters." I had my doubts. "Three, you can use common names for every letter except X, and only X will have the Latin name."

Maya squeezed her toy, not saying anything. Blue globs

of oil floated upwards. I second-guessed myself, triple-guessed myself, quadruple-guessed myself while I gently stroked through her curls. Maybe I shouldn't have given her a choice. Maya struggled with making decisions. But she couldn't go through life letting other people make her choices for her, could she? Maybe I should have given her only two options. But she was smart; she would know I had left something out. I wished I had a manual. Something to tell me how to be a perfect mom for the person I loved most in the world.

Autism is a spectrum, her doctor had said. *There are similarities between children but no one-size-fits-all approach.*

So many paths. So many ways to fuck up a kid who deserved nothing less than everything. So many mistakes I had already made—the biggest one being her dad, but somehow, I couldn't bring myself to regret it, not even a little bit. Because it brought me *her*.

"Option three," Maya said finally. She squeezed her toy again.

"Great," I said. "Xenopus coptodon it is." I knew this wasn't the end of it. When we got to X, Maya would struggle again. But that was a problem for future Janie. One thing at a time.

"Mother," she said. "I don't wish to alarm you, but I would never name an amphibian Xylophone."

5

———

JANIE

"My fucking brother got himself fucking shot."

Shit. My needle slid through the linen fabric and straight into my finger. I kept my head down as Essie stormed into the library multipurpose classroom with all the energy of a very grumpy tornado. You'd think I'd be a good liar by now, considering I'd been practicing since the day I found out I was pregnant with Maya. Unfortunately for me, I had never figured out how to let a falsehood past my lips without looking like my entire ass was on fire.

Fucking inconvenient, actually.

Mostly I solved that problem by keeping my mouth shut. It was better to say nothing at all than spill the truth. I might be a terrible liar, but I was great at keeping secrets. So I clamped my lips around my pulsing finger while my friends made a fuss over Essie's announcement.

"Is he all right?" James Campos was on her feet in an instant. She pulled Essie into a tight hug. James was engaged to Essie's husband's older brother, Adam. They also worked together at Lodestar Ranch training quarter horses for ranch work and the show ring.

"He's fine now, which is good because I want him in perfect health when I murder him," Essie grumbled. She tossed her rainbow-colored hair in annoyance and dropped her embroidery bag by the empty seat next to me. "It happened three months ago. Months! He was in the hospital for weeks and didn't tell us. Fucking *Jack*."

I clamped my teeth around my finger and focused on the pain so I wouldn't say what I was thinking. *He's not fine.*

"Wow." Chloe Adams rested her hand on her growing belly. "Is he home now? What happened?"

Essie dropped into her chair with a huff. "He just got back yesterday." I stabbed my finger again at Jack's lie. *Dammit.* "And he's already leaving again. Can you believe that?"

My head jerked up. "Jack is leaving?" I blurted out. "But —" *But he can't just give me the best orgasm of my life and walk away like it never happened.* I clamped my teeth so hard it was a wonder I didn't break a molar.

It was a one-night stand. I knew that going in. Had I checked my phone a hundred and twenty-seven times in the twenty-four hours since he'd left my bed, just in case I'd missed his call or text? Yes. And that meant I'd been disappointed a hundred and twenty-seven times. Which was stupid because I hadn't even given him my phone number. People didn't exchange phone numbers after a meaningless hookup.

Pull it together, Janie.

"Yeah, he's heading to Wyoming tomorrow. Mom is heartbroken." Essie's slumped shoulders told me Cat wasn't the only one hurting at Jack's quick retreat. "Apparently he has some friends with a ranch south of Yellowstone National Park. A bunch of old military buddies. He's going to stay with them for a couple weeks and be back for Christmas."

Hannah Bell, the librarian and ring leader of our sewing circle, pushed her glasses up the bridge of her nose. "Wait...Mercy River Ranch? Is that where he's going?"

"I think that's the name he said." Essie pulled out her embroidery project and settled it on her lap. "You've heard of it?"

Hannah nodded. "It's my brother's ranch. It's sort of a half-way house for ex-military. A lot of them struggle with returning to civilian life after leaving military service. Mercy River is a place where they can pause and take a breath while they figure it out."

"Huh." Essie's brows pushed together. "That's not Jack. He doesn't pause."

My throat itched. I knew, deep in my bones, why Jack was leaving again. He needed to take a breath because he had nearly squeezed the breath right out of me. "Everyone needs a break now and then."

"You're not wrong," Essie admitted. "But it's hard to picture Jack actually relaxing, you know? He's like a damn robot. He just *goes*." She sighed as she pulled a stitch taut. "And I miss him, that's all. I wish he would stay longer."

"He'll be back soon," Chloe reminded her. "This is a good thing he's doing. So many people in the military refuse to get help."

"So many cowboys, too," Hannah murmured, wrinkling her nose to fix her glasses because her hands were full of embroidery. Then she smiled. "Fortunately, they come to their senses with a little push."

Essie nodded. "The good news is that once Jack is home, he'll be home for good. He's fully discharged from military service."

I hunched over my embroidery project like it was the only thing that mattered. Jack Price could walk through that door right now or never come home at all. It was all the same to me.

My face burned. God, I was such a terrible liar.

Even when I was only lying to myself.

6

JACK

Five months later

MOM

Can one of you stop at the grocery store this afternoon?

ESSIE

Why am I on this group text? I don't live there anymore.

JACK

No problem. Text me your list.

MOM

Aren't you in town today, Essie? You could just swing by while you're doing your other errands. I only need a couple things.

JACK

Mom, I said I'd do it.

MOM

Essie doesn't mind.

ESSIE

Essie does mind, actually. Sorry, Mom.
Better ring the bell and warn the village
folks the monster is coming.

SHEESH. You make a grown man nearly piss himself one single time, and suddenly everyone treats you like a live grenade. So maybe I was—my temper was short-fused these days—but Chuck Gains was the dumbass who pulled the pin.

Maybe I should have felt bad that Chuck had bought me a beer, and I'd repaid his generosity by scaring him so badly he'd spilled his all over himself, but I didn't. If you're not ready to find out what it feels like to kill a man, then don't ask the fucking question. Chuck had been an asshole all through high school, and he was still an asshole now.

The only thing I felt bad about was that Janie wasn't at the Painted Cat that night. A good thing, it turned out, because if choking her in her sleep had her running scared, then witnessing that little display would have been a sign to keep right on running.

That had to be why she hadn't called. I'd left the ball in

her court that night, and if she wasn't interested, we'd leave it at that. But when she didn't call, that stung. We had something. A spark, chemistry, whatever the fuck it was that made two people home in on each other like magnets. We had it.

For months, I'd avoided the Painted Cat, not wanting to corner her while she was working. I'd figured we were bound to bump into each other at some point anyway. She was Essie's best friend, and Aspen Springs wasn't exactly big. But it never happened.

Fine. I had never been young enough to play those kinds of games. Janie Belmont wanted nothing to do with me. I could accept that. I didn't like it, but I could accept it.

I cruised past two Subarus squaring off over a prime parking spot and claimed a space in the empty row at the back of the lot. By the time I was parked and walking back to the store, Sarah Gottlieb and Jerry Wilson were out of their cars and still arguing despite the fact that they were both parked close to the door.

I popped the collar of my coat up to my jaw, pulled the brim of my ball cap lower on my face, and quickened my stride, but no such luck.

"Jack!" Sarah called.

I hunched deeper into my coat and kept going like I hadn't heard her. Undeterred, she jogged to catch up with me, arriving at my side out slightly out of breath.

"You look different," she observed. "I almost didn't recognize you."

Probably because I hadn't gotten a haircut since I was

discharged months ago. It was shaggier than the short military cut I'd been sporting since high school.

I grunted, not slowing my pace. She had to hustle to match her shorter legs to my much longer stride.

"Can you believe that guy?" she huffed. "He stole my spot. My signal was on and everything!"

Irritation made my muscles feel too tight for my skin. "There's plenty of parking," I pointed out.

She sniffed. "It's the principle at stake. I was there first and my signal was on."

"So?"

"So?" she echoed. "What do you mean, *so?*"

I scrubbed my hands down my unshaven jaw. I didn't have the patience for this. Transitioning to civilian life from the military was a rough adjustment for almost everyone, but especially for those who had served in the special forces. Life on the outside was different. Less structure, lower stakes. I had expected that.

But damn.

I hadn't expected it to be so fucking *stupid*.

"You can't let people get away with stuff like that, right?" she pressed.

It was the last straw. We were at the glass doors and if Sarah followed me around the grocery store, nagging at me, I would lose my shit. I needed to end this before someone called my mom.

"I don't fucking care, Sarah," I said impatiently. Her eyes widened. "You both found parking spots, and then you kept arguing about something that doesn't fucking matter. You wasted each other's time. You wasted your own time. And now you're wasting *my* time. Look at my face, Sarah. Do I look happy about you wasting my time?"

Her gaze darted around my face, and she licked her lips nervously. "N-no."

"So stop." I snagged a cart and pushed through the sliding glass doors, ignoring the whispers behind me. It was the same shit everyone had been saying behind my back since I came home for good.

He's not the same guy anymore. The military changed him.

He's dangerous.

He has PTSD.

He needs therapy.

I snorted and headed for the dairy aisle. They were wrong—on all of it. I was the same guy now as I was back then. The military didn't change me; it gave me an outlet. I wasn't dangerous, although I could see a day in the not-so-distant future when I might become so, if people didn't stop walking so damn slowly all the time. I had bad dreams sometimes, but I didn't have PTSD, and I saw a therapist once a month, thank you very fucking much.

I just couldn't make myself care. About any of it. It was like a gauze curtain hung down over everything. I could see the mountains and land and people I loved through the haze, but nothing felt real. Home was right there in front of me, but I couldn't touch it, no matter how hard I tried.

For the first time in my life, I was lost.

Mountains had a way of putting things in perspective. The Rocky Mountains that lined the horizon to the west of Aspen Springs had witnessed the end of dinosaurs and the rise of humans. Births and deaths, all the wars and shifting borders—the mountains had seen it all and did not give a fuck about any of it. Everything was small from the perspective of a mountain.

That was how I felt. Like a goddamn mountain. I had zoomed out so far I couldn't figure out how to zoom back in again.

I wanted to. God, I wanted to. I would give my entire bank account to fucking give a damn about *something*. Anything.

After putting away the groceries, I took off for a hike. It was April and there was still snow in the mountains, so I stayed at lower elevation and followed the river. Two miles in, where the river crooked, I sprawled out, leaning my back against a large boulder. It only took a moment for the cold granite to penetrate my coat. It should have been uncomfortable, but instead it was a relief. At least I felt *something*. I tipped my head back against the rock and closed my eyes.

I stayed like that, the babble of the river and the breeze in the aspens luring me closer to sleep, until the soft fall of footsteps jolted me from the brink. I cracked one eye opened and saw a haze of red.

"Are you dead?" a child's voice demanded.

I opened both eyes. A little girl, maybe six or seven, I wasn't a good judge of these things, stared back at me with mismatched eyes that made me squint a little to make sure I wasn't seeing things. Nope, they were definitely two different colors. Her right eye was hazel and her left eye was blue.

"Oh, you're alive." She shook her head, her red braid bouncing, looking crestfallen.

"Sorry to disappoint you," I said.

"It's all right," she said. "I'm sure I'll see a dead body someday."

That shocked a laugh out of me. "Do you *want* to see a dead body?"

"Yes. I don't think I'll like it, but it would be interesting."

"You'll see one eventually," I said. "Most people do." Of course, usually it was the body of someone you loved. A parent, grandparent, or spouse. Probably better not to mention that.

Her head tilted and she looked off to the side. "Have you ever seen a dead body?"

"Yes." Hundreds, probably. I didn't keep count.

She looked to the other side. "Did you like it?"

"No."

My fingers dug into my thighs as I waited for her next question. What the hell was I going to say if she asked me whose body, or how, or any of the other questions a little kid had no business getting answers to?

But she didn't ask. She just nodded like that was enough.

The breeze kicked up and she twirled away from me, her arms stretched out like wings. I stared at her red braid whipping in the wind. *Déjà vu.*

"Are you a bird?" I asked.

"Don't be ridiculous," she scoffed. "I'm a girl."

I laughed, but shit—she was a girl, and too young to be out here alone. "Are you lost?" I asked.

"No," she said.

I tried again. "Where's your mom? Or...your dad?"

She lowered her arms and slowly turned around again. She looked sideways, her eyes narrowed suspiciously. "I'm not supposed to tell strangers personal information."

"Maya! I told you not to go further than the rock. You scared me."

Red hair. Brown eyes. A mouth I couldn't stop thinking about.

"I'm at the rock." Maya pointed to the rock I leaned against. "I didn't go past it."

She looked, then did a double take. A flush climbed her cheeks.

A slow smile spread across my face as I looked up at her. "You finally found me, Ace. What took you so long?"

7

JANIE

That was twice now that Jack Price had stolen my breath. He didn't need a hand on my throat; his words worked just as well. *What took you so long*? The audacity.

I gaped down at him, my mouth flapping open like a hooked fish as I took in all six-foot-two-inches of leanly muscled, gorgeous man sprawled in front of me. That sexy little smirk playing in the corner of those full lips he had once pressed against my core and made me come undone. Blue eyes sparkling up at me like he was remembering it, too. And then he winked at me.

Winked.

It was a little much, to be honest.

I wrenched my gaze away with an aggravated huff. My gaze landed on the river and I blinked, suddenly disoriented as a memory surfaced.

This was my sanctuary, the place I ran to when I needed to cry or scream or just get my bad out. I had been coming here for so long that I had almost forgotten that it was also the place I had met Jack for the first time. Right there, where the wide, straight river curved in a deep bend like it had a sudden change of heart. I had stood right there with my arms stretched like wings, and—

"Speaking of salamanders, Mother, I'm going to look by those rocks," Maya said.

I shook off the memory and smiled at my daughter. *Speaking of* was her new favorite phrase, but she hadn't quite gotten the hang of it yet. *Speaking of*, she'd say, and then fill in the blank with whatever she wanted to talk about.

"Go ahead," I said. "Stay where I can see you." Maya had a habit of wandering off toward whatever interested her. Fortunately, she wasn't very quick about it.

I pretended I couldn't feel the weight of Jack's stare on me as I watched her amble to the rocks. My skin prickled. When I couldn't take it another second, I looked back at him. His eyes were sharp, all traces of laughter gone.

"Mother?" He tipped his chin. "Something you forget to tell me, Janie?"

"Yes. You're a father," I deadpanned. "Congratulations, daddy."

The shocked, stricken look on his face made me burst into laughter. "Did the marines not teach you math? Maya is almost eight, Jack. I'm pretty sure I'd remember if we'd had sex eight years ago." Sex with Jack wasn't something a woman was likely to forget. I felt sorry for every man who came after him, not that there would be one anytime soon. "You're off the hook. *This* time," I teased.

"Not a marine." He smirked. "Anyway, if you're going to smack me in the face with my worst fear, maybe you can forgive me for forgetting how reality works for a minute."

My head tilted. "Knocking up a one-night stand is your biggest fear?" Jack had been in the special forces. He had been shot, stabbed, and nearly killed, but being a dad was what scared him? It shouldn't have even made his top ten. Oh, lord, he was a commitment-phobe. Of course he was. The hotter the man, the bigger the douche. And Jack was really fucking hot.

"Not knocking up a one-night stand. Having a child I wasn't there for. That's my worst fear." He shook his head, tsking softly like he was disappointed in me. My stomach dropped. "Come on, Ace. You're friends with my sister. You know my dad walked out on us and didn't even bother to show up for her wedding."

"Shit," I mumbled. He was right. I *had* known that. Now I was the one who was a douche. "Of course you have daddy issues."

"Essie has daddy issues," he corrected. "I have something to prove."

"Oh." I looked away. Maya's red curls bobbed as she squatted by a boulder. My heart squeezed. Every child should have a dad like that, a dad hell bent on showing up for her. I swallowed the thickness in my throat and stole Maya's line. "Speaking of rivers, please excuse me while I go jump in one."

I spun away, not to go jump in the river even though that was what I deserved, but to hunt salamanders with Maya, but I didn't make it a single step before Jack wrapped his large hand around my ankle like a shackle.

"Hey!" I protested. Good lord, the man was quick as a snake and even more lethal. At least rattlers gave a warning before they struck.

"It took you seven months to find me. You think I'm letting you walk away now?" With a low laugh, he tugged me off balance. I tumbled backwards, yelping like a deranged poodle—and fell straight into Jack's waiting arms.

And that was the *third* time Jack had made me breathless. I sucked in air and glared at him like my stomach wasn't swooshing with butterflies. My hands curled around his biceps. There was no give when I flexed my fingers. Solid boulders. "You know, I'm getting really tired of you knocking the wind out of me," I groused.

He considered me with serious blue eyes. A girl could ruin her life over eyes like that, over the way they made her feel so seen.

I was so damn good at ruining my life.

But now there was so much more at stake. There was Maya. And I'd be damned before I let one of my bad decisions hurt her again.

"Is that why you didn't call me?" he asked. There was no defensiveness in his voice. No censure, either. It was just a question and, coming from him, it didn't have a right or wrong answer.

"No," I said honestly. "I didn't call you because it was a one-night stand, and because you ran away to Wyoming for a solid month without saying goodbye, and because you know what? *You* didn't call me, either, and…what are you doing?" I asked, because he had shifted our bodies as I talked, bending one of his legs so I was cradled sideways in his lap facing Maya's direction, his other leg as my backrest.

"Making sure you have what you need. A view of Maya and solid lumbar support."

"Solid lumbar support?" I echoed incredulously. I sounded offended. Like his consideration of my needs was a personal affront. It wasn't how I actually felt about it, but since the way I felt was marshmallow goo, offended was what I was going with. Safer that way. "I could just sit on the ground, you know," I pointed out.

He shrugged. "No need to get your jeans dirty."

"I'm out here specifically to hunt salamanders with a seven-year-old," I said. "Getting dirty is part of the whole mom gig." I moved to slide off him, but he held me still. I twisted my neck to glare at him.

His eyes glinted back at me with silent laughter. He raised an eyebrow. "You've sat on my dick, Janie. I think you can handle sitting on my lap for a couple minutes."

I bugged my eyes out and gasped theatrically, slapping my hand across my heart. "You can't say things like that to me. I'm a *mother*." But I couldn't keep a straight face and let out a loud cackle.

"She can't hear us." He squinted in Maya's direction

and shook his head. "You're a mom...shit. I didn't see that coming at all."

Annoyance stiffened my spine. Maya was the most important thing in the world to me, but that didn't mean she was the *only* thing. I was a mom, yes, but I was also a human being, dammit. "Why, because we had a one-night stand? Right. Moms aren't supposed to enjoy sex." I rolled my eyes. "I've got terrible news for you about how babies are made. Some kids even have siblings."

He snickered. "I think it was the nipple piercings, actually. Can't say I've met any moms with nipple piercings before."

"That you know of," I deadpanned. "I've always suspected Mrs. Christianson has a little *something* under her clothes."

Jack looked aghast. "Our old biology teacher? She's sixty."

"I'll let you in on a little secret, Jack." I put my face inches from his. "Grandmas have sex, too."

"*Janie.*"

I giggled and his gaze dropped to my mouth. The tip of his tongue swiped the center of his bottom lip. My whole body pulsed in response. Jack wasn't going to kiss me, not with Maya hunting salamanders a few yards away. He wasn't brash or irresponsible. He was a strait-laced tier one operator who followed the rules.

Me, on the other hand. I was a problem. I knew better than to trust myself that close to Jack's mouth.

I scrambled off his lap like it was on fire, pushed to my

feet, and lifted my hand to my forehead like I was shielding my eyes from the sunlight when I was really just trying to hide my flushed cheeks. "I wonder if Maya has found anything yet."

I heard him stand and the crunch of his footsteps behind me, but I still jumped a little when he said, "You know why I didn't peg you as a mom? You didn't mention Maya once. Most parents can't shut up about their kids."

Right. That. Slowly, I lowered my hand, but I still didn't look at him. "The situation with Maya's dad is… messy. But it's my mess and none of that is her fault. I don't want her to be punished for my mistakes. There's a lot I'm not allowed to say, so I tend to not say anything at all. It's easier that way. So, yeah, I didn't tell you." I blew out a breath and turned to face him, hugging my arms around my rib cage. "Does it really matter, though? I mean, it's not like we're dating. I get how that wouldn't be fair to keep that kind of secret if we were actually in a relationship. But it was just a one-night stand."

His head cocked. "Does it have to be?"

I blinked. "Well…yeah. Obviously."

"It's not obvious to me. So how about you explain it."

"Because I'm a *mom*."

"I've had it on good authority that moms have sex." He smirked. "I don't see a problem."

I threw up my hands, exasperated. "*Time* is the problem, Jack. Not sex. Do you know how long it had been since I'd had sex when you walked into the Painted Cat that night? Three *years*. I don't have time to date. I barely have time to brush my teeth. I *really* don't have time for a whole ass relationship."

His gaze flicked from me to Maya and back to me again, his eyebrows knit into a dark, heavy slash. "I like you, Ace."

It was a punch in the gut, how easily he said that. Showing his cards like he had nothing to hide. Maybe that was easy to do when you always had the winning hand. I imagined he didn't get rejected often. *Never* would be my guess.

I shook my head. "You don't even know me." Because he didn't. Not really. And if he did...well, he'd probably be disappointed.

"I know enough to know I want to know more." I started to speak, but he cut me off. "I'm not asking you on a date, so don't waste your breath turning me down. All I'm saying is let's hang out sometime. You. Me. Maya, if you're okay with that. The occasional one-night stand whenever you want." His lips quirked when I smacked his arm. "Casual. No pressure. We'll just get to know each other."

Get to know each other? I wasn't sure how I felt about that. I narrowed my eyes. "Are you friend-zoning me?"

He snorted. "I hate that phrase. We're not just friends, Janie. But if we can't even be friends, we sure as fuck can't be something more."

I considered that. "All right," I said finally, even though I wasn't entirely sure what I was agreeing to. Friendship with the hazy, far-off possibility of something more? A good dicking every once in a while? Sure, why not. It wasn't like I was irrevocably signing a contract while I was too hopped up on painkillers to hold the pen steady. I could handle Jack Price.

"Mother," Maya called. "I found one."

"Coming," I yelled back. I offered Jack a half smile. "Duty calls."

I headed for Maya without looking back. I heard him move and figured he was heading back down the trail.

"Salamanders, huh," he said, squatting down, and I realized he hadn't left at all.

He was right there beside me.

8

JACK

Mr. Owen Hitchins
Strawberry Rhubarb

WAS IT MY IMAGINATION, OR WERE THOSE TEENY TINY hearts over the i's? I narrowed my eyes at Mom's neat, precise handwriting on the label, then shifted to compare it to the pie label next to it. No hearts. Maybe I wouldn't have noticed, but Mr. Owen Hitchins had taken Mom out two weeks ago and she hadn't come home until ten o'clock. On a fucking *weekday*.

I knew Owen. He was about ten years older than me, which made him five or six years younger than Mom. A widower with a couple kids. Fuck that. She'd already raised kids. Now it was her time to have some fun. Without

Owen, preferably. Hell, she was enlightened, wasn't she? She didn't need a man to have fun. Maybe she could take up embroidery with Essie and her friends.

"Jack!" Mom's exasperated voice cut through my thoughts. "If you do something to his pie, I will turn you over my knee. You're not too big or too old. Now, get Anna McIntire's pie like I told you. She's always in a hurry and I don't want to keep her waiting when she gets here."

It didn't surprise me that she could read my mind. Mom always knew when I was up to something. With one last glare at Owen's strawberry rhubarb, I slid Anna's turkey pot pie from the shelf above and shut the refrigerator glass door with my foot.

"You're not going to spank me," I said, delivering the pie to her waiting hands. "You didn't even spank us when we were kids and deserved it. You're definitely not going to start now."

"Kids *never* deserve it," Mom snapped back. "They're still learning how to be decent human beings, and the one lesson they absolutely *don't* need is that might makes right. Adults don't have that excuse, and that makes them fair game for walloping."

I couldn't argue with that.

The bell over the shop door jangled and Anna, looking harried as was to be expected, given that she had three kids at home and a belly round with another on the way, rushed in. She halted abruptly when she saw me and ran a hand over her hair like she was trying to remember if she had brushed it.

She hadn't.

"Jack! Hi!" she greeted me.

"Hi, Anna."

I couldn't stop staring at her belly. We'd gone to school together—she had been two years behind me—friendly, but never all that close. It shouldn't hit me like this, seeing her pregnant. But, shit. She was on her fourth. Most everyone I had grown up with in this town had all settled down and popped out at least one kid.

Except me.

I didn't even want four kids, but I still felt left behind. Like I was all alone at an empty train station, waiting for the last train home. Disconcerting for a man who lived by the motto that if you weren't five minutes early, you were already late.

"Don't worry, I'm not due for another three weeks," Anna said as Mom rang her up, because it was becoming clear to everyone that her stomach was making me nervous. "My water isn't going to break all over your clean floor."

I laughed. "If I don't see you again for a while, congratulations. Your baby is beautiful."

I hated standing around, so I grabbed a towel to wipe down the tables. I knew it drove Mom batty that I was here at all, but the way I saw it, she could use the free labor at Sweetie Pies, and I needed something to keep myself occupied when I wasn't at Lodestar Ranch. Sleep only came easy when I had worn my body down to complete and utter exhaustion.

The door jangled again, followed by the tap of high heels on the wood floor and the soft scuff of sneakers. Nothing Mom couldn't handle on her own. I focused on the table, rubbing hard at a sticky spot.

I felt eyes on me and glanced up to find Janie's daughter considering me from the other side of the table, head tilted and eyes shrewd like I was a specimen under a microscope. "Maya." I scanned the room but only saw the back of a woman in a calf-length black pencil skirt, her ruddy brown hair tucked in a French twist. Definitely not Janie. "Where's your mom?"

"At work." Her eyes focused on my shoulder. "That's my grandmother over there with Miss Cat. She picks me up from school when Mom is working."

"I see." I swallowed my disappointment. "Are you here for pie?"

"Yes, but not for today. Miss Cat is catering our party next weekend."

I wondered what the party was for, but before I could ask, Maya asked, "What's your favorite dinosaur?"

"Bold of you to assume I have one," I said. At her crestfallen expression, I hastily said, "T-rex." It was the only dinosaur I could think of. Admittedly, my knowledge didn't run deep.

It was the wrong answer. Judging from her expression, the T-rex was worse than not having a favorite dinosaur at all.

"Oh," she sighed. "Boys always say that."

Clearly I had been found lacking. I suppressed a grin. "You don't like the T-rex?"

"I like all dinosaurs, of course."

"Of course," I agreed.

"But the T-rex is very basic."

Well, shit. That might have actually hurt my feelings.

"What's your favorite dinosaur?" I asked.

She straightened. "Triceratops."

"I know that one. The one with the shield and horns, right?"

"Right. It's for protection. They were vegetarians, but I bet they had a temper. Animals with horns tend to be ornery, I think. Like a rhinoceros." Her serious eyes, one hazel and one blue, darted to mine and then away again. "Don't ever fuck with a rhino."

A bark of laughter burst out of me, at this very serious child saying *fuck* like an adult while imparting wisdom I'd be unlikely to ever need. "I'll try to remember that."

She nodded crisply. "You should."

My gaze shot to the clock on the wall as something occurred to me. "What time does your mom get off work, Maya?"

"Five-thirty."

It was three-thirty now. That meant Janie would be at the Painted Cat for another two hours. I doubted she had many customers right now. Maybe she'd like some company.

Suddenly I was in the mood for a drink.

WHEN I SAUNTERED into the Painted Cat, Janie was bent over the bar as she doodled something in a sketchbook, her heart-shaped ass reflected in the vintage mirror. She glanced up as I claimed the stool in front of her.

"Jack." She straightened. Her gaze shifted to the clock near the door. "Long day?"

Most people who frequented the Painted Cat before 5 p.m. were either perpetually drunk or having a rough day. The farmers and ranchers of Aspen Springs didn't have time for a leisurely midday beer, especially not in the spring. "Nah. Thought I'd stop by and see my friend, that's all."

She glanced doubtfully at the four patrons, none of whom were sober. "Saul?"

"You, Janie."

"Oh. Hello, friend." She grinned and braced her arms on the bar. "What can I get you?"

"Whiskey. Neat. Mid-shelf is fine." With two hours to kill and no intention of wasting my time with Janie drunk, I'd sip it slow. My gaze fell to her sketchbook. "Frogs?"

"It's a Maya project." She grabbed the Maker's Mark and a glass. "She wants to write a kid's encyclopedia. *Amphibians A to Z*. She's writing it and I'm illustrating. We're up to D now. That's Darwin's frog." She jerked her chin toward the sketchbook as she poured. "I'm practicing."

I studied it in the dim light. It was a simple pencil sketch, no color, but incredibly detailed and lifelike. "What's with his throat? Is he eating flies?"

She laughed. "No. Those are his babies." She tapped the drawing with the eraser end of her pencil. "That's the cool thing about Darwin's frog. The males carry their tadpoles in their vocal sacs. Swallow them right in there, and then six weeks later, a bunch of baby frogs hop out of their mouths. It's a whole new angle on the spit or swallow question."

I nearly choked on my whiskey. "*Janie.*"

She blinked her big doe eyes back at me. "What? You know your mind would have gone there eventually. I just helped it along."

It didn't take much to get a man thinking about blow jobs, that was true. My gaze fell to her smirking mouth. *Spit or swallow?* She could do either and all I'd feel was grateful.

Janie pushed away from the bar and moved to the far end, where a grizzled farmer I didn't recognize had finished his beer. He watched her pour another pint from the tap, his leering gaze glued to her chest. I spun on my stool to fully face him and stared, hard, until he felt the weight of it and dragged his eyes from Janie's tits. And then I kept right on staring while he shifted nervously. There were twenty-seven bones in the human hand, and I wanted him to know I was thinking about breaking every single one. He hastily grabbed the glass Janie set down in front of him and buried his face in it, but I didn't let up until she was back at her sketchbook.

"Stop it," she hissed. "You're scaring the customers."

I glanced around. The energy had shifted. The same four men who had been relaxed and loose on their stools were now stiff and fidgety. Even old Saul looked like he was considering making it an early day. I couldn't say I cared. Some of the customers needed a little scaring to put them on their best behavior.

I turned back to Janie. "You work alone?"

"Only for the afternoon shifts. We're not busy enough for Brax to pay two people. Someone else is usually here to close with me on Friday nights."

"Usually." My eyes narrowed as I remembered. She had been alone here the night of the snowstorm. "But not always."

"Not always," she conceded. "It's fine."

"It's not fine because it's not safe. What if something happens?"

She made a big, dramatic show of looking around the room and then back to me with raised eyebrows. "Like what? Some drunk guy tries to cop a feel but only manages to fall off his barstool?"

My brow furrowed. "Did that happen?"

She gave a little shrug. "Maybe."

My blood pressure ratcheted up. "Janie—"

"Oops, that's my phone." She held up her finger to

silence me as she pulled her phone from her back pocket. "Gotta take this."

I glowered.

She flashed a teasing grin back at me as she cradled the phone between her ear and shoulder. "Hey, Essie. Your brother is being a menace at my place of work. Want to come get him?"

"Jack is there?" I heard Essie's voice loud and clear through the phone.

"Sure is. It would be great if you could change that for me." Janie twirled a lock of copper hair around her finger and twisted away from me, leaning her hip on the bar.

"Hang on," Essie said, and then her voice was too muffled to hear.

I folded my arms across my chest, eyes narrowed, as Janie murmured, "Ohhh, really? Who?" She straightened and mouthed to me with exaggerated, silent words. *Your mom has a date.*

I lunged across the bar. "Essie!" I barked into the phone. "Do not let Mom give him free pie! Do you hear me? No free—"

Janie snatched the phone back. "I'll handle him, don't worry—" She smacked my hand as I reached for her phone again and pivoted out of reach. "Gotta go. Bye!"

I had my own phone out before Janie turned around again. It went straight to Mom's voice mail. Frowning, I pushed to my feet.

"Sit your ass back down, Jack," Janie ordered. "Let your mom have some fun."

I made a face, but I sat. I didn't want to leave her alone here with no one but Saul for protection, anyway. "I don't like this guy. He's too young for her, plus he's a widower. He wants a maid, not a friend. Someone to help raise his two daughters. That, and free pie."

Janie snickered. "Have you seen your mom, Jack? She's hot. He's not there for the free pie. It's a different kind of pie he's interested in."

"*Janie.*" I took a deep swig of whiskey, hoping the burn would set fire to the image she had put in my mind, but no such luck. "What a terrible thing to say."

Unrepentant, she smirked at me over her shoulder before squatting next to the cabinet behind the bar. "I like it when you say my name like that. All disappointed daddy." My dick twitched. Her voice dropped a couple octaves as she growled, "*Janie.*" Then she giggled and slapped the deck of cards on the bar between us. "All right. What are we playing?"

"War," I said. I needed something fast-paced to keep my hands occupied.

Because right now, the only thing I wanted was to have my hands full of *her*. The trouble was, I already knew exactly how it would feel. I didn't have to wonder if her breasts would overflow my palms—I'd already tested it. I didn't have to imagine the noises she would make when I teased her—those little breathy moans were already ingrained in my brain.

We're just getting to know each other, I'd told her.

But my hands already felt like they did.

9

JACK

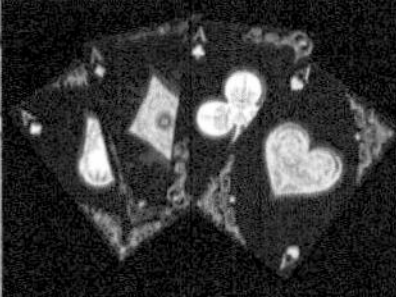

I WAS LIVING THE DREAM.

A horse beneath me and nothing but wide-open blue sky above me. The sweet smell of the Colorado mountains in springtime. Birds chirping, bees buzzing, cows lowing. Men I respected by my side.

This had always been my plan. Join the military, have the adventure and purpose I craved, and—when the time was right—return home to Aspen Springs, settle down with a family, do cowboy shit at Lodestar Ranch. Now here I was, doing exactly that. Living the dream. *My* dream.

I was bored out of my fucking mind.

I stared out at the valley. Hundreds of cows, doing cow shit. Eating, mostly. Occasionally wandering to another part of the pasture to eat some more.

Spring was calving season at Lodestar Ranch, which meant all hands on deck. Even Brax, who was employed by Lodestar as an attorney rather than a ranch hand, was here helping. Lodestar's main business was breeding and training quarter horses, both for ranch work and show-ing, but they kept a small herd of cattle to train the horses and for beef, if there was a surplus. I also suspected there was more than a little nostalgia in the decision, as well. Lodestar Ranch had been in the Hale family for generations as a cattle operation before Ted Hale, who had been like a surrogate father to me, switched to horses.

Horses. Cattle. I wasn't sure there was much of a differ-ence in the mind-numbing sameness of it all, to be honest. I almost wished I was a cow. I'd still be in this damn field, but at least I'd be happy about it.

"Jack!" Adam's voice cut through my thoughts with thinly veiled exasperation. "Did you hear me?"

Normally he reserved that tone for when his son, Ben, was testing his patience. He'd been even worse before James came along, but he was still a grumpy bastard. If Adam were a cow, he'd be the kind with horns. Ornery, like Maya said.

That tone would have had Ben hustling, but I—not being a twelve-year-old boy—took my time giving him my attention. It wasn't like the cows were going anywhere.

"What's your favorite dinosaur?" I asked him.

He stared at me like I really had turned into a cow. His jaw ticked, like he was physically clamping down his irritation at dealing with me. I wished he'd let it out. He'd never held back before. Now everyone tiptoed around me like I was one minor inconvenience away from a total mental breakdown, even the Hale brothers. I fucking hated it.

"Why the fuck are you asking me about dinosaurs?" he asked with strained patience.

"It's a T-rex, isn't it."

"Brontosaurus, as a matter of fact."

I was taken aback by how quickly he had an answer. "What's that? Do they have horns?" I asked.

"Nah. They're the long-necked ones. Traveled in herds." Adam leaned on his pommel. "They remind me of horses."

"Velociraptors are my favorite," Brax said, steering his gelding over to join the conversation. "Clever girl."

I knew what dinosaur he was talking about, thanks to the movie reference. All through middle school and high school—when Brax, Essie, and I had been an inseparable trio—we watched a movie together ever Friday night, and one of those nights had been a full *Jurassic Park* marathon. We still communicated through movie quotes to this day. It was like our own private language.

"Why are you smirking like that?" I asked. "It's creepy."

"Because I know you're not going to like what I say next."

"Then don't say it."

"Oh, but I'm going to." His smirk widened into a shit-eating grin. "I like velociraptors because I've always had a thing for brats. Taming them is a particular hobby of mine."

"I hate you," I muttered.

"Yeah, but your sister loves me, and that's the most important thing."

I would have offered to make my sister a widow, but Zack, the youngest of the Hale brothers, loped between us.

"What the hell is going on here?" Zack demanded, pulling his mare to a stop. "I'm busting my ass out there, and the lot of you are standing around yapping. I don't fucking think so. What are we gossiping about?"

"What's your favorite dinosaur?" Adam asked.

"You know, that's a good question." Zack rubbed his chin. "I'd have to say the pterodactyl. Imagine seeing one of those swooping over the Rocky Mountains. That would be cool as shit."

What the fuck. Everyone had a favorite dinosaur but me?

"How the hell do you all know so much about dinosaurs?" I demanded.

They looked at each other and shrugged. "Ben," they chorused.

"All right," Adam said. "These cows won't vaccinate themselves." The cows had already been vaccinated for scours four months ago, but now that they were two or three weeks away from giving birth, they needed a booster. "Zack, you're with me. Brax and Jack, go west."

He looked at us. "Ready?"

"Hell, yeah." Zack grinned, excitement radiating off him.

He looked so damn *awake*. Like he couldn't wait to get down there with the cows and do his job. They all did. Even Brax, who had never wanted the cowboy life, was grinning. Hell, the horses were starting to prance in place and toss their heads. They knew we were about to work them, and they were fucking eager for it.

Why couldn't I be like that? Just do the fucking job and be happy about it.

I was an ungrateful asshole, because I looked at those fields stretched out before us with all those fucking cows, and it felt like I was digging my own grave.

"WHAT'S YOUR FAVORITE DINOSAUR?" I asked as Janie slid a beer to me across the bar top.

Janie eyed me suspiciously. "Did Maya tell you to ask me that?"

Over the last week, it had become the best part of my day, this quick hour I spent at the Painted Cat sandwiched between working at Lodestar Ranch and Sweetie Pies. I'd grab a single beer, and we'd play a round or two of cards, if she wasn't too busy.

"No, but she asked me mine and wasn't too impressed with my answer."

Janie laughed. "She didn't like mine, either. I told her I liked the one from *Jurassic Park* that spit venom, and she said it wasn't even real and I should know better than to trust what I see on TV."

"Well, she told me the T-rex was basic." It still rankled, honestly. "I didn't even care about the T-rex before she said that. It was the only one I knew. But I looked it up." I took a swig of my beer, then wiped the foam from my mouth. Her gaze tracked the movement, pupils dilating slightly. I pretended I didn't notice.

I was getting good at that, pretending. Pretending we hadn't fucked on a snowy night six months ago. Pretending I wouldn't give my left nut to do it again.

"Apparently, the T-rex was smart as hell," I said. "Sure, they looked a little funny, with that big ass head and puny little arms, but they had giant brains. They hunted in packs like wolves. So, you know what? Hell, yeah, the T-rex is my favorite dinosaur and I'm standing by that. Tell Maya that for me."

"Sure," Janie said with a roll of her eyes. "Should I add a little neener-neener-neener and blow a raspberry, too?"

"She called me basic, Janie. I'm not basic." I leaned forward. "I'm *exceptional*."

"Please don't ask me to respond honestly to that. Your ego doesn't need stroking." She rolled her eyes again, but her cheeks pinked up.

Damn. I would have given her the password to my bank account to hear her thoughts out loud. My ego didn't need stroking, but something sure did.

She propped her forearms on the bar in front of me with a conspiratorial grin and tapped the back of my hand with her index finger. "I'll let you in on a little secret, Jack. Maya doesn't give a shit about dinosaurs."

"What?"

"Yeah." Janie nodded. "Maya cares about three things. Amphibians are her one true love. She also likes Princess Diana and flags, but not with the same intensity, and sometimes she forgets about Di altogether. The days when I don't have to listen to 'Candle in the Wind' on repeat, those are good days. Anyway..." Her voice trailed off with a little shrug. "Yeah, she doesn't care about dinosaurs."

"Then why did she ask me what my favorite dinosaur was?" I asked. I pictured her serious gaze studying me and shook my head.

"It's how she relates to people, I guess." Janie glanced around the room, noted the lack of clientele, and moved to the cabinet where she kept the cards. "When she wants to be friends with someone but doesn't know how, she asks them about dinosaurs. I honestly don't know where it came from, but somehow she got the idea that everyone loves dinosaurs. She's not wrong, that's the thing. It works a lot better than trying to talk to people about frogs. People really don't have much to say about frogs."

She dropped the pack of cards on the bar between us, her lowered gaze obscured by the dark sweep of her lashes. But I could see tension in her jaw and the firm press of her lips. Someone had hurt Maya's feelings, and Janie hadn't forgotten that. I had the sudden feeling that *I* wasn't going to forget it, either, and I hadn't even witnessed it. I wanted a name and an address so I could rectify whatever wrong had been done.

"She likes you," Janie said. Her dark eyes shifted back and forth between mine, like she was searching for an answer there.

"I like her, too," I said honestly. Mostly what I felt these days was annoyance. Boredom. Maybe a little bit of anger when people made their petty problems *my* problem. But I didn't feel that way about Maya or Janie. I felt...curious. Interested.

"Good. Because we can't be friends if you and Maya don't get along."

I tipped the bottle to my lips. "We get on just fine. She's wrong about the T-rex, that's all, and I need you to tell her that."

"Real mature, soldier." Janie rolled her lips together like she was holding in a laugh.

"Not a soldier," I reminded her.

"Oh, right. You're a cowboy now."

Cowboy. It didn't feel right, having that title directed at me. It didn't fit. I jiggled my knee. "Yeah," I said gruffly.

Janie studied me, head tilted, all that pretty copper hair tumbling over her shoulder. "You don't sound too happy about it."

All I could muster was a grunt. I didn't want to say the words out loud. I didn't want to be another whiny asshole venting his stupid problems to the hot bartender.

"Jack." She lightly flicked my knuckles.

"I get to watch the sunrise over the mountains every morning. I spend the day on horseback—which I love—in the fresh air. I work with people I care about and respect, and they're good to me." I stared into my beer. "Nothing to complain about."

"Hm." She fidgeted with the cards but didn't shuffle. "I get that. You have everything. A thousand people would trade places with you in a heartbeat, but they'll never get the opportunity. It feels ungrateful to say that this amazing life that you're so fortunate to have is maybe not for you."

The way she was able to so clearly articulate what was in my head made me look up. Her expression was open and curious. There was a softness in her dark eyes, but it wasn't pity. She looked at me like she cared. More than that, like she *understood*.

"Is that the voice of experience?" I asked.

She squinted at me quizzically. "I can't tell if you're being facetious."

I squinted right back at her. "What do you mean?"

"Jack." She sank her hands on her hips. "You know my last name is Belmont. As in, Belmont Ranch and Cattle. You know my family has more money than they could spend in five lifetimes. Are you honestly going to sit here in my bar and tell me you never once asked yourself why I was serving drinks instead of...oh, I don't know...literally anything else? I thought tier one operators were supposed to be observant."

"*Your* bar, huh?" I muttered into my beer, mostly to cover my shock. Because no, it had never occurred to me to wonder why Janie Belmont, of all people, was slinging drinks at a dive bar.

She pursed her lips. "Yes, Jack, *my* bar. Where I work. I understand that your best friend owns the place so you think it's yours, but I'm the boss here. Not you. But my point is that I expected better of you. Pay attention, Jack."

I loved that she was giving me shit right now. No one gave me shit except Essie, and even she had eased up since I'd come home for good. Everyone in this town either fawned over me like I was some kind of hero, or they were scared of me. But Janie didn't fawn over me, and she definitely wasn't scared of me—even though she was the only one who actually had a reason to be.

My eyes locked on hers. "I'm paying attention now, Janie. Tell me why you work here."

She stuck her tongue out like a bratty child. "Well, now I don't want to."

This time, I didn't pretend I was looking anywhere but right at her. "That's okay. It doesn't have to be today. We have time."

Days, weeks, months, years. For once, the thought of it didn't fill me with dread.

Because time meant more time with Janie.

10

JANIE

CLAIRE

If you don't walk through that door in 10 minutes, I'm coming to get you.

JANIE

Traffic! I'm almost there

CLAIRE

What traffic? Aspen Springs only has two traffic lights.

CLAIRE

You're still in the shower, aren't you.

JANIE

15 minutes, istg. Is Nisha coming with you?

CLAIRE

> Are you kidding? The terms of our prenup state two events a year. Any more than that is grounds for divorce. I'm not wasting one event on a frickin' garden party. I'm saving it for something that really makes us suffer.

MY SISTER HATED THESE FANCY FUNDRAISING PARTIES AS much as I did, but she was so much better at them than I was. It was such a joke that she was two years younger than me, because she was born with eldest daughter energy, whereas Mom still warned me to get my bad out first so I wouldn't embarrass her in front of her friends and Dad's business associates.

But this time, my parents would have nothing to complain about. I had stayed up late reading everything I could get my hands on regarding the farming bill that was scheduled for Congress before the August recess—that would make Dad happy. And then I had chosen an outfit that even Mom couldn't find fault with. *What would Claire wear?* I'd asked myself. Wide-legged tan trousers, point-toe flats, and a silk blouse in a deep aubergine that comple- mented my pale skin and red hair. I'd even tied my hair back in a low ponytail to imitate her nineties-era pixie crop.

"Oh, my god, are you cosplaying me?" Claire cackled. "I love it! It's like looking in a mirror."

I twirled so she could fully admire the outfit. "Mom is going to approve, right?"

"You look *gorgeous*."

"You have to say that. I look like you."

If I were three inches taller, ten pounds slimmer, had skin that never freckled, and hair shaded a sedate auburn instead of ostentatious copper, that might actually be true. But even if I had been born her carbon copy, I still wouldn't have her spirit. There was just something about Claire that made people smile.

Claire squatted down to greet Maya. "Hello, my love. Is it a hugging day?"

"No," Maya said bluntly without the slightest trace of empathy.

"Then I'll wave." Claire wiggled her fingers and then rose to her full height.

Most days were not hugging days for Maya. I had to hand it to my family. They might trample all over my boundaries, but they respected Maya's. Of course, we had never been a physically affectionate family anyway, so Maya's aversion to touch was an easy cross for them to bear. The days where Maya attached herself to me like Velcro were honestly much harder.

"You're late, Jane."

Mom glided into the foyer in a belted midi dress and low heels, her hair—the same dark-red shade as Claire's—tucked into an elegant chignon. It was only when she air-kissed my cheek that I got a faint whiff of her gardenia perfume. Mom had a holy horror of strong scents. *No one should ever smell you coming, even if you smell like a flower garden*, she always said. *It's gauche.*

"I'm not," I protested. Even the earliest guests—the ones hand-selected to arrive first with talking points memorized so that the VIPs would be entertained by a party in full swing from the moment they stepped foot on the property—wouldn't be here for another twenty minutes.

"You still have to get dressed, which means you *will* be late if you don't hurry. Maya, darling, Maria will be around, and she'll get you a snack when you're hungry. I left a puzzle and brand-new sticker book for you in your room."

Maya's face lit up. "Amphibians?"

Mom's nose twitched ever so slightly. She didn't approve of amphibians. "Princess Diana."

"Oh. All right." Princess Diana was another one of Maya's special interests, but this one my parents actually approved of.

Maya made a beeline for her room. Mom turned to me, seeming surprised to find me still standing there. "I laid out an appropriate outfit on your bed. Hurry, please. Guests will be arriving any minute."

"Mom, I am dressed." I gestured to the pants and blouse I had painstakingly selected with her taste in mind. "Look at me."

With an impatient sigh, she looked me up and down. "No. Go change."

My heart sank into my shoes. Dammit. I had actually tried this time. "What about Claire?"

Mom looked at Claire and smiled. People couldn't help but smile at Claire. "Lovely, as always."

Claire's eyes darted to me, her forehead pinched. "I'll come with you, Janie—"

"No." I shook her hand off my arm and turned back to our mother. "We're wearing the exact same outfit. The only difference is Claire's blouse is navy and mine is purple."

"Claire looks like Katherine Hepburn. You look like a hobo," Mom snapped. "Trousers don't suit you with those hips. Go change."

I wasn't going to win this one. I never did, when I went toe-to-toe with Mom. She didn't need to hold all the cards; she held the only one that mattered. Maya. Feeling like I was twelve again instead of a full-grown adult, I stormed up the stairs, Claire at my heels.

"At least Mom has good taste." Claire she shut the door behind us with a quiet snick. I would have slammed it. "I mean, whatever she picked out, it will be nice. She won't send you down there in yellow paisley or ruffles."

I ran my fingertips over the fine wool pencil skirt she had laid out on my bed. Claire wasn't wrong. The quality was impeccable. "I really did try to do it right this time."

"I know you did. You should just *stop*, you know? We're never going to make them happy. Don't bend over backwards for people who don't appreciate you."

The *we* was generous. Claire made them happy without even trying. Every boyfriend I brought home was worse than the last, but Claire? They were thrilled when she came out and absolutely beside themselves when she introduced them to Nisha. In their political circles, it gave them clout. I knew it made Claire feel like she needed to shower after fundraising events, but it could have been so much worse.

So, yeah. Claire made them happy just by being Claire. I, on the other hand, couldn't make them happy no matter what I did.

I tossed the trousers and blouse aside and grabbed the pencil skirt, holding it up at eye level. "It looks a little small."

Claire waved dismissively. "You always think you're bigger than you are. I'm sure it will fit."

I searched for a tag to verify that it was my size, but there wasn't one. With a sigh, I stepped into it. I had to wiggle it over my hips and suck in my belly to zip up the side zipper, but once everything was in place, it wasn't too bad. I could still breathe and move. The fabric held me in like a girdle, flattening my belly while enhancing my curves.

When I realized Mom had chosen a button-down top, I groaned. "Why would she do this? I'm not wearing the right bra for this shirt." I would have needed a minimizer to pull this off, but I'd gone with my favorite push-up. Button-downs and I did not get along. My chest always made the space between the buttons gape.

"Yeah, that doesn't look good." Claire eyed me with pursed lips. "Unbutton the top two. That should give you enough extra fabric that the rest of the buttons lie flat."

I did as she said, and she was right. The shirt fit perfectly.

Unfortunately, it made my boobs the star of the show.

Claire's eyes bugged out. "Shit, Janie, you look *hot*. God, I wish I had your cleavage. Just for a day," she said wistfully. "Nisha and I would have so much fun."

Normally I was a huge fan of my tits, but right now I wished I could flatten them. "Mom is going to be pissed if I walk out there like this."

"She has no one to blame but herself," Claire pointed out. "Anyway, maybe having your tits out will be a good thing! Chat up those old ranchers. Milk them for every cent you can." She gave a snort of laughter at her own joke. "Get it? *Milk* them?"

I made a gagging face. "Gross, Claire. I can't decide whether to laugh or puke. I don't want these people anywhere near my boobs."

"Suck it up, my love." Claire nudged me to the door. "With great power comes great responsibility. Use your tits for good."

I LOOKED at all the beautiful people and felt overwhelmed with gratitude that this wasn't my life anymore. There wasn't a single part of me that regretted walking away from all this. The money. The proximity to power. The status. From a distance, it all looked like a good time. But I had lived with it intimately and knew that money came with strings, power was abused, and keeping a high status was dependent on shoving someone else lower.

No fucking thank you.

I was happy with the life I had built. It might not come with a Chanel handbag, but at least it was bought and paid for honestly.

For the most part, anyway.

Jack was here somewhere. Sweetie Pies was catering the event and he had volunteered to help his mom set up. I oscillated between wanting to see him and *not* wanting him to see me. I didn't feel like myself here. But still, I kept my eyes peeled for him as I left the portico and crossed the lawn.

I did a quick turn around the garden with Mom, Dad, and Claire, greeting the early arrivals. Mom had taken in my excessive boobage with a cool nod that made me wonder if it had been her intent all along. *Icky*. Dad had said hello with his usual jovial smile, which he kept glued to his face while he told everyone how much he loved having me by his side every day at the ranch. No one at the party was local to Aspen Springs, and more importantly, they wouldn't be caught dead in the Painted Cat. They had no idea the idyllic picture Dad painted of our family life was a lie.

They didn't know a damn thing about me.

And they definitely didn't know about Maya.

11

JACK

Holy shit, the Belmont ranch was huge—and this wasn't even the part where they kept the cattle. Acres of grass that had no right to look this green and a sprawling house that was more suited to Beverly Hills, California, than Aspen Springs, Colorado. I had known that Janie and I came from opposite sides of the railroad track, but *damn*.

She had been raised with all this. What the hell was she doing at the Painted Cat?

With all those acres spread out before me, it hit me how absolutely ludicrous it was that I had never considered it until she had brought it up. But the truth was, she didn't act like someone who had money. She looked completely comfortable behind the bar in her worn-in Levis and scuffed boots. She handled rowdy customers and their less-than-hygienic bathroom habits without batting an eye—all right, she batted an eye and bitched a bit, but she still did her job. She dealt with whatever came her way. She never tried to shove the more disgusting parts on someone else.

She fit there. She didn't fit here.

At least, the Janie I knew didn't fit here. But maybe I didn't know Janie all that well, after all.

"You can set up the mini quiches over there, if you please, Cat," a woman's voice said.

Since I was holding two trays of mini quiches myself, I looked up. I recognized her from the other day at Sweetie Pies. Maya's grandmother—which meant she was Janie's mother. And behind her—

Shit.

I damn near swallowed my tongue.

Janie.

And her tits.

Janie's tits.

Tits.

"Do you mind if I grab one, Cat?" Janie asked, already reaching for it. "I didn't get a chance to eat before I came here, and I am *starv*—oh, hi, Jack."

Before this moment, I would have said that the hardest thing I'd ever done was BUD/S training. Now? Janie Belmont had raised the bar. Nothing in this world was as excruciating as prying my gaze from Janie's luscious cleavage. I was no better than that creep who had leered at her in the bar.

I dragged my gaze upwards and found her watching me, chocolate eyes glowing with amusement, her lips tilted in a full smirk. I cleared my throat. "Hi, Janie."

"Hi," she said again. She bit off half the quiche and her eyes rolled back. "Oh, my *god*, Cat. These are divine." She popped the rest in her mouth and made another sound of ecstasy.

Shit. My pants were uncomfortably tight now. I could only hope no one noticed I was sporting wood. Just in case, I lowered the trays slightly to block the view.

Mom put a second quiche on a cocktail napkin and offered it up. "Would you like another one before we hand them out?"

"Don't mind if I do," Janie said cheerfully, but her mother got there first, scooping up the quiche before Janie could take it.

"Nothing else is going to fit into that dress, Janie," Mrs. Belmont said. She didn't eat it herself, though. Instead, she folded the napkin around it and tossed it into the trash can behind the table.

Next to me, my mother inhaled sharply. Janie froze. Shock and hurt flashed across her face before both were quickly hidden behind a bland smile. She picked up a quiche and pushed the whole thing in her mouth. Mrs. Belmont's lips thinned as Janie chewed, each movement of her jaw slow and deliberate.

That's my girl.

She wasn't really my girl. It wasn't my place to tell her mother to go to hell, but *fuck*. I wanted to. Even though Janie had just proved she was more than capable of fighting her own battles, I still wanted to fight them for her.

"You look amazing," I said. "Beautiful."

Her eyes softened as she smiled at me. "Thank you. Maya says hello, by the way."

"Is she here?" I craned my neck to search the garden.

"No, she's—" Janie's eyes darted to her mother and she chewed the inside of her cheek. "This isn't really a child-friendly event. She's in the house."

There was a hint of anxiety in her expression. I glanced around the lawn again. Not a single child was present, and I wouldn't have expected there to be. Children weren't known for enjoying political fundraising parties. Janie was telling the truth. So why did it sound like a lie?

"You've met Maya?" Mrs. Belmont asked in tone that suggested she wasn't entirely pleased.

"We—" I started but was interrupted by a blonde server with a tray of drinks.

"Wine?" she asked brightly. "Beer?"

Janie swiped a glass of white with a small smile for the server. "Thank you."

Mrs. Belmont took one, as well. "Small sips," she murmured to Janie. "Remember to treat it as a decoration."

Janie rolled her eyes. "I'm not going to get drunk and embarrass you, Mother."

Mrs. Belmont ignored her and turned to me. "You were saying about Maya?" Her tone was perfectly cordial, but the way her nose wrinkled ever so slightly as she looked me over made it clear she didn't approve of me. "You're Cat's son, aren't you?"

Janie noticed it too, because her eyes narrowed on her

mother. "Mother, you know Jack Price. He was in the paper two years ago, remember? His team rescued the news correspondent who was taken hostage."

"Oh?" Mrs. Belmont's smile was genuine now. It was truly incredible how quickly she warmed up to me now that I was something other than the son of her caterer. She should have been ashamed of herself, but I doubted she was. People like that were never as embarrassed as they should be. "Jack. Of course. My husband will be delighted to meet you. I'll have to introduce you to him."

My stomach dropped into my shoes. The last thing I wanted was to be paraded around a party full of politicians and socialites looking for a photo op with a war hero.

"If I have time," I said. "But right now, I need to help my mother. Janie—"

I blinked at the empty space where Janie's tits had been just a second before.

Janie was gone. She'd escaped while her mother was distracted and fawning over me.

That shameless little hussy.

I MANAGED to dodge Mrs. Belmont for the next hour, but it was hard to hide from the hostess when you had to be literally out in the open with no cover, serving bite-sized hors d'oeuvres to guests who really ought to put something more substantive in their bellies to soak up all the alcohol. When she finally caught me, she and her husband spent the next eternity introducing me to all their friends like some damn show pony.

The worst part was, they were so fucking *nice* now that they had decided I was a worthwhile human being. But I saw how they treated the servers who carried trays just as I had. They weren't rude. They remembered to say thank you about half the time, even if they never looked directly at them. Mostly, the Belmonts and their guests treated the staff and servers like furniture. They were there to serve a purpose. They weren't actually *people*.

But Janie...she wasn't like that. She looked them in the eyes when she said thank you, and when she knew their name, she used it.

Her bright hair made it easy to track her around the party. My eyes went to her again and again.

I wasn't the only one.

Most of the glances going her way were furtive and quick. A few double-takes from men whose wives were quick to intervene. But one man in particular—he appeared to be a friend of her father's—was blatantly leering in way that put my hackles up. The least he could do was be subtle about it like a fucking gentleman.

I didn't like the way he watched her. But I fucking *hated* that he slung his arm over her shoulders like he had every right in the world.

Janie froze, her doe eyes round like saucers as she stared at her father in a silent plea for intervention. My blood pressure ratcheted up as I apprised the situation from a few yards away. Her father wasn't going to let this dickweed get away with that, was he?

Mr. Belmont's forehead knit in a frown. "I—ah—"

Apparently he was. Alarm bells rang in my head. *Are you fucking kidding me?* I strode forward.

Mrs. Belmont cleared her throat. "Charles, why don't you show Todd the stables?"

Mr. Belmont looked relieved. "An excellent idea! Shall we?"

Todd twisted to look at Janie. His nose grazed her hair. "What do you think, Janie?"

And then I watched him slide his palm over her bare cleavage, fingers curving inward along the undercurve of her breast. He squeezed.

I saw red.

Janie's expression went from distraught to shocked to furious. I had a feeling I was about to witness exactly what it looked like when Janie Belmont got her bad out, and as fun as that might be, I was too pissed off to wait for it.

"Remove your fucking hand or I will do it for you," I said lowly, enunciating every word carefully so his single brain cell would understand.

"Janie and I are old friends," he said. "Aren't we, Janie? She's fine."

Wrong answer.

I moved on instinct. I separated his body from hers by brute force, putting my own in between them, and shackled his slim wrist with one hand. A pathetic squeal spilled from his lips as I twisted his hand to an unnatural angle, just shy of making it snap, and drove him to his knees.

"Are you fine, Janie?" I asked, turning my head to look back at her over my shoulder.

She exhaled and dropped her forehead to my shoulder blade. "I am now," she said quietly.

In that moment, I felt it—the thing I had been missing ever since I was discharged. *Purpose.* Someone who needed me. It felt so fucking good.

"Janie," I said, but she didn't break stride as she made for the house like a woman on a mission.

I caught up with her as she pushed through the door. "Janie," I said again. I caught her by the elbow and gently turned her to face me.

"Hm?" she muttered.

The glossiness of her dark eyes made me want to do things. Hold her. Rearrange Todd's face. Possibly her parents', too.

"What the hell was that back there?" I asked. I scanned her face, searching for answers.

"You know what that was. An entitled man-child put his hand where it didn't belong and you corrected that for him." She looked away, her throat bobbing in a hard swallow. "Thank you for that, by the way. I was going to stomp on his foot, but your way was probably better." She gave me a wobbly smile that broke my heart.

"You say the word, Ace, and I'll break every bone in his body. But I'm talking about your parents. What the fuck was that about?"

"Oh." She curled in on herself, one arm wrapped protectively around her waist, the other across her chest. "Todd Yates is a big lobbyist in the ranching industry. My dad will do anything to keep him happy. And my mother... appearances are everything. She believes you don't make a scene. Ever."

I stared at her. "So they were perfectly okay with him touching you like that without your consent? What the fuck."

"They weren't *okay* with it," she said defensively. "They didn't know how to stop it without causing a scene or pissing him off."

"Janie."

"For what it's worth, I was absolutely going to cause a scene."

"I know you were, honey." I pulled her into my arms and rested my chin on the crown of her head. "I know you were."

For a moment all we did was breathe together. And then her hands dropped to my belt.

"Jack," she whispered. "I still want to cause a scene."

12

JANIE

THE LOOK ON HIS FACE AS I STARED UP AT HIM FROM MY knees was priceless. Absolutely fucking priceless. Hungry and desperate and so clearly fighting with himself to do the right thing.

I could not be less interested in doing the right thing.

I tugged his belt through the clasp, but his large hand descended on mine, stopping me.

"You don't ever have to get on your knees to thank me," he roughed out. "Not fucking ever."

"This isn't a thank you," I said, but I wondered if maybe it was, a little bit. I was used to sticking up for myself, with varying levels of success. Mostly I got smacked back down again because truthfully, I was never the one in a position of power.

But Jack. He had power, the kind that no one could take from him. It was carved into every fiber of his being, woven through the muscles and sinew and bone. And he had used it to protect *me*. No one had ever stood up for me before, not even Claire, who was more likely to broker peace than stand by my side in a battle. Watching him put that fucker on the ground made heat pool low in my belly.

"Then what is it?" he asked, his blue eyes finding mine.

"A fuck you to my parents."

The bulge in his jeans made my mouth water. With his hands still holding mine hostage, I used the only tools at my disposal. I nuzzled against him, dragging my nose up his twitching dick, then gently bit him through his jeans. The groan that ripped from his throat was downright feral.

I looked up at him from under my eyelashes as I dragged my tongue over the cotton. "I hope that's okay with you," I murmured.

His hands spasmed against mine. "Someone could walk in."

Well, look at that. I just got wetter. "I hope they fucking do. I hope they see their daughter on her knees, being a total slut for the man who protected her because they were too weak to do it themselves." I smirked. "Who knows, maybe they'll learn something."

"Fuck," he choked out. He caught my chin between his thumb and forefinger and turned my face up. "How can I be this turned on and also seriously worried about your mental health?"

I snickered. "Don't worry, soldier. I'm seeing a therapist." I licked my lips. "I really think sucking your dick could cure me, though."

"*Janie.*"

"Yes or no, Jack. Consent is important." My hands were free now, but I didn't move them while I waited for his signal.

He exhaled roughly. "Fuck. Yes."

"That's my good boy," I purred.

His head tipped back on a groan as I worked the buckle and zipper of his jeans. When I pulled them down, his enormous cock bounced free. Damn, I really hadn't imagined it. For months I'd wondered if I'd built that night up in my head. But no. It truly was a porn dick. I ran my tongue over my teeth and peeked up at him. His eyes were glowing like blue fire as he stared intently back at me.

God, I was going to enjoy making a mess of him.

I wrapped my palm around the heavy length of him and squeezed. His lips parted but he didn't break eye contact. I leaned forward, guiding his dick to my mouth. The head bumped gently against my lips and I felt a dampness there. I parted my lips and swiped the flat of my tongue over his slit, lapping up the drop of precum.

"Fuucccckkkk," he hissed, his hands going to either side of my head. His hips flexed, pushing the crown of his dick into my mouth.

But I wanted more. Palms flat against his muscular thighs, I sucked him deeper into my mouth, taking him so deep that I almost gagged. I paused to breathe, eyes watering, and then took him even further. His fingertips dug into my scalp, roughing up my sleek ponytail. It only spurred me on.

Let him make a mess of me, too. I wanted that.

I pulled back off with a wet popping sound that echoed against the marble floor. My eyes locked on his, taking in the way his broad chest rose and fell on heavy breaths. I leaned over his cock and spit, then rubbed my saliva around the crown with my thumb, loving the way he watched me like a man possessed. And then I went right back in, suctioning my lips to his dick with a hum of satisfaction.

And he fucking lost it.

Groaning my name, his hips snapped forward. "God, your mouth. So fucking perfect. You're perfect, Janie."

My mouth was too full of him to answer, but I sucked harder because I fucking loved hearing him say that. No matter how hard I tried, I could never be the perfect daughter. I wasn't a perfect mother, and god knew I had given that my all. But here, on my knees, Jack thought I was perfect.

Maybe a blowjob really could heal me.

His thrusts turned frantic, his breathing choppy. "Fuck, Janie, I'm going to blow. If you don't want my cum down your throat—"

But that was exactly what I wanted so I gripped his thighs for dear life and pulled him in. His cock twitched against my tongue and then it happened. One burst and then another and another. He growled my name as his cum filled my mouth. I swallowed down every drop. His thighs trembled as he slowly released my hair.

And okay, fine, it didn't actually cure me.

But I sure did enjoy the hell out of trying.

13

JANIE

CLAIRE

What the heck happened at the party yesterday?

JANIE

I didn't give a special forces operator a blowjob in the foyer, that's for sure

CLAIRE

I can't tell if you're joking. You're joking, right?

JANIE

winky face

CLAIRE

I still can't tell if you're joking

CLAIRE

Dad just paid a gossip columnist to kill a story. Is the story about a blowjob?

JANIE

No, that would be Todd Yates being an absolute piece of shit.

CLAIRE

That's old news.

THE PARTY WENT LATE, SO MAYA AND I SPENT THE NIGHT AT Belmont Ranch. Mother was her usual cool, collected self as she bid us good night. Neither of my parents said a single word about the incident with Todd, and when I tried to bring it up, Mother held up a hand to silence me.

"Not tonight, Jane. If anything needs to be said, it can wait until the morning. I'm simply too tired to deal with this now."

It was hard to say whether I was more relieved or angry at their lack of response. Remembering the feel of Jack thrusting into my mouth as he growled, *You're fucking perfect, Janie* helped a lot, though. I let it play over and over again in my mind as I got myself off under the silky Egyptian cotton Frette sheets that cost more than two weeks' pay.

The next morning, I discovered I had twin bruises on my knees, courtesy of the foyer's marble floor. Honestly, I wasn't mad about it.

Maya was awake and waiting for me when I slipped into her bedroom next to mine.

"Morning, ladybug," I said. "How did you sleep?"

"Good, but I want to go home now." She handed me her brush, her squeeze toy ready in her other hand.

"After breakfast, okay? Alice is making us French toast."

With a sigh, Maya nodded. It didn't take long to do her hair. I had braided it before she went to sleep, so it was easy to comb through and then redo the braid, Maya's preferred hairstyle. We arrived downstairs at precisely 8:01, a mere twenty seconds after Mom. Dad was already at his office. He didn't believe in weekends.

We murmured our good mornings as we sat down to plates already heaped with French toast and berries. Mom didn't deviate from her bowl of oatmeal and plain yogurt, with blueberries on top. She had eaten the same thing for breakfast every day for the last forty years. It was the secret to keeping her figure trim in middle age, and she never hesitated to remind me that it could do the same for me, as well.

"Yesterday's event was a success," Mom said as she spread a white linen napkin across her lap.

"That's great," I said automatically, concentrating on my food.

Mom took a dainty bite of oatmeal, then slid a white envelope across the table to me with two fingers. "Sign that before you leave, please."

"What is it?" I asked, wiping my hands on my napkin

before I picked it up. My eyebrows pushed together as I scanned the contents. My gaze shot to hers. "Mother... what is this?" I asked quietly.

"An apology." She took a sip of her tea, then dabbed the corners of her mouth with her napkin.

"I see that." The words came slowly as I struggled to contain my rage. "But *why* am I apologizing?"

"For the misunderstanding at the party yesterday, of course."

"I didn't do anything wrong." My voice shook. "Tell me you understand that."

Her lips thinned and she looked down at her bowl. For a terrible moment, I was afraid she would deny it. But then she sighed, and when she spoke, her tone was conciliatory. "I agree with you. Todd was out of line. He'd had too much to drink, and you were wearing that blouse—not that it excuses his behavior. But the fact of the matter is, he was humiliated. Men like Todd Yates do not enjoy being humiliated."

"Perhaps Todd Yates would be less prone to humiliation if he were actually a man instead of a whiny, entitled baby," I muttered.

Mom frowned. "When these things happen, they are dealt with privately. You made a spectacle of him."

Jack made a spectacle of him, actually. But I knew she would never say that. Jack was worth too much. I was merely a façade for my parents. A pretty picture with nothing of substantive importance underneath.

"Sign the card, Jane. We'll send it along with a

Williams-Sonoma gift basket. The whole thing will be forgotten before you know it."

I wouldn't forget it. Not ever.

I glanced at Maya, who was cutting her French toast into equal-sized triangular bites. Her head was tilted in that way she had that told me she was listening to every word. She didn't know what happened yesterday, but she'd know that today, her mom apologized to a man for something she didn't do.

I couldn't do it. I couldn't let Maya think that was an acceptable way to be treated.

"No." I pushed the card back across the table.

Mom's eyes flicked to Maya, and when she turned back to me, there was a calculating look in her narrowed gaze. "I am asking you for a favor, Jane. I would think you would be happy to do something kind for me, considering everything I do for you. Such as taking care of Maya while you're working this summer. It's not easy to find childcare for someone with her needs, is it? Not in Aspen Springs."

My chest tightened. No, it wasn't easy. It was damn near impossible, actually. "I thought you were watching Maya because you love your granddaughter and want to spend as much time with her as possible," I said, struggling to keep my tone light.

"Of course I love Maya. I love you, too, and I know you love me in return. We're family. Part of being family means looking out for each other and doing what needs to be done, even if it's uncomfortable." She sipped her tea. "Sign the card, Jane."

Not for the first time, I wondered what it would be like to have a family where love was just love and didn't come with a million strings attached.

14

JACK

ESSIE

Are you at Sweetie Pies?

JACK

Got here ten minutes ago. What do you need?

ESSIE

Is there any apple pie left? I picked Maya up from school today, and it's her favorite. I thought I'd drop by and get her a snack and then take her to the Painted Cat.

JACK

There's a slice left. I'll set it aside for her.

"Are you sure you don't mind?" Essie asked. Her gaze bounced from me to Maya and back again.

"I told you, it's not a big deal," I said. "I was going to the Painted Cat anyway. And Maya likes me. Don't you, Maya?"

Maya looked sideways. "You're all right."

"See? She thinks I'm fantastic."

"That's not what I said." But the look she sent her shoes was almost a smile.

Maya had finished her snack, and I'd been all set to offer to walk with them to the Painted Cat when Mom asked Essie to stay so they could catch up. I suspected Mom was trying to force me out the door a little early, but since extra time with Janie suited me just fine, I didn't mind. She didn't work Sunday, but I'd texted her yesterday. Her reply had been short: *I'm fine.*

Since I had never known a single person to say I'm fine and mean it, I was immediately concerned.

"You know, you've been spending an awful lot of time at the Painted Cat recently. I see your truck parked there nearly every day." Essie pursed her red lips, studying me. "You're not trying to self-medicate your PTSD with alcohol, are you?"

I blinked at her. Nothing subtle about my twin. "Jesus, Essie. I don't have PTSD. I told you that."

"Then why are you drinking in the middle of the day like a statistic?" she demanded.

"Maybe because it's the only place where no one treats me like I have PTSD," I snapped back.

"Hmph." She tossed her hair, the rainbow-dyed ends

gleaming in the afternoon sunlight. Her eyes narrowed. "Remember how you said you were going to sleep with one of my friends to get back at me for marrying Brax?"

I crossed my arms. "What of it?" I asked, though I suspected I knew. Essie was too observant for my own good. If she'd noticed my truck parked at the Painted Cat in the afternoons, then she'd also noticed I wasn't there on Sundays. Coincidentally, neither was her best friend.

"Maya, cover your ears," Essie instructed. Maya obediently placed her palms over her ears. "You know, there's a saying."

I sighed. "What's that?"

"Don't fuck with single moms."

"Or rhinos," Maya piped up, because hands over ears were not really an impediment to eavesdropping.

Essie laughed. "Words to live by, Maya." She wasn't laughing when she turned back to me. "All of them."

JANIE DIDN'T LOOK surprised as I pushed open the door to the Painted Cat and Maya walked in ahead of me. Essie must have called her to let her know the change in plans. Her cheeks flushed as our eyes met, but she quickly turned all her attention to her daughter.

"Hey, ladybug. How was the pie?" she greeted her.

"Good." Maya climbed up on a stool like she'd been

there before. "Cat said to tell you hello." She cocked her head. "Hello."

Janie smiled. "Thank you for relaying that message. I'll make sure to tell Cat you did so the next time I see her." She leaned over the bar, hand outstretched like she wanted to smooth Maya's hair, but when her daughter gave a brisk shake of her braid, Janie withdrew. "So. What are you in the mood for today? Do you want to go to the apartment upstairs and read a book, or do you want to stay down here with me?"

Maya looked around. It was quiet today, as it was most Monday afternoons. "I'll stay."

"Great." Janie pushed back from the bar, then squatted at the cabinet. When she popped back up, she had her sketchbook in her hand. "I practiced some axolotls this afternoon. Let me know what you think. Do you want a glass of water?"

"Yes, please. With my special straw."

"You got it." Janie filled a glass with water from the tap and topped it with a pink acrylic straw. "Here you go."

With Maya taken care of, Janie finally looked my way again. "Anything for you, Jack? Or are you just dropping Maya off?"

"I'll take a beer." I didn't specify which one as I slid onto my usual stool. I'd been a regular for a couple weeks now. She already knew. "I'm staying."

I watched her grab a Yeti stout from the beer fridge. She didn't seem like herself. Her shoulders rounded slightly; her chin drooped. Her normal energy was replaced with something much more subdued. The change made me nervous, considering everything that had gone down on Saturday.

She slid the bottle toward me without making eye contact. On impulse, I grabbed her wrist. She blinked up at me like she was surprised to see me sitting there. "Jack."

"Hey." I studied her. "What's going on?"

"Oh, you mean with Maya? My mom told me two hours ago that she wasn't available to pick up Maya from school. Luckily, Essie was on her way back into town from Lodestar so when I called Brax to tell him I might have to close the bar for an hour, she offered to help. I don't know what I'm going to do tomorrow, though. Or—" Her voice broke.

"I can pick up Maya. I leave Lodestar at two. That's plenty of time to get her from school. She can hang out with me at Sweetie Pies, or I can bring her here."

She stilled, her dark irises widening. "Are you serious?"

"Yeah. Of course." My eyebrows went up as I stared back at her from over the rim of my beer bottle. "Why wouldn't I be?"

"It's a lot of responsibility, that's all." She fidgeted with a loose thread on the cleaning rag.

"I happen to like responsibility." I wasn't just saying that. It was the truth. I enjoyed feeling a certain amount of weight on my shoulders. That weight was what made life matter. It meant *I* mattered. Without that weight, what was even the point?

She laughed softly but shook her head. "Thank you. I really do appreciate the offer, and maybe I'll have to take you up on it for tomorrow, but the truth is that if I don't fix things with my parents, I'm...fucked." She pressed her fingertips to her eyes with a disbelieving laugh. "God, I'm so *fucked.*"

"Ace, *tell me.*" I white-knuckled the beer bottle to keep myself from shaking the truth from her. I couldn't stand to see her like this. So worn down.

With a sigh, she pulled a white envelope from her back pocket and tossed it on the bar between us. I took a swig of beer, flicked open the flap, and pulled out a card with *thank you* embossed in gold calligraphy across the front.

Then I read the contents and the whole world flipped upside down.

I read it again to make sure I wasn't hallucinating.

"Janie." My gaze shot to hers. "What. The fuck. Is this?"

"It's an apology to Todd for the *misunderstanding*"— fury made her choke over the word—"at the party Saturday. My mother wrote it and handed it to me at the breakfast table. She intends to send it with a Williams- Sonoma charcuterie gift basket. Because we're *so* civilized." Her voice dripped with scorn.

My fingers tightened on the card and my forehead furrowed as I scanned the note again. "Your name is at the bottom."

"She reminded me that she will be watching Maya this summer when I'm at work. A favor for a favor, you know." Janie gave a derisive snort. "I told her no. So, today she let me know what it would feel like to be without reliable childcare."

"She threatened you?" I demanded. I couldn't imagine my mom ever pulling shit like this. Even my dad. He was a deadbeat, but he wasn't fucking *evil*.

"It's not a threat. It's quid pro quo. A favor for a favor."

"That's not how families work."

"That's how *my* family works." She was back to playing with the rag. Her teeth strummed her bottom lip as she pulled at the loose threads. "I signed it. I haven't told her yet, but I signed it."

Fury consumed me. "You can't."

"Well, I did." Her hand clenched around the rag so tightly her knuckles blanched. "Principles are great for people who can afford them, but you know what? They've always been too expensive for me. Maya is the only thing that matters. Everything else can be compromised. And... they know that. They know I'll cave. I always do."

The bleakness in her tone made me want to get in my truck, drive out to Belmont Ranch, and make her mom cry. But all I could do was sit there like a useless lump on a barstool. There was nothing I hated more than feeling helpless.

"It would be so much better if I could just skip the drama and not drag it out when we all know how it's going to end." Janie stared off into space, drumming her fingers on the bar. She sighed. "But I never do. I go down fighting, but I still go down. Just have to get my bad out first, I guess."

"I like your bad," I said.

She snorted. "You're the only one."

"There's no one else who can watch Maya this summer?" It was a desperate question. Janie wasn't stupid. If there were another option, she would have thought of it already. "Is it the cost?" A couple of my military peers were parents, and the amount they shelled out in daycare bills was sometimes more than a mortgage.

"Money isn't an issue," she said distractedly.

I blinked. How could money not be an issue? On a bartender's salary, I would have thought money was *always* an issue.

She shook her head. "Even if you picked her up every day this week—and again, Jack, that means a lot, seriously—summer vacation starts in two weeks." Frustration bled into her voice. "I've tried nannies before, but no one worked out. Maya is autistic. She's a level one on the spectrum, which is high functioning, but I haven't been able to find anyone who could handle her long-term. They're usually out at her first meltdown." She blew out a slow breath. "If I had more time, maybe I would have been able to find someone from out of town. Someone in Denver or wherever who had experience with kids like Maya. But it's too late."

Maya was autistic? Should I have known that? I didn't know much about autism, but it was hard imagining Maya having a meltdown of any kind.

Janie's gaze cut to her daughter at the end of the bar and her whole face softened. "She deserves the whole world. I can do this. I can swallow my pride and apologize. As long as I know the truth, isn't that what really matters?"

The words were quiet, spoken more to herself than to me. She wasn't looking for my agreement. I hoped.

Because she sure as fuck wasn't going to get it.

An idea popped into my head. Adrenaline made my heart pump faster, excitement coursing through my veins. *Operation Fuck Those Fucking Fuckwads.* God, I loved a mission.

She was still looking at Maya, all that love shining straight at her like a tractor beam, when I picked up the card and ripped it in half. Then I stacked the sides together and ripped it again. Shit, that felt good. Satisfying.

Janie paused like it had taken her brain a moment to catch up to what her ears had just heard, and then her head whipped toward me. She blinked down at the card scraps. Her mouth dropped open.

I took a sip of beer. It hit just right.

"Jack! What did you—why—what—" she sputtered.

"You can't apologize to that asshole, Ace. You know you can't."

She slapped the bar top with both palms. "For Maya, I can do anything." She leaned forward, dark eyes blazing furiously. "You have no idea what I'm capable of."

I had some idea, actually. Janie Belmont was a firecracker. And goddamn, I wanted to see her with her fuse lit. But not like this.

Never like this.

Janie deserved so much more than to burn herself up for someone else's wrongs.

"I told you I don't have another option," Janie hissed.

"Yes, you do."

"Yeah?" she huffed sarcastically. "What is it?"

I spread my arms wide and leaned back with a self-satisfied smirk. "Me."

15

JANIE

"No," I said. I didn't have to think about it. There was no way. It was too ludicrous to contemplate.

Jack looked at me like he had never heard the word before. Honestly, he probably hadn't. "Okay," he said, like he was agreeing with me, but I knew he wasn't. "Let's plan it out. Tell me all the reasons why it won't work, and we can settle them one by one. We need a battle plan, that's all."

He actually looked excited about it, like this was one of his special forces' missions to rescue an asset instead of babysitting duties. Why was that so damned hot? I looked away so I could focus on what was best for Maya instead of the way his biceps bunched as he folded his arms on the bar.

"In the first place, you have a job," I reminded him. "You're a cowboy, remember? I'm pretty sure Adam isn't going to let you have a seven-year-old tag along while you work cows."

"Nah, he'd probably be fine with it, actually. He's a single parent too, remember? Ben used to do that all the time."

"And even if he *were*," I bulldozed ahead, not letting him prove me wrong with things like facts, "Maya does not want to be chasing cows at sunrise."

"That's fair. I wouldn't ask her to."

Well. Okay, then. I'd expected him to try a little harder and not give up at the first impediment. "Good. So we agree it won't work."

"We absolutely agree that it won't work to mix Maya and cowboying," he said easily.

Too easily.

My eyes narrowed as I studied him. "You realize I'm saying no, right? Why does everything you say sound like you think I'm saying yes?"

He grinned. Smug bastard. He was so damn sure of himself. Truthfully, I envied his confidence. Sure, I was brash, but that was only because I knew the universe would put me in my place either way, so I might as well get a good hit in first. That wasn't confidence. That was stupidity.

"I can't be Maya's nanny and Lodestar's cowboy at the same time. All right. There's a solution to that. I'll quit Lodestar."

He couldn't be serious. Quitting his job to be Maya's summer nanny? That didn't make a lick of sense.

Or...maybe it did.

He wasn't happy there. I knew that much. He'd hinted at it without really saying it. On paper, cowboying at Lodestar Ranch seemed like a perfect fit for him. He hadn't shared why it wasn't, but it was clear that something was eating at him.

"Are you having a midlife crisis there, buddy?" I asked.

I caught him mid-sip, and he sprayed beer across the bar. "Buddy?" he choked out.

"I thought it would be mean to call you soldier. Like rubbing salt in the wound or something." I swiped the towel over the beer droplets, cleaning up the mess.

"It was still mean as hell, Ace. I'm not old enough to be having a midlife crisis. Take it back."

"Could have fooled me with all that gray in your hair." On impulse, I reached out and stroked his hairline at the temple, where silver strands almost outnumbered the dark brown. I liked it. Older guys had always made my stomach flip, unfortunately. Not that four years was much of a difference. "It suits you, though."

The way he looked at me...It was almost a kiss, that look. I could feel the warmth of it on my lips.

I pulled my hand back and cleared my throat. "So. Tell me what's going on at Lodestar."

"Nothing is going on. It's fine. They don't need me. There are a hundred other cowboys looking for work right now who would be more than happy to take my place." He rolled the beer bottle between his palms. "One cowboy is pretty much the same as any other. I'm replaceable at the ranch. But you need me. Maya needs me."

The stark vulnerability in his eyes made me pause. Jack had always been like an impenetrable fortress. Nothing could touch him. But it struck me that *this* was the chink in his armor. It wasn't enough for him to show up and get work done. He needed to be needed.

I chewed my lip, thinking. Maya wasn't paying us any attention at all. One hundred percent of her focus was devoted to my drawings. She was a self-motivated kid. It would be easy to look at her entertaining herself and think babysitting her would be a walk in the park. And mostly, it was—well, not *easy*, exactly, but it was fun and rewarding.

The hard days, though. The hard days were really fucking *hard*.

"Do you have any experience with autistic kids?" I asked dubiously.

"I don't have experience with kids, period. Tell me what I need to know."

I didn't beat around the bush. "Meltdowns. Have you ever seen a toddler having a tantrum at the grocery store? It's like that, but less crying and more outright shrieking and hitting. There is no reasoning her out of it. It's like she can't hear you. And she's not two anymore, so the looks people will give you are horrible."

He looked at Maya, head tilted like he was trying to imagine such a quiet kid going apeshit, and then turned back to me. "Okay. So what do I do about it?"

"Grab her," I said bluntly. "Use your body like a human

straitjacket. Maya doesn't like to be touched, but when she's sick or stressed out or doesn't feel safe, it's exactly what she needs. A weighted blanket will work too, but she prefers something with a heartbeat. You will feel all kinds of wrong at first—like you're torturing her or something—but it's the only thing that works. She relaxes almost immediately."

"Hand-to-hand combat." He pointed his beer at me. "I've been trained for that."

I pressed my lips together. "I don't know if I should find that funny or terrifying."

He stilled. "Are you worried about that?"

"Worried about what?" I asked, not following.

He stared at me for several beats, a steeliness in his watchful gaze. His jaw popped as he finally turned away. "Come on, Janie. I know what people say behind my back. I'm unstable. I have PTSD. I'm going to set something on fire." He met my gaze head on. "I nearly strangled you in your sleep. If you're worried I might hurt Maya, we need to talk about that."

That hadn't even occurred to me. Other than those fifteen seconds—an admittedly terrifying fifteen seconds—I had never felt anything but completely safe when Jack was around, and not just because he had never threatened me with harm. I felt safe *because* he was around.

"Has that...has that happened with anyone else?" Shit, this was awkward. I cleared my throat. "The nightmare strangling, I mean."

"No. But I haven't slept next to anyone since you."

"Oh." My heart fluttered. He hadn't slept with anyone since me. No, wait. He hadn't *slept next to anyone* since me. That didn't mean he hadn't had sex. He could have had sex with a different woman every night and it wouldn't change the truth of his statement.

His mouth quirked as he took another sip of beer. "Haven't had sex with anyone, either. Only you."

"I didn't ask," I said. But a hot flush scorched my cheeks.

"No, but you looked like you wanted to."

I huffed and crossed my arms while my pulse beat out a quick rhythm. *Only me, only me, only me.*

"Well, there was this one lady," he admitted. When I arched an eyebrow like I didn't care, he smirked. "Batshit crazy. Gave me the best blowjob of my life in her parents' foyer. I jacked off thinking about it last night."

I fell forward, stumbling over nothing but air and my own horny brain imagining Jack wrap his hand around his dick and pretend it was my mouth. He reached across the bar and steadied me.

"Janie," he said. All the humor in his eyes evaporated as we stared straight into each other's eyes, his strong hands the only thing keeping me upright. My knees had melted clean away.

"Yeah?" I breathed.

"The only time I'll close my eyes around Maya is to blink." His hands flexed around my biceps. "I swear I'll keep her safe. From everything. Even me."

"I believe you." I shook my head as he slowly released

me and eased back on his stool. "Honestly, it never occurred to me that you might not be safe for her. Maybe it should have. But I always feel safe with you." I looked at Maya and then back to Jack. "*Do* you have PTSD? It's not a dealbreaker. It's just something I need to be aware of."

He snorted. "No. Sometimes I have bad dreams. Not often, but sometimes. That's not enough to diagnose PTSD." He rubbed his jaw and contemplated the ceiling. "I wonder about that sometimes, though. What kind of psycho am I to have seen the shit I've seen and *not* have PTSD about it? But the truth is, it's not as common as you would think, considering how prevalent it is in movies and fiction. It takes a special kind of resiliency to get through combat dive training, and that same resiliency tends to protect us from PTSD, too, I guess." He shrugged. "I see a therapist, but that's to help me deal with the transition to civilian life. It's not because of trauma."

"Okay." I nodded. "I trust you, Jack."

His throat bobbed as he swallowed hard. "Thank you."

"But what are you going to do with a seven-year-old girl all day?" I pushed. "You're going to be so bored."

He chuckled. "I'm not going to be bored. We'll hunt amphibians. Does Maya ride? If she's up for it, we can go trail riding. Or the library. Maya strikes me as a library kid." His eyes cut to her and his lips tilted in a smile. "I could ask her what she wants to do. I bet she'll tell me."

"She will," I agreed. I exhaled slowly and rolled my shoulders, feeling a tiny bit of tension ease. Maybe this could really work. "She does best on a schedule. She hates change, unless she's the one leading it. We should do a practice day so you two can get to know each other better. Maybe Saturday? At my parents' house, we—"

Shit.

How could I have forgotten? I pinched the bridge of my nose.

"What?" he asked. "What's wrong?"

"We spend the night a couple times a week at my parents' house. Any time I have to close the bar. That way I don't have to get her up in the middle of the night and bring her home."

He tucked his tongue into his cheek as he studied me, amusement and something else—something hotter—dancing in his eyes. "So you're saying this is a live-in manny position?"

I groaned. "That's what would make the most sense, yes."

He was outright grinning now. "Sure, Ace. I'll move in with you." He dropped his head, a deep chuckle making his shoulders shake. "To be honest, my mom would be thrilled to get me out of her hair for the summer. I'm driving her nuts."

I stared at him, trying to make sense of how everything had unfolded. Nothing had ever just...worked out for me. I didn't trust it. "I can't believe this is happening. It's so *weird.*"

"It's *good.* Fuck Todd, and fuck anyone who says you need to apologize when some dickweed invites himself into your space." His jaw ticked again, but then his body twitched like he was physically shaking off the bad vibes. He swallowed the last of his beer and pushed to his feet. "I'll pick Maya up from school tomorrow, okay? We'll talk more then and take it from there."

"Okay," I said, still perplexed.

He paused by Maya on the way out the door. "Is it okay with you if I pick you up from school tomorrow?"

She looked up. "Can we get pie again?"

He looked at me. I nodded. "Sure," he said.

"Okay."

"Okay." He rapped his knuckles on the wood next to my sketchpad. "See you then."

And I watched my childhood crush turned one-night stand turned manny walk out the door.

What the hell just happened.

16

JANIE

I WAS AN ANXIOUS MESS.

I waited on my front porch, my hands wrapped around a steaming mug of coffee. I paced the length of the house. I sat on the swing and promptly stood up again. I paced some more. Maya sat on the third step, her knees snuggled to her chest, completely unconcerned that her mother was falling apart at the seams. She liked to give her whole being to whatever activity was at hand.

Waiting, in this case.

In about fifteen minutes, Jack was going to pull into the driveway, and everything would change. From the moment I'd discovered I was pregnant, it had been me and Maya against the world. We were a team. My whole life was built around her. I had no idea how Jack would fit into any of it. Our house, our routines, our lives.

But I was about to find out because Jack's blue pickup truck was rolling up my driveway ten minutes early. Of course he was early. The man had probably never been late to anything in his life.

He pulled up next to my eight-year-old Subaru and got out. Suddenly I had a whole new problem to consider. I gawked as his black work boots emerged first, followed by long legs and thickly muscled thighs encased in faded denim, and an ordinary white t-shirt that must have been made from literal magic because it had that perfect easy fit that somehow still managed to showcase every square of his six-pack.

Black aviators highlighted the way his nose crooked slightly, like it had been broken more than once. As if that wasn't hot enough, he'd added my own personal kryptonite: a backwards baseball cap, glints of silver peeking out near his ears.

Goddammit.

This man was going to live in my house. Eat, sleep, and shower mere feet from me. I couldn't even console myself with the comforting lie that men that hot were inevitably selfish in bed because I already knew that didn't hold true for Jack.

I was fucked.

Jack leaned over the truck bed and hauled two large suitcases over the edge like they weighed nothing. I suspected they weighed at least forty pounds apiece. I pressed my fingertips against my coffee mug like it would keep me from melting into a puddle of goo.

"Morning," he called.

I gurgled unintelligible babble back at him.

"Good morning," Maya said.

He made his way up the walk with a loose-limbed gait that reminded me of a lion, all casual strength and one-hundred-percent certainty of his place at the top of the food chain.

"Ready to have some fun?" he asked Maya as he reached the porch steps.

She considered. "Maybe after lunch."

My stomach clenched as I watched the scene unfold below me. I saw him take in her unsmiling face. There was no hug to greet him, either. I hope he didn't take that personally. The smiles would come in time.

She was actually excited he was here, but I knew how she looked to people who didn't know her very well. I bit my tongue against the urge to tell him that, to smooth their path to friendship and clear the roadblocks of misunder-standing. They needed to figure these things out for them-selves because they would be spending a lot of time together, just the two of them. I wouldn't be around to micromanage their relationship.

But Jack didn't seem to need my interference, anyway. He nodded and kept moving. "Sounds like a plan."

Two steps from the top, he stopped in front of me, putting us at eye level. He set the suitcases down on either side of me. Those full lips quirked as he took my mug from me and lifted it to his mouth. He took a sip and handed it back to me. "It's good. You got any more of that inside for me, Ace?" he asked.

Why did that sound so dirty? "If you...if you want." I couldn't see his eyes behind his sunglasses, and somehow that made me feel vulnerable because he could see every-thing in mine.

"I want," he said, his voice a little husky.

"Why do you call her Ace?" Maya asked. She had gotten to her feet and now observed us with curious eyes.

Maya. Jack's reason for being here. My reason for... everything.

The fog of lust dispersed from my brain at the sound of her voice. I cleared my throat. "We play cards at the bar sometimes. You know how my favorite cards are the aces? That's why he calls me Ace."

Jack chuckled softly as he pulled his sunglasses from his face and hooked them over the collar of his T-shirt. "You think so?"

What did he mean by that? I wasn't a snoop or a crack reporter, and I couldn't think of another reason he would call me Ace.

"I like nicknames," Maya said thoughtfully. "Mother calls me ladybug because of my red hair."

"And because you're cute as a bug," I said.

"That's an opinion. My red hair is a fact." She looked at me. "Do you have a nickname for Jack?"

"Not really," I hedged, not wanting the light of my life to discover what a petty brat her mother was. My cheeks felt hot.

Jack's assessing gaze swept over my face. "She calls me soldier."

"Because you're a soldier?" Maya guessed.

"Nope." He shook his head. "I'm not a soldier."

"Maybe she doesn't know that."

Jack's eyes crinkled in amusement. "Oh, she knows." He lowered his voice to a conspiratorial whisper. "I think that might be why she does it. Just to fu—uh, just to annoy me. She thinks it's fun to tease me."

Maya gasped. She *hated* being teased. She spun to me with an appalled expression. "That's not what nicknames are for, Mother," she chastised me.

My face felt beet red.

"But I like it," Jack said, his eyes on me.

"That's silly," Maya said. "No one likes to be annoyed."

Jack shrugged. "What can I say? I'm a silly guy," said the least silly man ever to walk the earth.

I pressed my lips together and he winked at me.

"Grab your bags," I said. "I'll show you your room."

I HAD SPENT the last week agonizing over the details of moving Jack into our yellow, three-bedroom Craftsman bungalow with as little disruption to Maya as possible. My bedroom was right next to Maya's; Jack would be down the hallway from us both. I moved Maya's stuff into my ensuite so that he could have the hallway bathroom all to himself.

I even cleared a shelf off in the pantry so he could have his own snacks and not feel like he had to share with us, although of course he could help himself to whatever we had available. Maya was particular about food and went through phases where she'd only eat two or three different things before she'd move on to something else, so I made sure he understood the system we had in place that ensured we never ran out of anything, because *whew*. An autistic meltdown was one thing. An autistic meltdown when Maya was hangry was something I wouldn't wish on my worst enemy.

"This is great. You have a really nice home," Jack said, and I could see the question in his eyes.

How did a single mom afford a three-bedroom house with a backyard view of the mountains on bartender tips?

He probably assumed my parents paid the mortgage. But he would be wrong.

"Thanks," I said. "I'll leave you to settle in and unpack while I make lunch. Grilled cheese and tomato soup okay?"

"Sure. Sounds great."

I eyeballed him, feeling unsure. How much did a man his size eat? If I got half a sandwich and three bites of soup into Maya, I considered that a win. I had the feeling Jack required a little more sustenance. "Like...one sandwich? Two?"

He laughed. "One is fine. I ate a big breakfast." He swung a suitcase onto the bed and flipped it open. He glanced up and found me still watching him. "Don't worry, Ace. I'm an adult. I know how to feed myself."

For some reason, I found that hilarious. Maybe because so many of the adult men I had known had no idea how to feed themselves. I doubted my father even knew where the pantry or refrigerator were—although that was partly because they looked exactly like every other cabinet in the kitchen—and it was a safe bet he'd need a map to find the grocery store, too.

"Okay. Are you going to help me, Maya?" I asked.

"No, thank you." She clambered onto the bed and sat cross-legged, her wide gaze glued to Jack like he was a fascinating new species of amphibian.

I lingered in the doorway. Maybe I should insist she come with me. Maybe Jack didn't want company while he got settled in. He rolled his eyes at me and flicked his wrist in a shooing motion. I got the message and headed for the kitchen.

The last thing I heard was Jack say, "If you tell me your favorite frog, I'll tell you mine."

"Fuck," I muttered.

Maya was going to *love* him.

I SAT on the porch swing with an iced tea and a deliciously smutty romance book Hannah had recommended to me, listening to my favorite sound in the world: Maya's happy voice. It was slightly higher pitched than her usual tone, and the cadence was faster. When she was *really* happy, it was hard to get a word in edgewise. Jack seemed to be holding his own, though, and I had to admit his deeper baritone still made me a little giddy.

Maya had insisted on taking Jack all over the yard after lunch. She showed him her favorite rock and the tree she liked to climb. He had seemed a little surprised at that, but in most ways Maya was a regular kid who liked to do regular kid stuff, even if some of that kid stuff was kind of a struggle for her. She saw a physical therapist twice a month for low muscle tone, and that helped. I made a mental note to mention that to Jack later.

There was so much he didn't know. Autism had been a part of our lives for so long that it was second nature now —even before her diagnosis, Maya had been Maya—and I didn't know how to adequately prepare him. It was trial by fire.

Maybe that should have terrified me, but honestly? It didn't. Jack didn't know how to fail. Whatever this summer threw at him, he'd roll with it. I knew there would be rough moments, but hell. Maya had had plenty of rough moments with me. We'd survived. So would Jack.

So far, so good.

Jack had picked Maya up from school every day this week after Essie pitched in on Monday. On Tuesday he took her for pie, but the rest of the days he'd brought her straight to the Painted Cat because I didn't want her to get used to having pie every day. They'd do a puzzle or read books. I took today off from work to get Jack moved in, and we still had another week before school let out. It was a good buffer before Jack became Maya's full-time manny. A low-stakes way for them to get comfortable with each other.

Part of me was still waiting for the other shoe to drop. I felt like I was actually getting away with something. Like I had misbehaved and been rewarded with chocolate cake instead of punished with a spanking. Which was stupid because I hadn't misbehaved—that would have been Todd and his roaming hand—and I sure as hell hadn't done anything I should apologize floor.

Other than defiling my parents' marble foyer, anyway. Which I wasn't one bit sorry about.

"Will you push me?" Maya asked, and I looked up.

They were standing by the huge old oak tree that had

probably been a sapling when the first gold miners had come through Aspen Springs. A couple summers ago, I had tied a tire swing to a sturdy branch. Maya loved that thing. She could go for hours if no one stopped her. It was almost like meditation for her. I pushed to my feet to warn him, but then I sat back down again. He'd figure it out.

"Sure," Jack said, and she climbed on, sticking her legs through the middle and holding the rope just above the tire. He gave her a gentle push to start.

"I don't have a dad," Maya said, like that was a totally normal conversation opener, and I jumped to my feet again, sending the swing flying behind me. "Essie said you don't, either."

The swing hit me behind the knees and I fell back onto it with a heavy thunk. Jack slid his sunglasses a fraction down his nose to peer at me over the rims, noted I was unharmed, and turned back to Maya.

"I have a dad," Jack said. "Not a great one, though. He doesn't come around a lot."

"Does that hurt your feelings?" she asked.

Kids really did just say whatever dang thought crossed their mind.

"It did when I was younger. But now…" He pushed her a little harder, let her go a little higher. "Now I think it's his loss. Someone who abandons their kid…that's not cool. That's a loser. I don't hang out with losers."

Maya's chin tipped as she considered this. "Am I cool, Jack?"

Jack caught the tire as it swung back to him and held it.

"Maya, you're the coolest kid I've ever met." Then he sent her flying.

My throat burned. Shit, he was going to be so good for her.

Her eyes closed in perfect bliss as the wind ruffled the curls that had come loose from her braid. My fingers itched to sketch the scene, so I took a quick photo with my phone to use as a reference later. I wished he could see the look on her face right then. How happy she was. How carefree.

He couldn't see it. But I saw it.

And I would do anything to keep it there.

"WALK ME THROUGH A TYPICAL DAY."

Maya had gone to bed ten minutes ago, leaving Jack and I to hash out the details of our arrangement. Jack relaxed on the swing, his arm stretched along the back but his body contained to his half, making it clear that there was room on the swing for two. I leaned against the porch rail, which happened to be conveniently out of touching, tasting, and smelling distance of the world's most tempting manny. Alas, I could still see him. No matter how much I tried to lock my eyeballs on the twilight blue sky, my gaze kept sliding his way.

"Maya is happiest when we follow a routine. We're not

rigid about it over the summer, but keeping regular meals and rest times helps prevent meltdowns. She's normally up between seven and seven-thirty. I make her scrambled eggs and toast with jam for breakfast. On Sundays we have pancakes. I don't have to be at the bar until eleven, so next week I'll take her to school as usual. You don't need to be on manny duty until pickup time at three."

"I don't mind taking her," Jack offered. "Yesterday was my last day at Lodestar. They've already found a cowboy to replace me, so I've got nothing else to do."

"Thanks, but I try to spend as much time with Maya in the mornings as possible because once I get home from work it's just a sprint through dinner and bedtime. Save your stamina for the summer. Trust me, you'll need it."

At the sound of his deep, rumbly laugh, my eyes darted his way again. Still mouthwateringly hot.

"Ace, I've got more than enough stamina to go around," he said, his voice threaded with laughter.

The memory of him lifting my body against the wall while he kissed me senseless and then tossing me on the bed where he then fucked me senseless made my breath stutter. Yes, the man had stamina. That was undeniable. I stared blindly at the darkening sky while heat scorched my cheeks.

"So what comes after breakfast, once school is over?" he asked, sounding completely unbothered by his accidental double entendre.

Apparently I was the only one with a dirty mind. I really needed to get a grip on the horniness. I couldn't be lusting after my daughter's manny. *Tacky*, my mother's voice whispered in my head. But it was Dad's disappointed silence and the way his gaze never quite met mine that hurt the most.

I folded my arms and pulled myself together. "Physical therapy. She hates it, but it needs to be done. When school is in session, we aim for three days a week. Over the summer, she should be going through the movements most days. She sees a therapist twice a month to check her progress and keep her moving forward."

Jack's forehead furrowed and he sat up straight. "Was Maya injured?"

"No, nothing like that. She has low muscle tone. It's not uncommon in autistic kids." I chewed my lip, thinking over how to explain it to a man who was so clearly physically gifted. "She's not weak, exactly. Her muscles are soft. Kind of, um, floppy? Like a stretched out rubber band. It means she has to work twice as hard as other kids to do things like sit up straight or write a letter by hand. Physical activity can tire her out pretty easily. I have a printout of her PT routine so you can look it over. It's a lot of planks, balancing on one foot, body weight squats, that kind of thing."

"I can do that." His gaze was serious. "I still have my own PT to do. We can do it together."

"Thank you."

He nodded. "Tell me about the meltdowns. What are her triggers?"

"Overwhelm, mostly. Especially when it comes on

suddenly. Like, loud noises, bright lights, lots of commotion. If she's overtired or overstimulated."

"So, fireworks on the Fourth of July is out."

"Definitely." I blew out a slow breath and rubbed the bittersweet ache out of my chest.

The Fourth of July had always been my favorite holiday. I fucking *loved* fireworks and parades, everyone cheering and clapping as we all enjoyed the spectacle together. It had been years since I'd done any of that. Now we spent the holiday inside, watching *Hamilton* for the millionth time. And it was great. I loved our tradition, too.

But I would always be a little sad that I couldn't share one of my favorite things with the person I loved the most.

It was one of the things I never said out loud. Having that thought at all made me feel guilty, like I was betraying Maya in some way.

"She has friends," I blurted out. Okay, that might have sounded a wee bit defensive, judging from the way Jack's eyebrows went up. "I just...I feel like I'm giving you all these reasons to not like her, but the truth is I think she's amazing. She's smart and funny and even though it's really hard for her to see someone else's point of view, she cares enough to try."

"You don't have to sell me on Maya, Ace." He stood and ambled toward me. "I like her. I've liked her from the moment she told me she wanted to see a dead body. I just want to make sure I'm taking care of her the way she needs me to. I want her to have a great summer."

"Okay." My voice wobbled.

He loomed over me, his arms bracketing my body against the railing. "I want you to have a good summer, too."

I could think of a hundred ways to have a good summer with Jack and every single one of them was a bad idea. He wasn't just my best friend's brother. He wasn't just the one-night stand who had a special talent for finding my clit.

He was my *manny*.

I was paying him to take care of my daughter, not to fuck me senseless. And sure, the distasteful power dynamics that came with a parent hooking up with their child's caregiver didn't apply here. I wasn't married. He didn't need the job. He didn't need me at all.

But I needed *him*. Maya needed him.

I couldn't fuck this up.

"Jack." I swallowed hard. "We need to set some ground rules."

"Like, no more than two hours of screen time a day, no dessert before dinner, that kind of thing?"

"No." I exhaled heavily. "Although yes to all of that, actually. But I meant ground rules about us."

"Dammit. I was afraid you were going to say that."

I couldn't help but chuckle at his crestfallen expression. "Because you know it's a bad idea. I can't have random hookups with my daughter's manny. Stability is so important to Maya's wellbeing. I can't risk it."

He studied me, his blue eyes dark in the fading light.

"Of course we can't do anything that would hurt Maya. I would never do that."

I tilted my head, my eyes narrowed. "You're doing that thing again where the words *sound* like you're agreeing with me, but your tone says you're not."

He laughed. "And you said you can't read people. You're doing great."

I huffed. "Jack. We can't—"

"I know what we can't do, Ace. But think of all the things we *can* do."

And then he left me there to think about it.

17

JACK

MATEO
When are you coming to Wyoming? Jay said he made you an offer a week ago.

JACK
September at the earliest. There's this girl.

MATEO
Yeah?

JACK
Red hair and the prettiest eyes you've ever seen. Cool hobbies. Makes me laugh so hard I cry.

MATEO
Bring her! I'd love to meet your girl.

JACK
I don't know how you do things in Wyoming, but here in Colorado, kidnapping 7 year olds is frowned upon.

MATEO

What the hell is going on at that ranch

JACK

Career change. I'm a manny now.

MATEO

Dude.

You're still seeing that therapist, right?

RIGHT??

TWO HOURS INTO THIS WHOLE MANNY GIG AND I WAS crushing it. Breakfast? Eaten. Dishes? Done. Janie? At work on time. Maya? Happy. Hell, she hadn't complained once when it was time for PT. This summer was going to be a piece of cake.

"Is there anything you want to do today?" I asked as I wiped down the wet spots on the kitchen counter. It was the first day of summer vacation and the possibilities were endless. Janie had warned me that Maya didn't always do well with wide-open questions, so I tossed out a few options. "We could go for a hike before the afternoon thunderstorms roll in. Or we could go to the library and pick out some books for the week."

Maya was walking circles around the kitchen table

while I cleaned, like she had nervous energy to work off. It was probably nothing more than the excitement of being done with school, but I'd mention it to Janie this evening, just to make sure.

"Can we go to Denver?" she asked.

Okay, that caught me off guard. "Why?"

"I need to start my summer project. It's the metamorphoses of an amphibian. I'm going to watch a tadpole turn into a frog, but the closest pet store that sells tadpoles is in Denver. Mom said it would have to wait until this weekend when she's not working, but I want to go now."

I hesitated. "That sounds like a cool project, but I think your mom might want to do it with you."

Maya shook her head emphatically, her red braid swinging from side to side. "No, she doesn't. She hates driving to Denver because of the traffic. She didn't want me to ask you because it would make you feel bad if you didn't want to go." Her eyes were big and hopeful. "I have the money to buy the tadpoles and the aquarium tank. It was a birthday present from Aunt Claire."

"Hm." Denver was a two-hour drive each way, and there was always traffic. It would be a waste of Janie's day off—I knew how important it was to her to spend quality time with Maya. Plus, we had switched vehicles so I could take Maya wherever she wanted to go, since Janie didn't like Maya riding in the front seat and my truck didn't have a back seat. It wouldn't be a problem to drive out to Denver.

"Please?" Maya begged. "Mom will be so happy. She does everything. I think she's tired."

Shit, this kid was such a sweetheart. Who could say no to a kid who cared so much about her mom? And she was right. Janie was exhausted. Her time with Maya was too precious to waste spending it in traffic.

"All right. Let's go." I tossed the sponge onto its little tray by the sink and wiped my hands dry on my jeans.

Maya jumped in the air, pumping a fist. It was awkward and clumsy and the cutest fucking thing I'd ever seen. "Yes!"

I laughed. "We leave in fifteen minutes. Grab your headphones and a book. I'll pack snacks."

"We have dart frogs," the sales associate said. He looked about sixteen. His nametag said Dave, but it was the third Dave I'd seen in the store and I suspected either no one was named Dave or the manager was. "We don't have any dart frog tadpoles in stock, but we have leopard frog tadpoles."

"I want a dart frog," Maya said firmly. "A blue dart frog."

I could forgive Dave for looking a little exasperated, since it was the third time she had said that.

"We have blue dart frogs. We do not have dart frog

tadpoles. If you want a dart frog tadpole, I can order it for you. It should be here in about two weeks."

Maya's lower lip trembled. "It has to be today."

"Look, kid, I told you. I have leopard tadpoles and I have blue dart frogs."

"I want a dart tadpole."

"Then I can order it for you. Two weeks."

"It has to be today. It has to be today. It has to be today," she chanted.

Shit, she was in a loop. Janie had warned me about this. Getting stuck in a loop could lead to a meltdown. Janie had given me a few tips on how to interrupt the cycle, and I'd watched her put those into action once last week. *I've got this.*

"Dave," I said, and it took him a beat to respond. Yeah, that definitely wasn't his name. "Give us a minute."

Looking relieved, Not-Dave disappeared toward the saltwater fish.

I spun to face Maya and dropped down to her level. "Maya." I squeezed her shoulders gently to pull her focus to me. I'd left her fidget toy in the car—a mistake I wouldn't make again. "Seven deep breaths. A color for each breath."

She breathed. "Red." Another breath. "Orange. Yellow. Green. Blue." Her gaze shifted to the frogs and I quickly squeezed her shoulders again. "Indigo." One more. "Violet."

"Okay. Now, we have two options. You can have a leopard tadpole today, or a dart tadpole in two weeks. If you don't decide in the next twenty seconds, we go home. Maybe your mom can help you decide."

She stilled. Her gaze went sideways. "Leopard tadpole today."

Well, that was easy. Too easy? Nah, I was overthinking it. I straightened. "Great. Let's get your amphibian."

THE TADPOLE AQUARIUM was set up and I had dinner ready to plate up by the time Janie got home from work.

She paused in the doorway of the kitchen like she didn't want to intrude. "You don't have to do that," she said.

"I had time, so I figured I might as well. You want something to drink? Wine? A beer?" I asked over my shoulder as I scooped enchiladas onto plates.

"Water." She made a face. "Something about working at a bar makes alcohol less appealing. I still like to drink every now and then, but it's not how I unwind at the end of the day."

I handed a plate to Maya to take to the table. "Yeah? How do you unwind?"

"Mostly it's a mug of chamomile tea. Sometimes I'll read in bed for a while. If I'm really keyed up, I like to sketch." She took the next plate from me and set it down across from Maya. "So how was your first full day?"

I grinned at Maya as I took the seat next to her. "It was

really good, right, Maya? This summer is going to be awesome. We're going to learn so much about frogs."

Maya's eyes went wide. "Tomorrow we're going to the library to get books," she said quickly. "That's how we're going to learn about frogs."

The way Janie's head whipped toward Maya, I knew something was amiss. "Sure, but we're also going to witness metamorphosis firsthand, right? Tadpoles to frogs."

Eyes closed, Janie pinched the bridge of her nose and pulled in a deep breath through her mouth. I had the feeling she was counting to ten. "How, exactly, do you plan to do that?"

My gaze darted from Janie to Maya and back again. What the hell was going on here? "Maya's summer project. We drove out to Denver to pick up the aquarium and tadpoles. It's all set up in her bedroom."

Janie's eyelids flew open and she stared daggers at her child. "Maya. I said no."

My mouth dropped open as I turned to Maya. "You tricked me?" I sounded shocked because I was. This sweet little girl with the mismatched eyes and the big heart had fucking *tricked* me? Assets trained in espionage couldn't trick me, but Maya had slipped right past my all my defenses.

Maya blinked rapidly. "You didn't say no, Mother. You said you couldn't keep another thing alive because you had your hands full with me and you. But Jack is here—"

"I said no," Janie interrupted sharply. "That should have been enough."

"I thought it would be okay!" Maya's eyes were big and suspiciously shiny.

"You tricked me, Maya," I said. "That is not okay. Now I can't trust you, and your mom can't trust me. She might even think I'm not responsible enough to take care of a seven year old."

Maya's lower lip trembled as she spun to her mother. "It's not his fault."

Janie twitched slightly as she rolled her lips together. Mad as hell but still struggling to hold back a laugh. "He should have known better." She cut me a disappointed look. "Seriously, Jack, you didn't think to call me?"

"It never occurred to me," I admitted. Rookie mistake, but shit. She'd lied right to my fucking face. The kid had zero tells. Janie couldn't lie to save her life, but apparently that trait wasn't genetic.

"I'm sorry," Maya said, not sounding all that sorry. Her furtive glance shifted between us. "But we can't return the tadpoles. The store said so. And you can't flush them down the toilet because you'd feel bad."

This kid actually thought she had me. Like hell was I going to be bested by a seven-year-old. "I'm sad, Maya. I was really looking forward to this project, but now it won't be fun. Since we can't return the tadpoles, they have to stay in my room now."

From the devastated look on Maya's face, this was a punishment she hadn't considered. "For how long?"

"Until your mother thinks we can trust you again."

Maya gasped. "But I lie a *lot*."

"Then I guess the tadpoles are mine forever." I cut into my chicken with feigned nonchalance. "I think I'll name them Thing One and Thing Two."

A suspicious sound from Janie made me glance her way. She had a hand over her face, hiding behind it. It took a moment, but she regained her composure. "Eat your dinner, Maya."

Maya ate her dinner, pouting the whole time. Neither Janie nor I paid her any mind. We kept a light conversation going about everything except tadpoles. The second Maya jumped up from the table and rushed to her room—to say goodbye to the tadpoles, I figured—Janie put down her fork and buried her face in her hands, her shoulders shaking with laughter.

"It's not funny, Janie. She told me she didn't want to make you drive out to Denver on your day off because you were so tired. I thought she was the sweetest kid I'd ever met." I was actually mortified.

Janie snorted. "Yeah, Jack. You got played." She dissolved into giggles again but fought her way through it to drive home her point. "Mr. Special Forces got played by a little girl."

God, she was pretty like this. Cheeks pink, eyes sparkling. I couldn't even be offended that she was laughing at my expense. "Well, if you're laughing, that means you're not going to fire me, right?"

"I'm not going to fire you." Her expression turned

serious as she considered me. "You're not going to quit, are you? She's a good kid. Lying is a phase most kids go through. She's not mean or vindictive. She's just..." Her voice trailed off as she searched for the word.

"Cunning," I supplied. "No, I'm not going to quit. I like cunning. It keeps things interesting." I rubbed my hands together.

Janie rolled her eyes. "Famous last words, I guess." Her smile was quick and bright. "She's going to drive you crazy this summer. A good kind of crazy, I hope, but still crazy."

Just like her mom.

"Bring it," I said. "I'm ready."

18

JANIE

day. She wasn't much for physical affection these days, but at bedtime she still wanted to rest her head on my shoulder while I read to her from her favorite baby books even though she had graduated to chapter books a couple years ago. I knew these moments wouldn't last forever, so I soaked up every bit of it. These were the memories I wanted to hold tight to—not the meltdowns and tears, the exhaustion and feelings of guilt and failure.

Although I planned to cling to the look on Jack's face when he realized that he had been tricked by a little girl until my dying breath. Priceless.

Still grinning to myself, I padded to the kitchen for some chamomile tea, pulling up short when I realized he was at the table, with a deck of cards laid out in a game of solitaire. "Oh. Um, hi."

He looked up. "Hi."

I shifted my weight from one foot to the other. "I didn't realize you were still up."

"It's eight-fifteen, Janie. I'm not *that* old."

My gaze slid to the digital clock on the oven behind him just in time to see the numbers flip from 8:14 to 8:15. No watch, no phone. Seriously, how did he *do* that? Time was so slippery to me. I was always running late or trying to catch up. Twenty minutes might pass and I'd think it was only two. But Jack? He just *knew*.

"I meant, I thought you were in your room," I said, slightly disgruntled, as I filled the kettle from the tap and put it on the stove to boil.

"I'm out here most evenings until about ten o'clock. Which you would know if you weren't always hiding in your room," he teased.

"I'm not hiding. I'm..."

"Janie." He gave me a look that said he saw right through my bullshit. "You're hiding."

Okay, maybe I was. Jack had been living here for ten days now, and I was still on edge about it. I wasn't avoiding him. I was just avoiding being *alone* with him. Maya made a good buffer. As long as she was around, I wouldn't be tempted to rip his clothes off.

"Whatever," I muttered. "Do you want some tea?"

"That depends. Are you going to stick around and drink it with me, or are you going to hightail it back to your room like a scared little rabbit?"

"Is that your way of saying you want company?"

He chuckled softly. "I want *your* company, Ace. I've

barely seen you since I moved in. I used to stop by the bar every afternoon just to play cards and hang out with you. Remember that?"

Was that really only two weeks ago? It felt like forever. I missed it, truth be told. I missed that thrum of anticipation that shivered through me every time he walked through the door of the Painted Cat. We had been on the cusp of something *great*. I had felt it in my bones with every not-so-accidental brush of his hand against mine, every look, every tease.

I was glad he was here. I needed him here. Maya needed him here.

But damn. It was like being sucker punched in the face with a bucket of ice water.

I knew I couldn't have him the way I wanted, but that didn't mean we couldn't still be friends, right?

I pulled two mugs down from the cabinet. "Deal me in."

He scooped up the cards, knocking the ends against the table until they all lined up in a neat pile. "What are we playing?"

"Your choice."

The kettle whistled. I poured the boiling water over the teabags and brought both mugs to the table, setting them aside to steep.

I looked at him expectantly. "So?"

"Poker." His smile was slow and suggestive, but there was nothing lazy in the sharp gleam of his blue eyes. "Strip poker."

I gave him my best *I don't fucking think so* look. Being Maya's mom, I'd had a lot of practice. "I'm not taking off my clothes in the kitchen with my daughter sleeping twenty feet away. No, scratch that. *You're* not taking off your clothes in the kitchen with my daughter sleeping twenty feet away."

He laughed. "We're not taking off clothes. We're taking off secrets."

I was instantly intrigued. "What do you mean?"

"You lose a hand, you tell a secret. A real secret. None of this, *oh, I don't actually separate whites and colors in the laundry* bullshit."

"I don't separate whites and colors. That's not a secret."

"Good. Then you understand the rules. You in?"

"This is dumb," I complained. "I can't bluff. I can't read people for shit. You're going to win every hand and the only person spilling secrets will be me."

"Maybe. But all the skill in the world can't fix a bad hand. A lot of poker is luck. I could lose." He rocked back in his chair, balancing on the two back legs, hands clasped behind his head, smirking. "I have a lot of good secrets, Ace."

God, that fucking smirk. He knew I couldn't resist. I wanted to smack it off him. Or kiss it off him.

"You're the luckiest person I know," I grumbled, giving my teabag a good dunking. "Anyone else with wounds to match your scars would be dead by now."

His grin widened. "Are you in?"

My stare was withering. "Obviously."

"Excellent." The front legs of the chair met the tiled floor with a gentle thud. "Five card draw."

"We need chips. The only kind I have is chocolate." I grabbed the bag from the pantry, dumped the chocolate chips into two small glass bowls, and brought them to the table. "Pretend they're even."

"Works for me." He pushed the card deck toward me. "You deal. Then you'll know it's fair."

"Exactly." I pushed it back. "If I'm going to lose, I need a scapegoat and I prefer not to direct my ire inward. It's uncomfy."

Laughing, he gave the cards one last shuffle and then dealt.

I studied my hand. Crap. Of course it was crap. An ace, a three, a seven, a jack, and a nine. Nothing remotely matched. I heaved a sigh before I remembered I wasn't supposed to be making this easy on him. My gaze shot to his. He was already watching me, his lips tilted in a wry smile.

"Make your bet, Ace."

I tossed down three chocolate chips. "Why do you call me that?"

"It's a secret," he murmured, matching my bet. "Win a hand to find out."

I blew a raspberry at him and slid him four cards, keeping only my ace. I got back two jacks, a four, and a five. Dammit. I groaned. A pair was better than nothing, but shit. If I'd kept that jack, I'd have three of a kind—not great, but decent.

"Raise," I said, adding three more chips to the pot.

He snorted. "After that groan, you don't really expect me to fold, do you? Call."

I turned over my cards. He turned over his.

All diamonds. A flush.

His eyes glinted at me. "Take off a secret, Janie."

I didn't have a lot of secrets. Really just the one big one. I chewed the inside of my cheek. Maybe I could break it down into smaller bites. That was fair, right? No one removed both shoes at a time playing strip poker.

"What do you want to know?" I asked carefully.

He didn't even have to think about it. His response was instantaneous. "Why do you work at the Painted Cat? I saw your diploma in the closet with the Legos. You have a degree from Georgetown University in public policy. Why aren't you using it?"

I lifted a shoulder and reached for my tea. "Those are two different questions. Pick one."

"Why are you working at the Painted Cat?"

I was actually relieved. That was the easy one. The other question...well, it opened a whole other can of worms. "It's the only place in Aspen Springs without any ties to my parents. They own most of the real estate on First Street. They're the bank's biggest client. They donate more money to the schools and library than everyone else combined. There's literally nowhere in this town that doesn't owe my parents *something*, even if it's only a favor."

He stared at me, aghast. "They wouldn't let anyone hire you?"

"No, it's not that. I'd definitely get any job I applied for —they'd make sure of that. And then that job would come with strings, and they would absolutely pull those strings. I refuse to be their puppet." *Even when it's in my best interest.*

He stared at me, his fingertips white where he gripped his mug. A muscle ticked in his jaw.

"But they don't have anything to do with the Painted Cat. They don't own the building or the land. Brax bought it free and clear. He doesn't even have a mortgage. He said something about an investor, but as long as it's not my parents, it doesn't matter to me. It might not pay a lot, but at least it's really mine. No strings. They can't touch me there."

"But you still talk to them. Even though they pull this shit. Even after everything with Maya." That muscle in his cheek popped again.

"Well, yeah. I mean, they're my parents. They love me, even if the only way they know how to show it is by exerting control. And they love Maya. So." I shrugged. "It is what it is. They came through for me when I needed them most. That counts for something."

He opened his mouth, but I shook my head. "No more questions. I gave you my secret. If you want more, you have to win another round."

Which I was absolutely not going to let happen. I couldn't cheat any better than I could lie, but I could toss my cards on the table and storm away like an angry toddler, and by god, I would do it if I had to.

Something of that must have shown up on my face, because he bumped his foot against mine. "Play fair, Janie."

Making a face at him, I shuffled and dealt. A queen, three eights, and a ten. When he bet five chips, I matched him and traded my ten for another queen. Full house.

"Great," I mumbled. "Now you're going to think I cheated."

"*Janie.*"

I peeked up at him over my cards. "What?"

"Jesus. You really can't bluff." He pinched the bridge of his nose, then shook his head and tossed his cards down. "Fold."

"Wait, does that mean I win? You have to take off a secret?"

"That's how this works."

I reach for the chocolate chips and pop a couple in my mouth. "I didn't cheat, you know."

His lips quirked. "I know you didn't. So ask your question. You want to know why I call you Ace?"

I stopped chewing. The weight of his gaze made my whole body hum. The intensity of his eyes as he leaned closer. He *wanted* me to ask. He wanted to tell me.

And I wanted to know. So damn badly. But it would shift something between us. Even not knowing his reason, I knew that much. It wouldn't be a secret if it didn't mean something.

The question was there, on the tip of my tongue, but I

swallowed it down. I didn't want my world shifting beneath me. I needed solid ground.

"Tell me about the turtle," I said.

The look he gave me was part disappointment, part resignation. His head tilted. "What turtle?"

"I don't know what turtle. That's why it's a secret." I took another mouthful of chocolate chips and washed them down with tea. "It's what you said that night, when you were having a nightmare. Turtle."

"Hmm."

I narrowed my eyes at him. If he lied to me right now, would I even know the difference? "Don't fuck with me, soldier. I'll know." *No, I wouldn't.* I never knew. That was the problem.

"I wouldn't fuck with you. Not like that, anyway." His gaze dragged over me, making me wish he would fuck with me a different way. God, being a responsible mom really took the fun out of it sometimes.

I pretended I couldn't feel the flush in my cheeks. "You're stalling."

"Yeah." He exhaled roughly and hunched over his mug, frowning into it. "I've never told this story to anyone. I don't know why. It's not even bad. I've seen way worse. Hell, I've done worse. But somehow, this is the thing that sticks with me. A fucking turtle."

"You don't have to tell me. It's just a game." I pushed to my feet. "It's fine."

"Sit your ass down. Of course I'm going to tell you. I want to."

I slowly sank onto my chair again, my eyes never leaving his. "Okay."

"I have to be vague with the specifics. It's all still classi-fied." I nodded. He tipped his head back and contemplated the ceiling like the story was painted there. "We were in..." He rolled his lips. "A country that has turtles. One of our guys had been captured and was being held as a spy. They were absolutely going to torture him. But their government and ours came to an agreement. They would release him and in exchange we would take care of a problem for them."

"A...problem?" My forehead furrowed. "You mean...a person? An assassination?"

His chin dipped. "I had my orders. I was fine with it. This problem—he was a really big problem, Janie. He was a monster. The world is a better place without him in it."

"I understand," I said, and I did. I felt a little sick about it, but I understood.

"He always had bodyguards around him. There was never an easy shot. I tracked every move he made for weeks and it never lined up. And then one day he was out walking with his granddaughter. Both surrounded by bodyguards. No clear shot. There was a turtle in the road. And he...he did the stupidest fucking thing, Janie. He made his guards stop traffic. He ran out into the street and grabbed it, brought it safely to the other side. His grand-daughter was clapping for him. He was laughing and smiling as he rescued the fucking turtle. And I put a bullet in his brain."

I didn't know what to say. Words all sounded trite in my head, every last one of them. I stretched across the table, tentatively sliding my hand next to his. His fingers flexed at the contact, and then his pinky wrapped over mine.

"I'm not sorry about it. Our guy came home, and a monster was put down. But I think about it a lot."

"Because no one is pure evil? It would be easier to do that job if you could believe there was nothing good in the people you had to..." I cleared my throat. "Um, take care of?"

"He literally skinned a man alive once. I don't care if he rescued the last sea turtle from extinction, he needed to die," Jack said bluntly. "It's not that all monsters still have a shred of humanity in them. What bothers me is that only humans can be monsters. No other species would help a turtle across the road, but no other species would do the shit we do to each other. Other animals are just trying to survive, but that's not good enough for us. We make depravity a fucking hobby. That...I don't know. It eats at me."

It wasn't just our pinkies now. Somehow both our hands were tangled up together.

"Jack." I stared at our hands. "This probably won't make you feel better, but have you heard about dolphins?"

He gave me a blank look. "Dolphins?"

"Yeah." I nodded vigorously. "They're fucking psychos."

"But I love dolphins."

I swallowed hard. "Oh. Then, yeah, that definitely

won't make you feel better. Sorry. Don't do an internet search, okay?" I heaved a sigh and shoved another small palmful of chocolate chips in my mouth. "God, I'm sorry. You wanted a fun game and I bummed you out, didn't I?"

His shoulders twitched in a half-hearted shrug. "I'm all right."

I stopped eating my feelings and studied him. "You're not sad?"

"About the dolphins? I'm going to pretend you never said anything. About the other stuff..." He shrugged again. "Not so much. It felt good to talk about it. Like an itch deep in my skull finally got scratched." His thumb rubbed over my knuckles and I realized we were holding hands again. "Was it hard for you to hear about it?"

"Well...yeah. But that's okay. I don't mind hearing hard things or ugly things. At least it's honest. You had to live those experiences. It's who you are. If you want to talk about it, then I want to hear about it. I don't mind getting a little heavy so you can feel lighter. That's what friends are for, right?"

His eyes were dark and fathomless as they met mine and held for a long, quiet moment. "Right. Friends."

Why did it feel so disappointing that he agreed with me?

19

JACK

BRAX

We riding today or what?

JACK

Fuck yeah. I'll be at Lodestar after lunch. I have a breakfast date with Maya.

BRAX

I thought today was your day off?

JACK

Janie was so tired when she came home last night. I thought it would be nice to let her sleep in for once. We need to have a talk about that, by the way.

BRAX

Yeah, fine. Park behind my cabin when you get here. I'll have the horses saddled and waiting.

JACK

> You make it sound like we're sneaking around.

BRAX

> We are. If Adam sees us, he'll put us to work.

"BLUEBERRY PANCAKES AND TWO SLICES OF BACON, COMING right up." I slid the plate in front of Maya, who was ready to go with a fork in one hand and a knife in the other. I put my own plate down across from her and took a seat.

"Thank you, Jack," she remembered to say after the first bite was already in her mouth.

"You're welcome, scamp."

She grinned at that, showing me a little too much of her food, but I let it slide. Normally her table manners were impeccable—her grandmother was a stickler about it, according to Janie—and anyway, I didn't want to spend every moment correcting her. That would exhaust us both. Better to pick our battles. No one wanted to fight a war on a Sunday morning.

"Scamp," she repeated with a mischievous giggle that reminded me of her mom. Maya loved her nickname—

maybe a little too much. I hoped she didn't feel the need to earn it every day.

I watched her saw clumsily at her pancakes while I tucked into mine. Her fingers and hands were so small that using a fork and knife together was unwieldy for her, but she was getting it. The first few times I had tried to jump in and help, but Janie had put a stop to it. Now I knew that I should give Maya a chance to do it herself. If she needed help, she'd ask.

"What are we doing today, Jack?" Maya asked around a bite of bacon.

I swallowed my own food before replying, then took a sip of orange juice. "Well, it's Sunday, so that means your mom doesn't have to work. She's going to take you with her to the library for her embroidery club, and I'm going to go for a ride at Lodestar with Brax."

"You're going to Lodestar?" Maya's eyes went wide. "Will Essie be there?"

I wasn't surprised she asked. Kids loved my sister. Essie was colorful and loud, and that tended to make her a favorite. "No, she's part of the embroidery club, remember? So you'll see her at the library."

Maya nodded. This time she waited to swallow her food before speaking. "Right. Okay. And then you'll come back home? Here?"

The anxious note in her voice made me squint. "Of course. I live here, remember? All my stuff is here."

"Okay." She stuffed another bite into her mouth and

chewed, those unusual eyes of hers darting this way and that. "Even though I tricked you about the tadpoles?"

That was what she was worried about? The tadpoles had been in my room all week since we moved them there Monday night. Maya had been great about changing the water and feeding them to prove she was responsible. She'd been scrupulously truthful. Too truthful, even. I didn't need to know that my shirt was ugly and my singing along to the car radio made her want to rip her ears off.

But then I remembered what Janie had said. None of Maya's babysitters had lasted very long. She was a smart kid. Observant. She had to have known why they left. I could only imagine how that made her feel.

I leaned back and rubbed a hand over my mouth. "Are you kidding? I'm having a great summer with you. I'm not happy you tricked me, but you're not going to do that again. Right?" I added pointedly, and she nodded vehemently. "Good. So I'm staying. You're stuck with me until September, scamp."

"I don't mind," she said. She finished another bite and hopped to her feet. "Can I go look at the tadpoles now?"

"Sure, go ahead." I didn't mind her in my room. I'd left my firearms at my mom's place, and there wasn't anything else for her to get into.

She darted from the kitchen just as Janie entered. "Pancakes, Mom!" she shouted as she made for the tadpoles.

Janie blinked her dazed doe eyes at me. Her copper hair was piled on top of her head with a silvery blue scrunchie that matched her miniscule silky pajama shorts. Bare feet. No bra.

No bra.

I knew she wasn't wearing a bra because her perky tits had that soft, floaty look to them and her goddamn nipple piercings were outlined clear as day against the white cotton T-shirt that was sliding off her shoulder with not a bra strap to be seen.

I blinked back at her, feeling as dazed as she looked.

"Pancakes?" she echoed. She looked around like she expected them to appear out of thin air.

I jolted to my feet. "Right! I put a plate in the oven for you to keep them warm. I wasn't sure when you'd be up."

"What time is it?" She shuffled over to the coffee maker with a yawn.

"A quarter to nine."

"Nine?" she yelped, spinning around on her toes. "Why didn't you wake me up?"

I arched a brow at her. "It's not my job to wake you up. Anyway, you looked wiped when you came home last night. I figured you could use the rest."

"Maya usually wakes me up around seven to make her breakfast. I'm so sorry. I know it's your day off from kid duty." She looked genuinely distressed.

"Hey, don't worry about it. I'm an early riser anyway. Can't shake military hours no matter how hard I try. It was fun." Making pancakes with Maya hadn't felt like work. It had felt like a great way to start a day that I was really looking forward to.

She kept staring at me with that baffled, sleepy look, her body blocking me from my second cup of coffee. Instinctively, I squeezed her hip to encourage her to move. That was a mistake. I'd spent a lot of time since I moved in struggling to keep my hands off her, and now that I was actually touching her, I didn't know how to stop.

"Jack," she said plaintively. I thought she was going to push me away, but instead her forehead met my chest with a soft thump. "I'm just so fucking *tired*. Thank you."

I traced soft circles on her lower back. "I know you are, honey. Go sit down and I'll get us both a cup of coffee, okay?"

It felt so good to take some of the weight she caried like she had done for me in our poker game. So right. Like we were in this together. I hadn't felt this kind of comradeship since I'd left the military. And somehow I'd found it here, in the unlikeliest of places, with a precocious kid who had wiggled her way into my heart and her mother I couldn't make myself stop touching.

"How's the mannying going?" Brax asked as we moseyed down a trail where Adam was unlikely to follow. "You surviving okay?"

"More than surviving. I'm having a blast."

Brax turned in his saddle just enough to give me a look of pure disbelief over his shoulder. "With a seven year old."

"Yeah. Maya's great."

Brax faced forward again, shaking his head. "I have to say, I thought you would be bored to tears, but as long as you're having fun, it's not a bad summer gig until you find something permanent. You deserve that. Have you started thinking about what you're going to do when summer is over?"

"Maybe," I hedged.

Truthfully, I'd been avoiding thinking about that at all. Not because I didn't have options. Mercy River Ranch was a possibility. I hadn't given Jeremiah an answer yet because I was still waffling on it.

Mercy River was a different kind of ranch than Lodestar. Both raised cattle and horses, but Mercy River was a nonprofit with a mission to give former military men and women a healing place to ease back into civilian life. Most of them had physical trauma or PTSD to work through.

Horses, mountains, and a cause I cared about. It should have been a no-brainer. So why was I still hesitating?

"I have to ask you something," Brax said.

"Go for it." We came out of the copse of trees and the view opened up. There was no better place to admire it than between a horse's ears, in my opinion. Shit, I'd missed this. I nudged my gelding into a quick trot to pull even with Brax. "What's your question?"

"Is something going on with you and Janie?"

I stared him down. "Why do you have to ask me that?"

"Essie said I have to."

"Well, it's none of your damn business."

"So, that's a yes?"

"It's none of her damn business, either."

Brax sighed. "Yeah, that's definitely a yes."

Shit. "Don't tell Essie that." I scrubbed a hand over my jaw. "Nothing is going on. There was a time when it felt like we were heading in that direction, but she put a stop to that when she hired me."

Brax nodded. "Makes sense. Can't go around fucking your kid's nanny. That's the rule." His gaze tracked over my frown. "Maybe it's really more of a guideline than an actual rule."

I grunted. Some people chafed at rules. Felt caged in by them. That wasn't me. My whole life, I'd been a rule-follower. Rules weren't a cage, to my way of thinking; they were freedom. People concentrated so hard on the one thing they couldn't do that they never opened their eyes to all the other possibilities. Rules established the fence line. But I was damn good at finding a gate.

I hadn't found a gate through Janie's rule yet, that was all.

But right now, I wanted to have a different conversation with my friend.

"You know she doesn't get home until two-thirty or three in the morning after her shifts on Friday and Saturday?" I asked.

Brax shrugged. "I never thought about it, but it makes

sense. The bar closes at one, and she still has to clean up before she can leave. That's why she needs a live-in nanny, right?"

"She's fucking exhausted. It doesn't matter what time she gets to bed, she still has to get up at seven to take care of Maya. Closing two nights in a row is too much. She looked like a zombie this morning."

Brax tugged the reins, signaling his mare to stop. He turned to me, eyes narrowed. "What's with the tone? She asked for those shifts, and I gave them to her because I like her. She works six days a week because that's what she wanted, but most of the money she makes comes from closing the bar Friday and Saturday. That's when she gets the good tips."

"She can't keep burning herself out at both ends," I insisted.

Brax threw up a hand. "What do you want me to do about it? She's never said a word about wanting different shifts."

"Take her off the closing shifts. She can work Monday through Friday and be home by six. Give her the manager position."

Brax rolled his eyes. "There isn't a manager position. *I'm* the manager."

"You're barely there," I argued. "Who makes the schedule for the other employees? Who does the inventory so you know what to order?"

"Janie," Brax admitted. He sighed. "All right. The bar is

doing fine. We can afford it. I'll talk to her about it tomorrow."

"Good." I nudged Captain with my heels and we moved forward.

Brax scratched his jaw. "It's a good idea, actually. I hate all that paperwork shit. Did Janie come up with it? She could have asked me herself. She's never been afraid to speak her mind to me before."

"I don't think it occurred to her, and I figured I'd see if it was even a possibility before I got her hopes up. If she doesn't want the manager position, she'll tell you."

"Huh." Brax eyed me speculatively. "So you figured you'd get yourself involved in something that isn't your business."

"The bar is my business."

And so is Janie. But since that was more a feeling than a fact a reasonable person would agree with, I kept it to myself.

20

JANIE

MOM

Don't you think your little tantrum has gone on long enough?

JANIE

That's a funny way to say "I'm sorry."

MOM

I've done nothing to apologize for.

JANIE

Neither have I.

MOM

You seem to forget who approves the distributions.

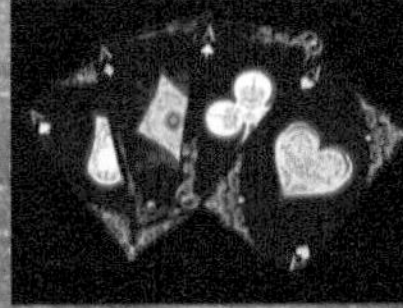

"This is the first time I've left the house in two weeks and I haven't had a drink in eleven months," Chloe announced as she bellied up to the bar. "Stand back world. Tonight I'm pumping and dumping."

I laughed and lined up four glasses of water—one for each of my friends, who had all shown up to celebrate my last time closing the bar. "What can I make you?"

"Can I have a margarita on the rocks? I've been dreaming of it for months." Her pale green eyes were wide and hopeful.

"Of course. One margarita coming right up." I pivoted to the agave-lime juice mix—we didn't do things fancy at the Painted Cat—and grabbed a tumbler. "Salt?"

"Yes, please."

"You should have brought Grayson with you," I said as I stirred all the ingredients over ice. "I miss the baby phase."

"Do you?" Chloe laughed. "I've lost all sense of time since he was born. Has it been forever or just a day? No one knows. Much as I love him, I've felt like I'm just an extension of him, like an extra arm or a leg."

"Or a boob," Essie suggested. She was flanked by Hannah on one side and James on the other.

"Definitely a boob," Chloe agreed. "That's all he wants, really, to eat and cuddle. It's nice to get out and feel like a full human being for a minute. I'm my own person again. Anyway, Steven practically shoved me out the door. Said it would be good for me. I think he just wants Grayson all to himself."

"They're so cute together. Gray has that man wrapped around his little finger." James sipped her beer and shook her head in disbelief. "Sometimes I still can't believe that it's *Steven* we're talking about."

"You know what? I'm not all that surprised." I pushed Chloe's margarita to her. "He came to the bar one night last November, and it was the funniest thing. He was obsessed with your shoes. And flowers. Mostly, I think, he was just obsessed with *you*." I gave her a teasing grin.

With a happy hum, Chloe pulled the tumbler closer to her and took a sip. "Mmm. Delicious." She licked the salt from her lips. "Was that the night Jack was here? Apparently he gave Steven some advice. It worked...for about a week." Her lips quirked in a self-satisfied smirk.

Essie looked up from her wine. "Jack was here? In November?"

Oh, *shit*. She still didn't know about that. I squinted at the ceiling like I was trying to remember. "Um, well, I don't...hmm."

"He was definitely here. There was a snowstorm that night, remember?" Chloe said.

I picked at my cuticle. "Was he? Hm."

"But that doesn't make any sense," Essie said slowly. "Jack was only here for, like, twenty-four hours in November before he bailed on us for Wyoming and Mom didn't let him out of her sight for one single second except when he was sleeping or pissing."

Hannah made a disgusted face. "Ew, Essie."

Essie rolled her eyes. "Everyone pees, Hannah. I'm just saying. Jack couldn't have been here."

Chloe furrowed her brow. "Am I losing my mind? I swear it happened. It was a Friday night. I'm sure of it."

"But Jack got here on a Saturday and left on Sunday," Essie argued.

The suspense was killing me. Any second now they were going to figure it out.

Any.

Second.

Now.

Four pairs of suspicious eyeballs latched onto my guilty face.

And there it was.

A hot flush crept up my neck. My cheeks prickled. "It was a snowstorm," I said feebly. "What else were we going to do in a snowstorm?"

"That's valid." James bobbed her head. "It's like, what else were we going to do when the hotel only had one bed because the rodeo was in town? Sex happens." She grinned at me in solidarity even as she gave Essie a sympathetic pat on her back.

Essie dropped her face in her hands. "Noooo."

"Isn't Brax Jack's best friend?" Hannah pushed her glasses up her nose and stared at Essie. "You can't complain when he has snowstorm sex with your best friend when you have all kinds of sex with his."

"I can complain," Essie muttered. "He said he was

going to sleep with one of my friends to get back at me, and I told him not to fuck with single moms."

"In his defense, all your other friends were taken," Chloe said soothingly. She took another slurp of her margarita.

"And he didn't know I was a single mom," I defended. *And he wasn't fucking with me.*

Essie huffed in disapproval. "Well, he knows now. He's your *manny*, for fuck's sake."

"Well, now we're not fucking at all," I said flatly. "So it's fine."

"What?" Essie looked truly appalled. "What do you mean? Why aren't you fucking? You two would be so great together. We could be sisters-in-law."

"Because he's my manny, for fuck's sake." I repeated her words back to her, enunciating slowly and carefully while I exchanged bug-eyed looks with James.

"Pfft." Essie waved a hand dismissively. "That rule only applies when there's a power imbalance, or the guy is really old and gross. You and Jack are both young and hot. That makes it legal."

"You're giving me whiplash, babe. I need you to pick a side." Noting a customer flagging me down, I pushed away from the bar. "I'll be back."

There was a low hum as they immediately started rehashing the whole thing behind my back. It didn't bother me. I knew them all well enough to know that the gossip we shared with and about each other was never cruel or malicious. But I still wanted to hear what they were saying.

Essie gifted me with a magnanimous smile upon my return. "I've decided. You may fuck my brother."

I rolled my eyes. "Gee, thanks."

Essie pursed her red lips as she regarded me, her eyes narrowed to blue slits. "What, Jack isn't good enough for you?"

"No. *No.* That's not what I'm saying." I laid a placating hand over hers. "Jack is *too* good for me. He's—"

"He's not," Essie interrupted. "I promise you he's not. He's a jackass a solid sixty-three percent of the time. When he found out I married Brax, he flew all the way here from wherever the hell he was just to punch him in the stomach."

I squeezed her hands in mine and leaned in so we were eyeball to eyeball. "Again, Essie. Whiplash."

She blinked at me. "But I love both of you. I don't know who to defend."

I laughed and retreated to the fridge so I could get refills. With a beer in one hand and a bottle of white wine in the other, I pivoted back to my friends. "You don't have to defend anyone. It's not like we had a painful breakup. We had a very adult conversation and decided this was for the best."

"Ugh, that's so mature." Chloe made a face. "I mean, I'm really proud of you."

I snorted. "Yeah, I hate it." The truth was out of my mouth before I could stop it.

"Oh, honey. Of course you hate it. He's living with you and he looks like *that*. It's not fair." Chloe winced. "Trust me, I know how it feels."

"Okay, but seriously," James said. "Why can't you be together? So he's the manny and people will talk. Who cares?"

"It's not that." Well, it wasn't *just* that. People talking about us meant people talking about Maya, and that made my skin crawl with foreboding. But that wasn't my only concern. "What happens if we got together and it didn't work out? It's not like there's a dozen people lining up to be Maya's babysitter. And Maya *loves* him."

"Janie." Essie leaned back, her expression serious. "Come on. You know Jack would never leave you in the lurch like that. If things didn't work between the two of you, he'd still show up for Maya and do his job. That's who he is."

I wanted to agree with her, but I knew better than anyone that people weren't always what they seemed. Hell, some people didn't even know *themselves* until they had been truly tested. I trusted Jack. I did. But I'd made that mistake before. I couldn't risk it again. Not with Maya's happiness on the line.

But no way could I say that to his protective twin sister, so instead I said, "That's what I'm afraid of. Imagine having to face the source of your heartbreak every damn day. Watching him be all hot and sweet with your kid? No, thanks. Anyway, it's fine. We're friends."

That didn't satisfy Essie, but Hannah cut in to save me.

"I can't believe this is our last Friday night closing down the bar together. It's the end of an era."

I looked around. We were all busy, but my friends had made a point to stop by at least one or two Fridays a month to hang out. They never asked for free drinks and they always tipped because they weren't assholes. We'd laugh and talk and they'd drink and be silly. Some of my best memories were right here at work, as crazy as that sounded.

"It's good, though," I said. "The hours are so much better, and the raise will make up for the lost tips."

Essie tipped her wine to her lips. "Brax is thrilled you said yes. The last thing he wants to do after all his lawyer shit is more paperwork."

"I don't mind." Was managing a dive bar a dream come true? No, of course not. But then, neither was bartending, and I'd been happy enough doing that for the last few years.

The truth was, I hadn't spent a whole lot of time contemplating what I wanted to do when I grew up. The second I had a positive pregnancy test, boom. I was a grownup. My dad had wanted me to go into public policy, so I'd been on that track until it all turned upside down, but when it imploded, I hadn't really felt like I'd lost all that much. That dream hadn't been mine to begin with.

Bartending had been a placeholder. I was doing it until my *real* career started, whatever that would be. Accepting the management position made me feel like I was locked into someone else's plan all over again.

That was silly, right? Brax wasn't going to chain me to the bar against my will. It was just…inertia was such a powerful force. It kept you moving along a path even when that path wasn't right for you. Dread had curdled in my belly when I said yes because I couldn't shake the feeling that yes now meant yes forever. I'd never figure out what I truly wanted from my life.

But I knew what I *didn't* want. I didn't want to miss all those moments with Maya because I was too tired to pay attention. I didn't want to miss putting her to bed with a snuggle and a book. And I sure as fuck didn't want my parents to have veto power over every dime I spent.

Maybe that was enough. I would make it enough. I had to.

JACK WAS at the kitchen table when I got home, a steaming mug of chamomile tea waiting for me. He set aside the book he was reading and smiled sleepily when I plopped into a chair across from him.

I pulled the mug closer to myself, wrapping my hands around the warmth. I always got a little chilly when the sun went down, even in summer. "Thank you."

"You're welcome." He yawned and stretched. His shirt rode up, exposing a couple inches of muscled torso and a trail of sparse hair that disappeared into the waistband of his jeans. I tried not to stare. I didn't succeed. "How was it with the girls? Did you have a good time?"

"Yeah. It was great," I said around a yawn of my own. "I should warn you, though. That night in November? The snowstorm? Essie knows you didn't go straight home."

He chuckled and rubbed his belly, then tugged his shirt back down. That shouldn't have been sexy, but it was. "Oh, I'm aware. My phone has been buzzing nonstop since you closed the bar."

"Sorry. Chloe let it slip and I couldn't..." My voice trailed off and I shrugged.

"You couldn't lie." He laughed again. "Don't worry about it. I don't care if she knows. The only reason I cared back then was because I didn't want her to come get me. I wanted to stay with you."

I didn't know what to say when he was sweet like that. I took slow sips of tea so I wouldn't have to say anything.

"So what are you going to do with your weekend now that you don't have to work?" he asked.

"Hang out with Maya, of course." I covered another yawn with my hand.

"Sleep in tomorrow. I'll handle breakfast."

I shook my head. "You're officially off the clock. If I have weekends off, so do you."

He blinked, his forehead furrowing. "I hadn't thought of that. Maya asked if we could go for a ride tomorrow afternoon. I said yes."

He didn't look especially pleased about it, either. I eyed him over the rim of my mug. "I'll take her." He still didn't look happy. I squinted. "Do you want to come with us? It's totally fine if you want to make other plans—"

He cut me off. "I want to go riding with you. That would be great."

"Okay. And I'll make breakfast tomorrow."

That not-very-happy look was on his face again. "I'll make breakfast. You should sleep in."

"You're up just as late as me," I pointed out. "It's your day off. *You* should sleep in."

"I'll sleep in Sunday." When I opened my mouth to argue, he leaned across the table and pressed his thumb against my lips, silencing me. "Let me be clear. If I see you out here before eight-thirty, I'm carrying your sweet ass back to bed and trust me, I *will* find a way to keep you there. Nod if you understand me."

My eyes darted over his face. *Oh*. He was serious. I nodded.

"Good girl," he said approvingly. He scraped back the chair and pushed to his feet, collecting our empty mugs as he went. "Sweet dreams, Ace."

All right, so there was one thing I knew I wanted.

It was such a damn shame I couldn't have it.

21

JACK

BRAX

Essie says I get to punch you in the stomach.

JACK

Wouldn't it make more sense for Essie to punch Janie in the stomach?

BRAX

That's never going to happen. Essie says this will be more fun.

JACK

You're welcome to try, I guess.

BRAX

Thanks, but I kind of like having all my teeth inside my head.

If she asks, tell her I was brave.

JACK

For the record, I didn't hit you for sleeping with my sister. I hit you because you tricked her into marrying you instead of telling her you'd been in love with her your whole life.

BRAX

I know.

JACK

It sure did feel good, though.

"I DON'T WANT TO GO TO THE GROCERY STORE." MAYA GAVE me a disgusted look, like I'd suggested eating worms for breakfast.

"Guess what? No one likes going to the grocery store. Not even adults. But it still has to get done or we don't have food to eat."

Maya hit her thighs with her little fists. Once, twice, three times. "I don't care."

I sighed. Maya was in a *mood*. It had already been a long day, and it was barely past lunch. Maybe she hadn't slept well, but more likely it was just a crappy day. It caught me off guard, coming on the heels of a fantastic weekend. After spending most of Saturday with Janie and Maya, I'd made myself scarce yesterday and headed for the mountains. I hadn't gotten back until Maya was in bed, but Janie told me they'd had a great time working on their amphibian book.

Today she suddenly wanted nothing to do with me. First, she'd refused to do PT in the morning. When I'd threatened to bar her from my room—and the tadpoles —until she did it, she'd given me the most disgruntled face and told me I couldn't do it with her. She hadn't wanted me to push her on the tire swing or eat lunch with her. I'd taken it all in stride because what was I going to do? Call her mom and whine that Maya didn't want to be my friend anymore? It hurt my feelings, but I had my pride.

Everyone had a bad day now and again. She just needed space. Or...something. I didn't know, and that frustrated me.

"It's Monday. We always go to the grocery store on Monday," I said. It was part of our routine, so that Janie didn't have to waste weekend time food shopping.

"I'm not going." Maya's lower lip stuck out.

"You are going," I said as patiently as I could. "I know it sucks being a kid sometimes when adults make decisions for you, but I can't leave you here alone." I squatted down so we met each other at eye level. "I'll tell you what. We'll get the grocery shopping done, and later we can go to the library."

"I don't want to go to the library *with you*."

My jaw nearly hit the floor. Maya was *vicious*. "Fine." I straightened. "But we're still going to the grocery store."

MAYA'S MOOD did not improve at the grocery store. Neither did mine.

With Janie's grocery list in my phone, it didn't take long. The list never changed much week to week and we knew where everything was. Maya stomped along like a little thundercloud while I grabbed items off the shelves and tossed them into the cart. Even her red braid bounced like it was angry and she glowered at the checkout lady who rang up our groceries.

When I gave her an apologetic grimace, she just shook her head. "Don't you worry about it. I feel that way most Mondays."

We made for the exit, slowing down as we neared the cookie case. There was one chocolate chip cookie left— Maya's favorite—and the rest were sugar cookies. The cookies were free, on the honor system that customers would take no more than one apiece. It was our tradition to grab one on our way out as a little treat for surviving our least favorite chore. I had never conditioned it on anything like *you can have a cookie if you're good*. It had never occurred to me, and I'd never needed to.

A mean little part of me wanted to hurt her feelings the way she'd hurt mine, but come the fuck on. I was an adult. I wasn't going to punish her for not wanting to go to the grocery store or for being in a bad mood. That wasn't fair, and the only lesson she'd learn was that she had to fake being happy around me and hide her real emotions.

"Get a cookie if you want one, Maya," I told her.

She bit her lip and tilted her head, looking exactly like her mom. My chest ached even though I still wanted to strangle her a little. "Do you want one too? A sugar cookie?" Because even if she was willing to make peace, she wasn't going to be a martyr about it.

"Yes, thank you." I didn't really, but I couldn't say no to the first nice thing she had said to me all day.

She didn't smile but she looked a little happier as she reached into the bin with the tongs and pulled out the last chocolate chip cookie.

And then everything happened so fast. A boy—maybe four years old—grabbed the tongs from Maya before she was ready, and his mom took his shoulders to redirect him with a gentle "Wait your turn, Andy," but it was too late. The chocolate chip cookie fell to the floor and ended up under his foot.

Maya *screamed*.

The boy's mouth flapped open in shock. He clamped his hands over his ears and stared wide-eyed at Maya. Maya kept right on screaming like a tornado siren. Her arms flailed at her sides.

"Maya!" I reached for her. She fucking *hit* me. I recoiled in shock.

The mother looked at me. "Your child is out of control."

Out of control. That was exactly what this was. Maya wasn't in control of herself right now. She was having a meltdown.

I sank to my knees and enveloped her small frame in a full-body hug, pinning her flailing arms to her sides. Her teeth sank into my trap muscle, but I held on tight.

"What's wrong with her, Mom?" the boy whispered.

"She's having a tantrum, honey. Thank you for setting a better example."

Hot rage prickled the back of my neck. *Judgmental bitch.* But I tuned them both out and focused all of my attention on Maya. Right now, Maya needed me to hold us both together. Nothing else mattered.

"Maya," I said softly in her ear. "Maya."

Her body slackened and she pressed her damp face into my neck. I braced for another bite, but she just let out a deep, shaky breath. I pushed to my feet with Maya still in my arms and found the cashier two feet away.

"My nephew is the same," she said. "If you want to carry her to your car, I'll bring your cart."

"Thank you," I said over the thick lump in my throat.

I got Maya safely to the car, where I held her for another ten minutes before I decided it was safe to drive home. The whole time, I had one thought in my head.

I have to fix this.

"WHERE'S MAYA?" Janie's voice was calm but brisk as she jogged up the porch steps, her gaze flicking around like she expected her daughter to pop out from somewhere.

"Inside. She fell asleep on my bed while watching the tadpoles. I know she doesn't nap, but I thought she needed one after everything."

"I'll wake her up. I want her to be able to sleep tonight." She didn't pause as moved past me to the door. "I'll be right back after I check on her."

I took that to mean she didn't want to have this conversation in front of Maya. I had figured as much. That was why I was waiting for her on the porch. I rubbed my palms on my jeans. Shit, shit, shit.

"Maya's up." Janie pushed through the screen door, startling me. "She's playing her video game in the living room now."

I slowly got to my feet, my heart in my throat, as she faced me.

"I'm sorry," I said, at the exact moment she said, "You okay, soldier?"

We blinked at each other.

Her forehead furrowed. "What are you sorry for? What —" She reeled back a step. "Are you quitting? I told you—"

"No, I'm not quitting." I grabbed her elbows to steady

her. "I just need you to know, it was my fault. The melt-down. It was my fault."

Janie cocked her head, her gaze traveling over my face. "Walk me through it."

I blew out a breath. "She was in an off mood all day. You probably noticed it before you went to work." I paused and Janie nodded. "I didn't know what was wrong—I still don't—but I knew she wasn't feeling like herself. I made her go to the grocery store anyway, even though she told me she didn't want to. I didn't listen."

Janie squinted at me and rolled her lips. "Okay. And then what happened?"

"I told you. A little kid grabbed the tongs out of her hand and she dropped the cookie. Immediate meltdown." I shook my head. "I should have listened to her," I muttered. "I set her up to fail."

"Jack." Janie's hands settled on my chest. "You didn't set her up to fail. Yes, she was in a bad mood. Yes, in hindsight it looks like it would have been better to go grocery shopping tomorrow. But that's not how this works. Not every bad mood ends in a meltdown. Maya is perfectly capable of understanding that she doesn't get everything she wants. It's not like you took her to a parade, which she is *not* capable of dealing with. Anyway, it was my fault, too." She chewed her lip and her gaze faltered.

My hands went to her hips like it was the most natural thing in the world. "How so?"

She sighed. "Yesterday she was a little bit anxious about the shift in my hours at the bar. She thought it meant you wouldn't live here anymore since I don't need a babysitter late at night. Honestly, that hadn't even occurred to me until she asked me about it. I told her I didn't know. There wasn't time to talk about it this morning, so I figured it could wait until I got home from work."

I stilled. Moving out hadn't occurred to me, either. "You want me to leave?"

Her hands spasmed on my shirt. "I didn't say that." She didn't lift her eyes from my throat. "But you *are* leaving, right? In September. Maya will be back in school, and you'll—" Her eyes finally met mine with a question in them.

A question I still didn't have an answer to. "I could stay. For the rest of summer, I mean. It doesn't make a whole lot of sense to move out now when everything is working. It's easier to stay."

"Right." She nodded quickly. "Right. Okay."

Her mouth was close enough to kiss. Holding myself back felt unnatural. She wanted that kiss as much as I did. It was there in the way her breath quickened, her gaze dipped to my mouth, and she licked her lips. She wanted it —but she wasn't going to take it.

So I thought.

But Janie always did surprise me.

She rolled onto her toes and pressed her lips to mine, quick and fleeting. "Thank you," she whispered.

And then she darted inside, leaving me standing there with my heart banging against my ribs.

22

JANIE

CLAIRE

How would you feel about Maya spending a few days with her aunts? We're going to spend July 4th at the cabin, and we thought it might be fun for Maya to come along and avoid the fireworks. We don't see much of her now that you're never at the ranch.

JANIE

How long are you going to be out there?

CLAIRE

Three days. We'll pick her up the morning of July 4th and bring her home Sunday night. Come on, you know Maya loves it. So many amphibians!

JANIE

You mean frogs. There are frogs. We happen to have frogs here, too, you know.

MAYA'S REACTION TO A LONG WEEKEND WITH HER AUNTS FAR away from the dreaded fireworks was an immediate yes. She had her bags packed and ready to go before she went to bed that night.

"You're not leaving yet," I told her as we settled onto her bed to read a book together. "Claire isn't picking you up until Friday. You have a birthday party to go to tomorrow, remember?"

"Sam." Maya nodded, snuggling deeper under the blanket. "I got him a Lego Minecraft set. Do you think he'll like it?"

"I know he will."

"Are you taking me to the party?"

I smoothed a stray wisp of her braid that was tickling my cheek. "I have to work, ladybug. Jack will take you, and I'll meet you both there the second I get off work."

Maya fidgeted with the silky trim of her blanket. "Jack will still be here?"

"Jack will still be here," I said firmly. "He's here until September when you go back to school."

My chest ached. She had asked me that question last night, too. And this morning before I left for work.

And after dinner, she had given him a quick, fierce hug before running to my bathroom to brush her teeth and get ready for bed. Maya was not a hugger. My breath had caught in my throat as I watched him hug her back with so much tenderness in his face.

She thought he would leave because of her meltdown. I knew he wouldn't, but all the assurances in the world wouldn't convince her. She had been left too many times before. The only thing that would prove it to her was time.

Fortunately, Jack was willing to give her that.

We read three books and then I turned out the light. She let me kiss her forehead, which was a small miracle. She was always a little more tolerant of affection in the days following a meltdown. Even meltdowns had a silver lining, and I would take her hugs and kisses while I could get them.

Jack was scrubbing the lasagna pan when I came in for a glass of water. "You don't have to do that. I pay you to watch Maya, not to do all the chores. Leave it to soak. I'll take care of it in the morning." I grabbed a glass from the cabinet and made for the sink.

"I don't mind. You cooked dinner. Dishes are a fair trade."

"Well, thanks. But that pan will take you all night. Just soak it, seriously." I stood there, holding the empty glass, waiting for him to take the hint and get out of my way.

He cocked an eyebrow. "Need something, Ace?"

"The sink." I held up the glass. "For water."

"Go ahead. It's all yours."

"You're still scrubbing the pan," I pointed out. Was he fucking with me?

"Yeah, but I'm not using the faucet. I've got all the soap and water I need. Go for it." His mouth quirked.

Oh, he was *absolutely* fucking with me.

I gritted my teeth. "You're in my way."

"What are you talking about? There's plenty of space." He tilted his head thoughtfully. "You sure are trying your best not to touch me. What's the matter, Ace? Scared you might be tempted to kiss me again and then run away and refuse to talk about it?"

"I'm always tempted to kiss you, you giant dingbat," I snapped.

Oh.

Oh, *no*.

I slapped a hand over my traitorous mouth, but the damage was done. My admission hung there in the air between us.

We stared at each other.

"Janie." His eyes never left mine as he wiped the soap-suds from his hands onto his jeans and took the glass from me and set it aside. "You can't say something like that and expect me not to do something about it. If you don't want me to kiss you, you need to walk away. I'm going to count to three. One. Two—"

I didn't walk away.

I ran.

MAYBE ONE DAY I'd act like an adult instead of three juvenile raccoons in a trench coat, but yesterday was not that day. Neither was today, quite frankly. What was it about Jack that made me feel like a hormonal teenager again, desperate for his attention and simultaneously terrified of it?

A mature adult would not have kissed her manny on the front porch while her daughter was asleep in bed. A mature adult would definitely not have run away—twice! —instead of having a conversation about it.

Don't kiss the manny. Don't even think about fucking the manny. That was the bare minimum of being a good mom. I knew that, but I remained on the precipice of getting my bad out, one accidental brush of our hands away from falling over the edge.

And Jack knew it. Facing his knowing smirk across the breakfast table was intolerable—and humiliating. He seemed to have no trouble keeping his hands to himself. It was all me.

But at least I wouldn't have to deal with this birthday party alone. If there was an upside to having a ridiculously hot manny who happened to be your teenage crush, that was it. Birthday parties were at the top of my least favorite parenting responsibilities. Yes, I was thankful Maya had friends who seemed to view her differences as a good thing instead of plain weird. Yes, I was grateful to adults who ensured she wasn't left out of parties when every other classmate was invited. But ugh. I hated them.

It was such a relief to have Jack in it with me. I had expected him to be nervous about bringing Maya anywhere only a couple days past her meltdown, and children's birthday parties weren't known for their calm, low-stress atmosphere, but Jack had only shrugged and said whatever happened, the world wouldn't stop turning.

I'll handle it, he'd said.

Sexier words had never been spoken. It was a miracle I hadn't leaped over the breakfast table and jumped his bones right then and there.

I headed to the party straight from the Painted Cat, but it was already half over by the time I got there. There was a bouncy house set up in the backyard—my heart sank because Maya had a tendency to treat bouncy houses as an existential crisis. She loved them but hated taking off her shoes. It was unlikely to cause a meltdown, but she could get stuck in a loop.

Then I saw Maya across the yard and breathed a sigh of relief. She had her shoes on and her face was free of tears.

My relief was short lived. Something was wrong. Her braid was half undone and...shorter? I squinted. What the hell? But it was Jack's expression that had me breaking into an anxious sweat. He slowly turned to the nervous-looking kid behind him and the adult—Sam's dad, Glen—at his side as I crossed the yard at a jog. Shit, shit, shit. I knew that lethal look in his eyes. He had looked at Todd the exact same way before he removed his hand from my body.

"All he wanted was a hug," Glen said. "It's his birthday. It wasn't right, but Maya is fine. Couldn't have gotten more than an inch. It's just hair. Boys will be boys, right?"

My vision went redder than the lock of hair clenched in Sam's fist.

23

JACK

I might have let him keep walking if he hadn't said that. At the very least, I would have let him keep his hair.

The switchblade I kept in my pocket was in my hand before the thought had fully formed in my brain. My body acted on instinct. One quick swipe of the blade was all it took. Feeling the sudden lightness, Sam's dad froze, then turned around with a shock-slackened face.

I held up his two-inch ponytail like a trophy. "It's just hair. It will grow back. Boys will be boys, right?"

"You're a psycho." He jabbed his finger in the direction of my chest while backing up a step because he wasn't stupid enough to put an appendage within grabbing distance of me.

"Maybe I am." I shrugged. "Something you might want to consider before you hurt someone I love."

I looked at Sam, who stared back at me with round eyes. I didn't feel great about that, but the kid needed to learn to keep his hands to himself. "That's not yours," I said, pointing at Maya's hair in his fist. He'd cut it right above the black hairband that kept her braid from coming undone. "Give it back to her."

Looking thoroughly chastened, he handed it over to Maya. "I'm sorry," he whispered.

Maya looked at it and shrugged. "Okay."

Okay? I blinked.

"You need to do something about your manny," Glen said, and I realized Janie was behind me.

"Oh, I plan to," she said.

And she was *livid*.

"I'M NOT GOING TO APOLOGIZE." I faced Janie in the soft glow of the porchlight with my arms crossed defensively over my chest. "You know how kids who slice open animals turn into serial killers? Well, kids who cut little girls' hair because they won't hug them turn into date rapists. If his dad isn't going to teach him how not to be a little piece of shit, then someone else has to. I did the world a favor."

Maya was asleep, completely untraumatized by her forced haircut, her hair freshly washed and braided. She'd spent the car ride home yapping about the party and how she couldn't wait for her aunts to pick her up tomorrow. I was closer to a meltdown than she was.

"I'm not asking you to apologize. Trust me." Her voice turned wry. "I'm the last person who would make anyone apologize to a man who hasn't learned to keep his hands to himself. Anyway, his hair was stupid. Growing a ponytail in the back doesn't make balding in front any less obvious."

I shifted restlessly. Cutting Glen's hair wasn't enough. I still had all that adrenaline in my system with nowhere for it to go. I needed to hit something. Or...fuck someone. I tried not to let my gaze linger where the hem of Janie's skirt met her pale thighs. She had her knees pressed together as she faced me from the swing. I kept waiting for her to relax, for her knees to drift apart enough to give me something to jerk off to tonight, but she kept her thick thighs locked tight.

I wasn't proud of it.

But I pushed that shame aside and peeked again.

"Maya still wants to be friends with Sam, so I'll need to do some damage control," Janie went on, completely unaware that I was trying to eye-fuck her and completely unhelpful about it. "I'll give them a few days to cool off and then invite Glen and Cheryl for coffee or something to clear the air. They can't honestly be mad that you cut his hair when Glen was totally fine with Sam cutting Maya's. That would be so hypocritical."

I sighed. "I hate to shatter your rose-colored glasses, honey, but people are often hypocrites."

Her lower lip fell open and she blinked at me.

"What?" I said.

"Nothing." She didn't just shake her head. She shook her whole body. "It's been a while since you called me honey, that's all. It surprised me."

I speared my fingers through my hair and tugged. "It's hard as hell keeping myself professional around you. You're sitting there thinking up ways to be a good mom to Maya, and I'm trying to look up your skirt."

She snorted and looked away, her cheeks pink. "You're trying to look up my skirt, and I'm pressing my thighs together because I get wet every time I think about the way you stood up for Maya." She rolled her eyes. "I'm such a good mom," she muttered sarcastically under her breath.

Like hell was I going to let her talk shit about herself.

Like hell was I going to let her keep her thighs together.

I was kneeling in front of her before she got the last word out. "In the first place, you are a fantastic mom, and trust me, I know what a fantastic mom looks like because I have one myself." With a hand on each of her knees, I stared her straight in the eyes. "In the second place, how wet?"

I watched her struggle with herself. I watched her relent. I hope she didn't feel like she lost the battle, because it felt like winning to me.

She ran her tongue over her bottom lip, leaving it glossy. "Find out for yourself."

Bad Janie was back. Thank fuck. It was a mystery to me

why she kept this part of her locked down tight, but goddamn, it was beautiful when it rose to the surface. Fucking glorious.

There was no resistance as I pushed her knees apart. My palms slid up her inner thighs with slow, ruthless intention, giving her every opportunity to stop me. When I got to her core, I paused, tracing the lace hem of her cotton underwear with my thumbs. Goosebumps broke out on her soft thighs and her breath hitched.

She watched me with hooded eyes. "Are you going to sit there petting me, soldier, or are you going to find something useful to do with those fingers?"

"Honey, I've got nowhere to be. I'll be taking my time here, thank you."

But my thumbs apparently had a mind of their own, because they met in the middle. I could feel her damp heat through the gusset of her underwear and I had my answer. Very wet. She was very fucking wet.

I groaned. "Fuck, Janie. You're soaked. Is this all for me?"

"All for you," she whispered.

I slipped one thumb under the cotton and ghosted up her seam, wet and warm and silky. She shifted toward my touch with a sharp inhale and my gaze flicked to hers. "Pull up your skirt. I want to see."

Janie caught the hem with her fingertips and slowly dragged her skirt up her thighs, teasing me. My dick twitched with every new inch she exposed. When she lifted it past the blue triangle of her underwear, she widened her legs a smidgeon more. Fucking tease.

"Show me." My voice came out husky and raw.

"Hm. Should I?" she wondered. Her hand went between her legs and she toyed with the lace there. "I don't know."

I swallowed a groan, watching her fingers drive me insane. "You should. You definitely should."

With a little laugh, she hooked an index finger under the hem and pulled her panties to the side, shivering as the cool night air hit where she was hottest. I covered my mouth with my fist and leaned back on my heels for a better view. Copper curls and pink flushed skin.

"Damn, you're pretty. Like a sunrise," I murmured. "What am I going to do with you?"

Her laugh was breathless and strangled. "Fuck me, I hope. Otherwise I'm going to feel pretty awkward about flashing my pussy at you."

"Oh, I'm going to fuck you, Janie," I promised darkly. "I'm going to fuck this pretty pussy every way I can. With my fingers." I pushed two inside. When I pumped them in and out, she moaned softly. "With my tongue." Still pumping my fingers in her slick pussy, I leaned in and swiped her clit with my tongue. She gasped, her fingers diving into my hair. "With my dick." Impatient for all of it, I dragged her panties down her legs and tossed them aside.

"Yes," she whimpered. "Yes."

I loved her like this. My lips curved into a smile and I pressed every word to her pussy. "I'm going to make such a mess of you, honey. Because that's what you do to me. You turned me inside out, made me break my own rules, made me want things I don't know how to want."

I kept at her with my mouth and fingers as she writhed against me. Her nails dug into my scalp, a sharp flick of pain that kept me steady. I added a third finger and stretched her wider. Her breaths came on loud pants now as she pushed closer and closer, her pussy tightening around my fingers. I didn't draw it out. Didn't make her wait. I latched my lips around her clit, sucked hard, and sent her flying. She soaked my fingers, my tongue, and I lapped up everything she gave me.

"Jack," she muttered as I grabbed her wrists, taking her with me as I pushed to stand. "Jesus fucking Christ, give a girl a minute."

"I don't have a minute. My dick is so hard the wind could make me blow right now. On your feet, honey."

She swayed against me with a soft chuckle. Her hands cupped my face, squishing my cheeks a little, eyes dark and sparkling as they met mine. "You literally made my knees weak, soldier. Good job."

No commendation had ever felt so good. "I'm happy to repeat it any time you ask. Hands on the rail, Ace."

I spun her away from me so she faced the inky velvet sky and flipped her skirt up. She shivered, her hands tightening on the rail. I unzipped my jeans and groaned with relief when my cock sprang free.

"The stars are out," she said.

The only stars I cared about were the ones in her eyes

when she told me over her shoulder, "I've always wanted to be fucked under the stars."

"Happy to oblige in making all your sex fantasies come true." I lined myself up at her entrance, dragging the weeping head through her wet slit so she knew I was there, and then slammed home.

For a moment, all I saw was stars but not a single one of them was in the sky.

"Oh, my god," she whispered. "Oh, my *god*."

I couldn't move. I was dangerously close to spilling on the first thrust. I blinked and forced myself to focus on something other than the warm, soaked pussy clenched around me like it was made to take my cock. The constellations above us. There was the frying pan. One of the dippers. Hard to tell if it was big or little without the other one to compare it to.

"Jack," Janie commanded. "*Move*."

I moved, pulling out slowly and then snapping my hips flush to her ass again. "Like that?" I teased. "Or..." I pulled out again and this time only pushed halfway in again, thrusting in rapid, shallow thrusts. "Like this?"

She groaned. "All of it. I want all of it."

"All of what, Janie?" I was merciless, taunting both of us with what we wanted.

"All of *you*."

I slammed into her so hard, so deep, that we both cried out. "You want me? Or you want my dick?" I leaned over her back, caught her chin in my hand, and forcibly turned her face to mine as I fucked us both to the edge. "Tell me."

"Both." Her eyes were dark and luminous in the moon-light. "I want both."

And then she braced against the rail and pushed back against me, meeting my thrusts with thrusts of her own, and I lost my ever-loving mind. I pounded into her with feral fury. My fingers dug into the soft flesh of her hips and when I finally felt her pussy clench around me, her orgasm took me over the edge with her.

I collapsed over her, holding my weight so I wouldn't crush her against the rail, and breathed into the sweat-damp curve of her neck. "You can have it," I roughed out. "All of me. You can have it."

"Mmm." She reached behind us to rub the back of my head and gave a happy little laugh. "Good. I'll take it. I'm claiming you for the next two months, soldier. You're mine until September."

September.

Because that was when I was leaving.

I had thought that was what I wanted. To escape a life that had made me feel claustrophobic since the moment I had pulled into town back in November.

I didn't feel claustrophobic now, with Janie's warm, sated body beneath me and the whole Colorado sky above me.

Two months wasn't enough. I wanted so much more.

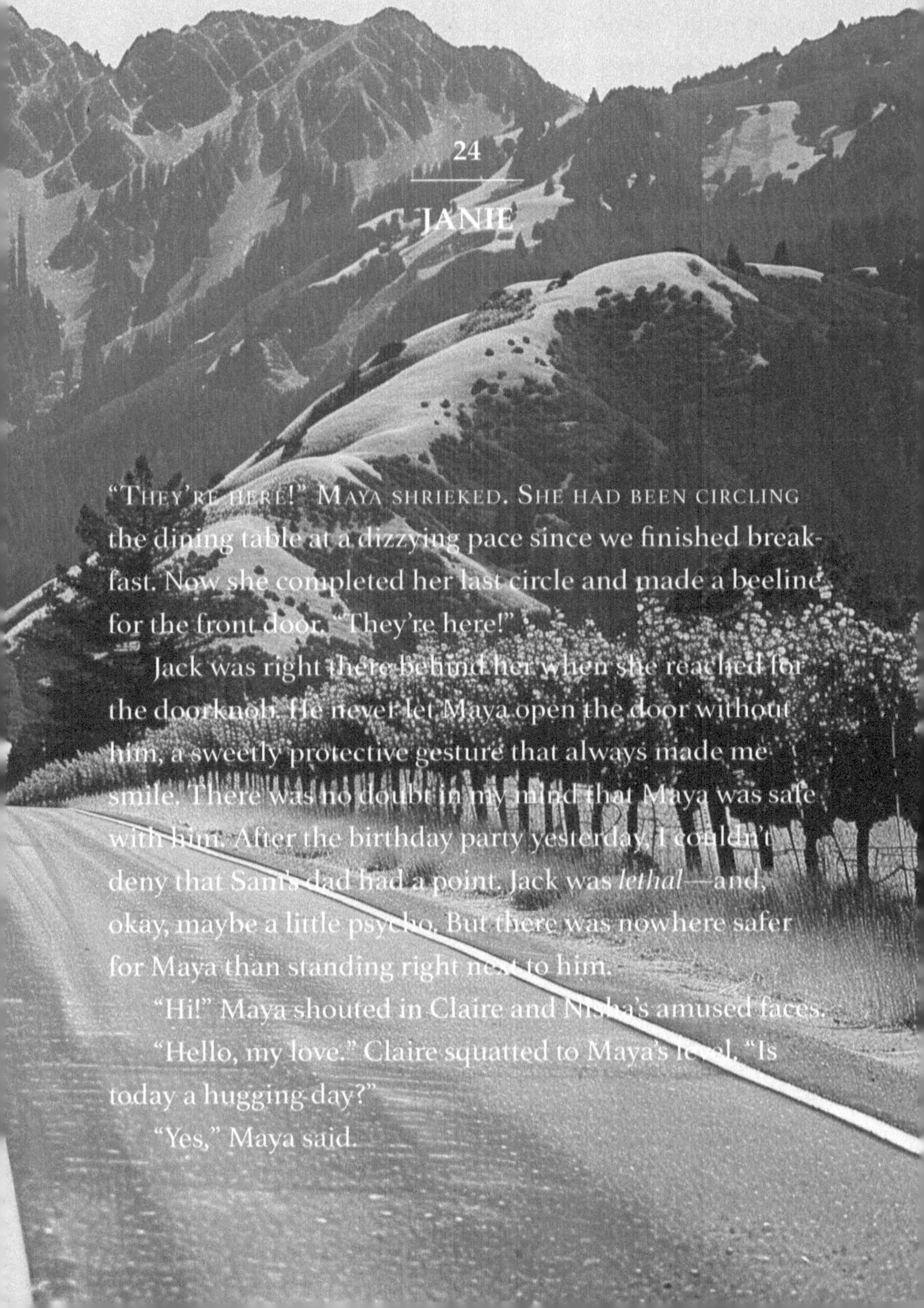

24

***

JANIE

"They're here!" Maya shrieked. She had been circling the dining table at a dizzying pace since we finished breakfast. Now she completed her last circle and made a beeline for the front door. "They're here!"

Jack was right there behind her when she reached for the doorknob. He never let Maya open the door without him, a sweetly protective gesture that always made me smile. There was no doubt in my mind that Maya was safe with him. After the birthday party yesterday, I couldn't deny that Sam's dad had a point. Jack was *lethal*—and, okay, maybe a little psycho. But there was nowhere safer for Maya than standing right next to him.

"Hi!" Maya shouted in Claire and Nisha's amused faces.

"Hello, my love." Claire squatted to Maya's level. "Is today a hugging day?"

"Yes," Maya said.

"Wonderful." Claire didn't miss a beat, but her gaze shot to mine over Maya's head as she wrapped her in a brief, tight squeeze. *Meltdown*, I mouthed, and she nodded. She straightened and Nisha claimed a hug of her own.

"All packed?" Nisha asked.

"Since Wednesday," Jack said drily. "Maya is super excited."

Claire looked at Jack, her expression openly curious. "You must be the manny."

"Jack Price." He extended his hand for a shake. "We met briefly at your parents' garden party back in May. My mom was catering the event."

"He's my manny and a Navy SEAL," Maya piped up. "Mom calls him soldier even though he's not a soldier. I think Mom shouldn't tease him, but Jack says he likes it when Mom is a little mean."

My chest felt hot. "Jesus, kid. Way to sell me out," I muttered.

Claire and Nisha turned to me with identical fascinated expressions.

"Is that so?" Claire said. "A special forces operator who happened to be at the garden party. You don't say. Did Janie by any chance show you the foyer, Jack?"

Jack quirked an eyebrow at me, his blue eyes glinting with amusement. "What do you want me to say here, Ace?"

"Nothing." I shot daggers at him with my eyeballs. "You say *nothing*."

"Yes, ma'am." Jack saluted with a cocky grin. "Come on,

Maya. Let's say goodbye to your tadpoles while your mom helps Claire and Nisha get your suitcase in the car."

"Great!" Maya bolted down the hallway.

Jack shot me a wink and ambled after her.

Nisha grabbed Maya's purple suitcase and made a big show of hefting it off the floor. "Oof! It's *so* heavy. Thank goodness you're here to help, Janie. I don't know if I could carry all five pounds of this by myself."

I rolled my eyes.

"Forget the suitcase," Claire said. "I don't know how long it takes to say goodbye to tadpoles, but I think that hot manny of yours has bought us five minutes, tops. What do we need to know?"

"I texted you a copy of Maya's insurance card in case of emergencies, along with the contact information for her primary doctor. Maya had a meltdown on Monday. She actually hasn't had many issues this summer. A boy cut her hair at a birthday party yesterday, and I thought for sure she would have the biggest meltdown we ever saw, but no. Let's see, what else..." I mused. This wasn't Claire's first weekend with Maya, so she knew what to expect.

"Great, but that's not what Claire meant," Nisha said. "What is going on with you and your manny?"

I played dumb. "What do you mean?"

"Janie," Claire said in her best kindergarten teacher voice. "You cannot fuck your manny."

"I know that," I huffed like I wasn't, in fact, fucking my manny. Because I did know that, in the way that people knew a third glass of wine was a bad idea. Knowing and resisting were two very different things. "But what if I fucked him *before* he was my manny?"

Claire served me a look. "Oh, like a blowjob in our parents' foyer, you mean?" She rolled her eyes. "Yes, this is a mature adult relationship that won't cause any problems for Maya. I can see that." She sighed like it came from her soul. "I love you, Janie, but you make terrible decisions when it comes to men."

My head snapped up. "One terrible decision. *One*. And no one will ever let me forget it."

"Having an affair with your child's caregiver would be another," Claire said gently. "I think you know that."

She made it sound so...gross. "He's only here for the summer. Jack is leaving in September." I said it to remind myself as much as my sister.

"That doesn't change the fact that Maya needs him now. What happens if things go wrong with you two? Relationships are messy. You know that. The last thing Maya needs is mess."

She wasn't saying anything I hadn't said to myself a hundred times already. God, I was an awful mom. So fucking selfish. Maya deserved better. What was I thinking, putting her happiness and well-being at risk? And for what, good sex with a man who would be out of our lives before the first frost?

Really, really, *really* good sex. Mind-blowing, soul-shattering, life-altering sex.

But it was still just sex. It wasn't love. Even if it felt like maybe it *could* be, someday, like that was where we were heading—we were never going to get there. We had an expiration date. If we kept going like this, I was going to be hurting as much as Maya when summer was over.

Claire took me by the shoulders. "You *are* a good mom, Janie. But I need you to look me in the eyes and tell me nothing is going on with your manny."

"Nothing is going on with Jack," I lied in a voice two octaves above my usual tone.

Claire rolled her lips together like she was suppressing a laugh. "You always were a shit liar, my love. Also, your underwear is on the porch. You might want to pick them up before your daughter sees them."

My face went up in flames. I hadn't spared a single thought for the ruined panties Jack had stripped from my body before eating me on the porch swing. There had been the nagging feeling that I was forgetting something while I showered and changed into my pajamas, but I figured it was just my guilty conscience. Not my underwear. Jack had truly fucked me stupid.

"It's going to be okay." Claire gave my shoulders a sympathetic squeeze. "If this thing with Jack is only temporary, then...you know...wrap it up." She circled her wrist impatiently. "You have this whole weekend to get him out of your system. Get your bad out, Janie."

I stilled, certain I had misheard her. "Get my bad out?"

"Yeah. Oh, don't look at me like that. I don't mean it like

Mom does. You've been a single mom since you were barely old enough to drink. Of course you want to cut loose once in a while, and even I can see that if you're into men, you're definitely into Jack. He's hot. So use this weekend to do that. Get your bad out, and then you can settle down again. I don't want you to get hurt, that's all. I don't want Maya to get hurt, either."

25

JACK

BRAX
Essie and James have a spot staked out for the fireworks. Parade first?

ZACK
Hell yeah. The library is closed for the holiday, so Hannah says we can park there.

ADAM
Meet there at 5 pm?

ZACK
We'll be there. You in, Jack? We can walk down to the bar and buy you a drink to thank you for your service.

BRAX
The Painted Cat is closed.

ZACK
Yeah, but I hear you have the key. ;)

BRAX

What have I told you about using me for
free drinks?

ZACK

But it's for Jack. He's a hero. Are you
going to say no to a hero?

JACK

No one's buying me a drink. You know I
hate that shit.

See you at 3. Janie's coming, too.

"So, um, are you going to be around this weekend?" Janie fidgeted with the seatbelt as I started the truck. Since Janie only fidgeted when she had something on her mind she wasn't saying, it caught my notice.

We hadn't had a chance to talk about last night. Frankly, I hadn't thought it was necessary. Everything thing we needed to say, we laid it all out under the stars. I knew where I stood, and I thought she did too. Clearly I was wrong about that, or she wouldn't be asking such a ridiculous question.

"Of course I'll be around. Why wouldn't I be?" I asked, shifting into reverse and backing out of her driveway with one hand on the back of her seat.

"You officially have weekends off now that I'm only working at the bar Monday through Friday. I thought maybe you would want to go see your mom or use one of the Lodestar cabins. Not that you *have* to leave," she added hastily when she caught sight of my expression. "You live there, too. I just figured that weekends are your time now, so there's no reason to stay."

"You're my reason, Janie."

Her head whipped to look at me. "Yeah?"

"Yeah."

It really was that simple. I loved hanging out with Maya, but having Janie all to myself for a few days? That was too good to pass up. The second I had learned she would be staying with her aunts for the weekend, I'd cleared my schedule—not that there had been much to clear, but I had briefly considered heading to Mercy River for a long weekend. And that was *before* sex on the porch. If we spent the whole weekend fully dressed, playing cards, then that was fine with me. I'd take Janie any way I could get her.

Not that I was going to put that offer on the table. I planned on getting Janie naked as much as possible this weekend.

I reached for her hand across the console and threaded my fingers through hers, leaving our palms clasped on her thigh.

"We probably shouldn't make a big deal about it. If it's just sex—"

I stopped the truck right there in the middle of the road. No one was behind me, but people in Aspen Springs were used to dodging cows. They could dodge my truck just as well.

I twisted in my seat to look at her. "What do you mean, *if it's just sex*?" I demanded. "It's never been just sex with us. Not even that first night in the snowstorm. I thought we made that pretty clear last night when you said you wanted all of me." Something was happening in my chest. It felt like a fucking heart attack. I didn't like it.

"That's not what I—" She tried to tug her hand free, but I didn't let go. She gave an exasperated huff. "I don't mean that there aren't feelings involved. Of course there are feelings. I like you, Jack. I like you *so much*. But with you leaving in September, we can't have a real relationship. If I call you my boyfriend, Maya will get confused. She might think you're staying. I know it's going to hurt her when you leave either way, but I'm trying to minimize the damage here." She squeezed my hand. "Can you understand that?"

A car honked. I rolled down my window and waved them around. Idiots. They couldn't figure that out themselves?

"I can understand that," I allowed. More than understand.

The thought of hurting Maya made my whole body physically ache. I *hated* it, even though I knew it wasn't something I could or even *should* protect her from. People moved away, friendships disintegrated, family members passed away. Heartache was human. But I didn't want to be the cause of Maya's heartache. I wanted to be the one comforting her through it.

I shifted into drive. "You're right. We probably shouldn't make a big deal of it around Maya. That's fair. But she's not here now, and I don't think any of our friends are going to rat us out."

Apparently we weren't the only ones with the bright idea to use the library parking lot because by the time we rolled up, it was crammed full of cars. We texted the group to let them know we'd catch up with them when we found a spot and ended up parking a couple blocks away.

I strode around the front of the truck to open her door and found her still buckled. With a laugh, I unclasped her seatbelt and helped her out. Then I pressed her up against the door and kissed her because it had been a whole thirty minutes since I'd had my mouth on hers and that was way too fucking long.

"Jack," she protested, my name smothered between our mouths. "Someone will see."

I pulled back to look at her just in time to see her pupils flare with heat. She liked a little danger. "Good. I hope they do." I leaned in to kiss her again, but she twisted her face away and slipped under my arm, laughing. I snagged her wrist and hauled her back. "Don't run from me, Ace. There's nowhere for you to hide."

She made a show of looking at all the buildings,

people, and cars, then back to me with raised brows. "Are you kidding? With this crowd? You'd never find me."

Her words hit like a struck gong. A low thrum of excitement vibrated through me. "Careful, Janie. Hunting people was my specialty. I might take that as a challenge."

"I dare you," she taunted, her eyes laughing.

I caged her against the truck. "Are you sure this is a game you want to play, honey? I've been chasing you for months now. You know what that does to me, living under the same roof as you, so close and so untouchable?" My fingertips ghosted her soft cheek, traced her jaw, found her throat. She swallowed, her throat bobbing under the light pressure of my palm. "I'm out of patience. If you run, I'll chase you. And when I catch you, I'm not letting go."

Her lips parted as she stared up at me with blown pupils and flushed cheeks. "What happens if you don't catch me? I don't want to watch the parade alone."

I laughed. "Be serious."

That triggered her competitive streak like I knew would. Her eyes narrowed. "I want a thirty-second head start."

"Baby, you can have a whole two minutes." My muscles were already waking up, ready for the hunt. I hadn't felt this alive since I'd almost died.

"You're on." She was as gleeful as a kid on Christmas morning. Walking backward, she taunted, "Call me when you're ready to admit defeat."

Then she spun on her toes, preparing to run.

She made it two steps before I caught her with an arm

around her chest and hauled her back against me. Her whole body tensed, ready to fight. This was going to be *fun*. I nuzzled her hair. Breathed in her scent.

"One more thing, Janie. I'm going to fuck you where I find you, so don't stop running until you want to be caught."

26

JANIE

ASPEN SPRINGS LOVED A PARADE. THE WHOLE TOWN WAS here, lining the one-mile stretch of First Street to watch the parade go by. Everything was red, white, and blue. The overflowing flower baskets hanging on the iron lampposts, the bunting decorating the storefronts, the middle-aged dads in their Uncle Sam hats. It made it hard to get my bearings on the congested sidewalk.

But I didn't need to get my bearings. I was perfectly safe. Jack was not going to fuck me in the middle of a literal parade on First Street with all of our friends and family in attendance. He'd hunt me, always letting me stay one step ahead of him, and then when I was ready, I'd lead him home and let him catch me.

What we were doing, it was just a game.

But, god, it was fun.

Excitement shivered down my spine as I weaved through the crowd. All the familiar and unfamiliar faces blended together until it was all a blur. Four rows of men in kilts played *America the Beautiful* on bagpipes as they marched down the middle of the street—half the families of this town had Scottish and Irish ancestors that had come to Colorado during the gold rush, and even those that didn't often claimed they did.

I squeezed between a man holding a sign that said NO KINGS SINCE 1776 and a woman rocking an American flag bandana as a top. My two-minute head start had ticked down to a minute. *What if he can't find me in this mess?* The thought drew me up short. I twisted, trying to see over the throng. Where was he?

Thirty seconds.

Maybe I should go back, just to make sure he didn't lose track of me. The noise of the crowd pitched higher as the float with the Golden Nugget rolled by. Mr. Willis waved from the front, decked out in his best suit, tossing beaded necklaces like it was Mardi Gras on Bourbon Street. The float paused. A knot of people surged into the street, taking me with them.

Twenty seconds.

I ducked under the outstretched arms and retreated to a doorway. My shoe was untied, and I needed a second to plan my next move. Keep going, go back, shelter in place?

Time's up.

After a quick glance around—still no sign of Jack—I dropped to the ground to tie my shoe, my back to the store door so at least he couldn't sneak up behind me. Like he could even find me in all this chaos. Sure, he was ex-special forces, but what did that mean, really? It wasn't like—

A prickle of awareness on the back of my neck made me look up suddenly. All the air froze in my lungs as I tried to make sense of what I was seeing underneath the float.

Jack.

There he was, across the street, his big body crouched on the ground like he was mimicking my posture, just waiting for me to notice. Our gazes locked. A slow grin spread across his features, and he tipped his chin like a predator scenting its prey. My eyes widened as the truth banged in my chest.

Oh.

Oh, *shit.*

That man was going to catch me, and he was absolutely going to fuck me right here in the middle of a parade on First Street with all our friends and family looking on. How had I believed for one second that Jack was safe? He had promised to fuck me where he found me, and since I had as much will power when Jack's hands were on me as Cookie Monster at a bakery, I was in very real danger.

Run, my brain screamed.

But instead I froze like a scared little rabbit.

The wheels turned as the float moved forward. They blocked my view of the street, but I kept my gaze locked on the spot where I had seen him. The wheels passed and—

He wasn't there.

Shit, he wasn't there.

I shot to my feet, my head pivoting like a weathervane

in a bipolar storm, eyes frantically roving the crowd. Where the hell was he?

There.

Jack moved through the crowd like he was pushing aside paper dolls instead of real people. My heart beat so hard I could feel it in my eardrums. My breath came in shallow, rapid pants.

He's coming.

I was fucked. Figuratively and soon to be literally. Adrenaline tunneled my vision and made my limbs shake. My belly fluttered like a million butterflies had taken flight. Fear. Arousal.

Run! my brain shrieked again.

This time I listened.

My eyes locked on his determined face, I scrambled backward, bumping into people as I went, one step, then another—oh, god, he was gaining on me—I squeezed between two women and let their bodies protect my own.

I whirled and ducked, fighting my way through the throng. The crowd was too tight for me to truly run, and frustration made me clumsy and stupid. But there—a break in the bodies. Freedom. I bolted toward it, toward the alley beyond it. I was so close! I could make it. My feet moved faster, buoyed by hubris.

I never stood a chance.

Right before I veered into the alley, I turned around. Just to see how close the danger really was. Too close, it turned out. Jack lunged forward. All the breath left me in an audible whoosh as his arm wrapped around my waist and lifted me off my feet. He spun us in a dizzying circle, moving us deeper into the alley, almost like we were dancing, until the momentum landed me against the store wall.

My ass hit the brick with enough force to make me wince. My head would have done the same, but his hand got there first, protecting me from the worst of it.

I was surrounded by him, effectively caged in by a hard wall and a body that might as well have been a hard wall. Honestly, I would have a better shot at knocking down the bricks than moving him. We matched each other breath for heavy breath as we stared at each other, my breasts brushing against his muscled chest with every intake of air.

And, god, I was so *aware* of it—aware of everything.

The scratch of brick against my bare calves. My hard nipples straining against the soft cotton of my bra. The hot, slick feeling between my legs. And the gentle stroke of his thumb against the nape of my neck.

It was that tender touch that made my bones turn to water.

"Hurt?" he asked curtly.

I shook my head. "How did you find me so fast?" The words came out grumpy, but I couldn't help it. If I had known he meant every word, this wasn't the place I would have chosen to be caught. Sure, knowing someone could walk by and see us at any second was a turn on. But it smelled like pee.

"I never lost you." He squeezed my nape and then slowly skimmed his hand down the curves of my body like he was taking inventory of what was his. "You're all I see, Janie. I couldn't look away from you if I tried."

It was threat and promise, danger and safety, all rolled into one. I shivered in the sudden chill as the shade of the building enveloped my damp, overheated skin. His jaw clenched tight, a muscle popping in his cheek, as his gaze roved over my face.

"I was very clear on the rules, Ace. I fuck you where I find you." He hooked his index finger in the waistband of my shorts, his thumb running over the metal button, toying with it. Toying with *me*. "Were you ready to be found?"

"No," I admitted.

His fist closed around my waistband, pulling the fabric taut until the seam wedged between my pussy lips. I gasped and then whimpered as he shifted even closer. Outside the alley, the noise of the crowd pitched higher. My heart damn near pounded out of my chest with it.

Jack's eyes were shards of blue ice as he looked down at me, his grip still tight on my shorts. "Tell me you're not wet." He lowered his head to mine and nipped small, sharp bites along my jaw. I tilted my face to give him better access because even here, like this, I couldn't resist his touch. "You can't, can you? Because it would be a lie, and you're a terrible liar."

I fisted his shirt in my hands, but even I didn't know if I intended to push him away or pull him closer.

"God, I want to fuck you. I *need* to fuck you." His voice was hoarse and frayed. "Tell me I can. Please."

Everything snapped into focus. The fear, adrenaline, and arousal were all still there, but so was a heady rush of something else altogether. Something I had experienced precious little of in my lifetime. I felt *powerful.* This incredible, strong, lethal man was under my control. He would never hurt me, not as long as he had breath in his body.

I was prey. He was the hunter. But the hunter would starve without the prey, and I had never seen a man as hungry as Jack was right now.

"No," I said. "Not here."

A tremor wracked his body. He slapped his palm to the bricks next to my face with a guttural groan. I didn't even flinch—I only got wetter. For a moment his hand tightened on my waistband like he had no intention of letting me go. And then slowly, so slowly I knew it cost him something, he set me free. His breath ghosted my ear in a single word.

"*Run.*"

27

JACK

I CONSIDERED MYSELF A PATIENT MAN. WHEN I HAD A target, I would wait as long as I had to. I never pulled the trigger before I had the perfect shot.

But it took everything I had not to haul Janie back to me by her hair and fuck her against this wall like I had promised I would. I watched her sprint away with the last vestiges of my self-control, red hair streaming behind her like a banner, and something primal in me roared to life.

You can run Janie, but I'll run faster.

And this time, when I caught her, there would be no stopping me from claiming her. She understood that now. But just in case, I gave her another head start. For me as much as for her. Frustrated need coiled in my gut, making me feel like a drawn bow waiting for the release. I needed to run.

I needed to *chase.*

Pure adrenaline surged through my veins as I counted

down. I could see her copper head bobbing and weaving amongst the crowd as she headed away from the parade. A minute passed, and then two. I trailed her at a slow jog, keeping her in my sight without getting too close. She was heading home, I figured. Somewhere she felt safe.

And then she veered left.

My brow furrowed. Where the hell was she going? There was nothing in this direction except an old hay farm. I quickened my pace. She slowed suddenly, and a twitch of her shoulders told me she was about to look behind her. I ducked behind a car so she wouldn't see me. Her gaze swept past me in a wide arc, and she bit her lip. Nervous that I was there? Or nervous that I wasn't?

I'm right here, honey. Any time you want me.

With another long, sweeping look over her shoulder, Janie crossed the street and made for the fence at a quick jog. Beyond that was a maze of first cut hay bales nearly as tall as she was. The perfect place to hide.

She ducked between the rails and then paused to catch her breath. She leaned on the gate post and tilted her face to the sky like she was admiring the sunset. My eyes narrowed. The sunset was spectacular, I'd give her that, but she was a little too comfortable right now. A little too smug with her own power. She owned me and she knew that. The knowledge made her feel safe and in control. But my girl was about to find out just how dangerous it was to keep a wolf on a leash.

I picked up a pebble and with a flick of my wrist, sent it skipping across the asphalt.

Plip, plip, plip.

Her shoulders shot up to her ears and she froze. I ducked into a shadow just as she turned around. Her head pivoted this way and that as she searched for the source.

"Hello?" she called, nervousness making her voice thin and shrill.

I didn't move.

She shook the tension from her shoulders and faced the field again. I stepped out of the shadows, not even trying to muffle my footsteps. A twig cracked under my boot. She whipped around again and I swear to god, she stopped breathing.

We stared at each other across the open space. The road and fence were between us, but neither of them could keep her from me. I watched her weigh her options. The haystacks were about a hundred yards from where she stood. She might be able to make it before I caught her, but it was doubtful.

"You could just let me take you now," I offered.

Her eyes narrowed. "You can try," she dared.

I grinned.

And then she flew. *Snap.* There it went, the last tether of my self-control. Every cell in my body was consumed with the need to catch her and pin her down. I tore after her. Shit, she was fast, adrenaline spurring her on.

But I was faster.

She glanced over her shoulder just in time to see me place my hand on the top rail of the fence and vault over it. Her eyes widened and she stumbled. *Fuck.* But she quickly righted herself and picked up speed. *That's my girl.*

Ten yards and I was gaining.

Five yards and she didn't give up.

Two yards and she slipped into the maze with a breathless, triumphant laugh that made some inner beast inside me rage with frustrated hunger. I followed her in, squeezing my body between two round bales, and then paused, listening. There was no sound of footsteps. Either she was tiptoeing on the grass, or she was hiding in place.

I closed my eyes, letting my other senses heighten. The aroma of sweet summer hay was almost cloying, but beneath that, the faintest hint of her shampoo lingered. The sound of the breeze rustling the grass mingled with something more rhythmic. *Her breath.* She was close. I matched mine to hers so that if she were listening she'd only hear one set of inhales and exhales. *Closer.*

My eyes popped open just as Janie made a mad dash from one bale to another. Her copper hair glowing in the fading light might as well have been a red flag waving in front of a bull.

Mine.

Her big doe eyes went wide as I barreled toward her. She backed up on instinct, flattening her body against a haybale. Like it could offer her even a modicum of protection against me. I was a man possessed, half-crazed, fucking feral for a taste of her. I hit my knees with three feet left to go and slid the rest of the way home.

"Jack!" she gasped.

There was genuine concern in her voice—for me, not herself—and I knew I was going to feel every year of my age in the morning, but right then the only thing I cared about was getting my mouth on her. Nothing could stop me now except her telling me no. But all I heard from her was an eager, breathy *yes* as I tore at the zipper on her shorts like a fucking animal.

I dragged her shorts and underwear down her hips, past her milky thighs with their freckles like scattered sunshine, and let them drop to her feet. I didn't even let her step out of them before I pressed my face between her thighs and took the deepest breath I've ever taken. Something settled inside me as her scent surrounded me. Her musky arousal, clean skin, a hint of sweat. Janie. My Janie.

I had fucking *earned* this pussy.

Unable to stand another second not tasting her, I delved my tongue between her lips and licked her entrance to clit. She was soaked.

"*Jack*," she said again. But this time there was no fear in her voice. Only need. Her hands gripped my hair like she thought I might change my mind. Like I wouldn't give my right hand to stay right here, on my knees for her, forever.

My dick strained painfully against my jeans. I didn't stop licking her while I unzipped to relieve the pressure. I ran my palm over the heavy weight of it once, twice, before returning all my attention to the meal in front of me.

Delicious. So goddamn delicious.

Her hips canted into my mouth and we both groaned. I

nipped at her, payback for making me wait so long, and then sucked her clit. She cried out and yanked at my hair. She was already teetering on the edge, her nerves at their breaking point from our chase.

"Fuck," she whispered. "*Fuck*."

Her legs trembled violently and then her knees gave out altogether. She would have hit the ground, but I caught her, taking her with me as I rolled onto my back. We landed with her thighs bracketing my head, me staring up at the most beautiful thing I'd ever seen. Her pussy, her breasts, her face. What a goddamn *feast*. I grinned up at her.

"Sit," I ordered.

She made a sound of protest, but I ignored that and dragged her down to my hungry mouth.

28

JANIE

Jack's mouth made me see fireworks. My god, the thing this man could do with his tongue. That was *talent*.

My head fell back on a moan as he gripped my thighs and pulled me down harder on his face. A distant boom felt like it echoed my heartbeat. Red, white, and blue exploded behind my eyelids. Actual fireworks, not the magic of Jack's tongue. The celebration had started.

And then Jack sucked my clit again, his low, deep hum of satisfaction rumbled through me, and this time the bright bursts of light were all our own making. I came so hard I forgot where I was. I pressed my hips down hard as I rode out the pleasure, but all he did was hold me tighter.

I collapsed over him, spent, but I didn't have time to catch my breath before he hauled us both off the ground. I clung to him like a monkey, laughing softly, my legs wrapped around his torso.

"Honey, there is nothing funny about the way I need to fuck you," he said, his voice strained.

I pulled back enough to get a hand between us. His dick was hard and heavy and suddenly I was ready to go again. "Oh, I see," I murmured. "Poor baby." I ran my thumb over the leaking tip and licked my lips.

His gaze dropped to my mouth and he groaned. "No time for that," he grunted before spinning us around.

He braced his shoulder blades against the hay bale, hips tilted forward, grabbed my hips in a bruising vise, and slammed me down on his cock. I cried out at the heady rush of pleasure and pain. For a moment, neither of us moved as I sat fully impaled on his dick. Our breaths sawed in and out as we stared at each other.

"Take your tits out for me," he ordered roughly.

It occurred to me I was about to be stark naked in some farmer's field, while Jack was still fully dressed, but that didn't stop me from whipping my shirt off and tossing it aside. Feeling wanton, like one of those women who used to dance at the Painted Cat back in the gold rush days, I kept my eyes locked on his while I unhooked my bra behind my back and shimmied it off my shoulders. He bit his lip as he watched me play with my studs through half-hooded eyes. His cock jerked inside me and his hands flexed on my hips.

"Put it in my mouth." His lips parted in invitation.

I tilted forward. The straw scratched my palm as I tried to keep my balance. With a little smirk, I dragged my nipple across his cheek, stopping at the corner of his mouth, teasing him with what he wanted.

"Brat," he said, so adoringly that it felt like the highest praise. Then he turned his face and caught my nipple between his teeth, flicked his tongue over the stud, and drove his hips straight up.

"Fuck!" I shouted. I grabbed his shoulders for balance, my nails digging straight through the thin cotton of his t-shirt. He was going to have ten little crescents marked into his skin tomorrow, but I didn't care. At this angle, his pelvis hit my clit just right and I saw sparks.

"Ride, Janie." His voice was rough against my ear.

I rode—*hard*. I dug my heels into his ass, squeezed his hips with my thighs, bore down on his shoulders, and moved my hips faster and faster. I had never felt so alive. So safe.

"Attagirl, Ace. Let your bad out."

Let your bad out. One word made all the difference. Like he didn't mind my bad. He welcomed it. He wanted it. He wanted *me*. All of me. The messy and the loud and all the things that made me too much for other people made me just right for him.

And so I gave it to him. I came on a frantic sob, pleasure and emotion swelling to a crescendo, echoed by the *boom boom boom* of fireworks exploding in the sky. My pussy was still convulsing when he lifted my hips and slammed me down on his dick, again and again and again, using my body to pleasure his.

I felt filthy and used in the best possible way, treasured

and needed. This was Jack like I had never seen him. Jack when he was cool and calm and in control made my knees weak. But *this* Jack—frayed and feral and fucking me like the sky could fall down around our ears and it wouldn't stop him—this Jack ripped me apart and put me back together again like I was made for him.

He shouted my name as he spilled himself inside of me with punishing thrusts, tremors wracking his body like an earthquake.

I held on for dear life, until finally, finally, the tension drained from his body and we slowly slid to a tangled heap on the ground.

I smooshed my face against his neck with a happy, satisfied sigh. He tucked me closer and smoothed my hair behind my ear.

"You done running from me now, Ace?" he asked against my forehead.

I searched my soul. It didn't take long, not with the truth blooming like a sunflower in my chest. We weren't a mistake.

"Yes," I whispered. "I'm done running."

My body moved with his as he let out a deep breath. His throat bobbed as he swallowed hard.

"Good," he said, his voice thick. "It's about damn time."

29

JACK

MOM

You should come to dinner sometime next week. Bring Janie and Maya, too. Won't that be fun?

JACK

I don't know, Mom. It might be just me. Janie might be tired after a long day at the bar.

MOM

Then she'll be thrilled not to have to cook. How about Thursday?

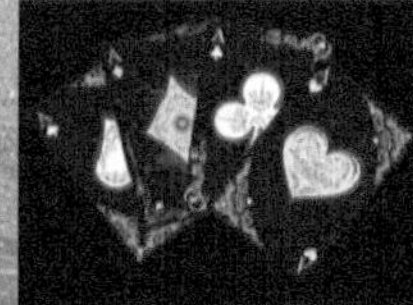

"Are we lost?" Janie put her hands on her hips as she came to a halt at what appeared to be a dead end on the trail.

"We're not lost," I assured her. "I know these mountains like the back of my hand. Essie, Brax, and I used to come up this way all the time."

I snagged a fistful of her shirt just under her chest and pulled her in close, because to my way of thinking, if we weren't walking, we might as well be kissing.

She didn't look convinced. "This trail wasn't on any of the maps."

"That's because elk don't tend to draw maps. No opposable thumbs." At the nervous look on her face, I chuckled and brushed another kiss against her mouth. "Trust me?"

She tilted her chin to consider me, beautiful brown eyes searching mine. Whatever she found there cleared away the worry. "I trust you, Jack."

Damn, that felt good. It was something I valued in myself, the ability to come through no matter what, and it mattered to me that people I cared about saw me that way, too. No one had warned me that the pieces of myself I valued most would be almost worthless in the low-stakes civilian life. But somehow it didn't feel like low stakes when Janie was the one I needed to come through for. It felt like the most important thing in the world.

"Good." I dropped a kiss on her damp forehead. It was hot out here in the midday summer sun, even with the thick-leafed aspens giving us shade. "We're almost there. Listen."

I cocked my head and we let the silence stretch around us until it wasn't silent anymore. The birds called to each other, the wind rustled through the leaves. And there, underneath it all, was the low thunder of tumbling water. "Hear that? It's the falls."

When Janie had suggested going for a hike, I'd known exactly where I wanted to take her. An easy two-mile hike led to a secluded waterfall and swimming hole. It wasn't the biggest waterfall around here and there were plenty of others that were easier to get to, which meant almost no one came here. We'd have it all to ourselves.

"This way." I took a hard right, ducking under the gnarled bough of a fir tree and lifting it so it wouldn't smack Janie in the face. Janie followed me through and then I took the lead again.

Another quarter mile in, the trees yielded to the river. It babbled over rocks before plunging straight down in a ten-foot waterfall.

"Oh, we're at the top of the falls!" Janie exclaimed, her eyes wide with surprised delight. She peered over the edge, holding onto a rock for balance. "Is there a way down to the pool?"

I nodded. "Follow me."

It was a sketchy scramble over wet boulders to reach the bottom. I kept Janie behind me so that if she slipped, my body would break her fall. *Be careful* was on the tip of my tongue, but I bit the words back. Janie wasn't dumb and she had hiked enough to know that the spray from the falls made the rocks slick. She would be careful without me reminding her like she was a kid.

This was why fraternizing was frowned upon in the military. Watching someone you loved put themselves in harm's way was fucking terrifying. Even when it was just a hike.

Love.

The word snagged my brain and my toe snagged a rock. I would have taken the rest of the way down on my ass if Janie hadn't grabbed my pack to keep me on my feet. I immediately braced against a boulder so we wouldn't take each other down.

"What did I tell you?" I sent her an impish grin over my shoulder. "Girl Scouts. Always good in the clutch."

She jerked in surprise. "You remember that?"

"When it comes to you, Janie, I remember everything."

Her gaze shifted sideways, mouth quirking, like she was remembering something herself. "Not everything," she murmured.

Now I was curious. "Oh, yeah? What do you think I'm forgetting?"

"We're not having that conversation here." She flicked my shoulder. "Eyes forward, soldier, and maybe you'll make it to the bottom in one piece. Can you imagine the obituary if you fell here? *Former Navy SEAL who survived gunshot wounds and underwater espionage dies on three-mile hike because he wasn't paying attention.*"

I faced forward again, laughing. "No chance. You'd have to make up a story about me saving you from a grizzly bear or something. Can't have Maya defending my honor on the playground."

"There are no grizzlies in Colorado."

I grinned. She was rolling her eyes behind my back. I could hear it in her voice.

We were at the bottom now, safe and sound. I took her hand to help her down the last drop, and she allowed it even though we both knew it was unnecessary. I just liked touching her, and from the way her fingertips trailed my palm before letting go, it was safe to say she liked touching me, too.

Keeping our hands off each other when Maya came home tomorrow was going to be fucking torture.

Janie dropped her pack and yanked her shirt off over her head.

"You going in?" I asked. A stupid question when she was standing there in her sports bra and underwear.

My mouth went dry. Her pale, creamy skin was as blindingly bright as fresh fallen snow reflecting a winter sun. Good fucking god, it almost burned to look at her but I didn't care. Scalded retinas were a small price to pay for all that beauty.

She flashed me a cheeky grin. "Of course I'm going in. Isn't that why you brought me here?" She dipped a toe in the water and immediately pulled it out again with a little yelp. "Christ, that's cold!"

"Yeah, have fun, Ace. I'm staying here where it's warm and dry." But I peeled my shirt off, because I had the feeling she wasn't going to allow that.

Sure enough, she gave a tinkly little laugh. "You're getting in, soldier. I need your body warmth."

I had stripped down to my boxers by the time she wrapped her arms around my waist. I protested, laughing, as she walked to the edge, taking me with her. Our bodies pressed together, thigh to thigh, belly to belly, chest to chest.

"Don't do it," I warned, as though I couldn't stop her right this second if I wanted to. The truth was, I'd follow her anywhere. Even if it meant freezing my balls off. "There will be payback."

A mischievous smile flashed across her face. "Oh, I'm counting on it."

She didn't pull me in. She didn't have to.

We jumped in together.

"YOUR LIPS ARE BLUE." Janie pushed the words through chattering teeth.

I rubbed the towel I'd stowed in my backpack over her goose-bumped arms. "So are yours." I pressed my numb lips to her numb lips in a clumsy kiss. She giggled.

"Careful," she said against my mouth. "I can't feel my lips. I might accidentally bite you."

"What makes you think I wouldn't like that?" I said back.

The only answer I got was the sharp nip of her teeth. And fuck yeah, I liked it.

We toweled off. Muttering to herself about skin cancer and sunscreen, Janie pulled on her clothes. I was still damp so I draped myself over a rock like a lizard and let the sun do its thing. My eyes drifted closed. I heard Janie unzip her pack—probably looking for a snack.

"Can I draw you?"

I cracked open an eyelid and found Janie with her sketchpad balanced on her knees, tapping a charcoal pencil against the paper.

"You want to draw me? Now?" I was still fully naked, scars and all.

She nodded slowly as her gaze swept over me. There was nothing sexual in the way she assessed me. She scrutinized every inch of me, fingers twitching like she was already imagining how she'd direct the pencil.

"I want to draw you just like this. It's perfect. The contrast of it all. Hard rock, soft skin, hard muscles, soft sunlight. Plus you have the body of a Greek god. It would be criminal not to draw you. Straight to jail."

"Shit, I'm blushing." I really was, a little bit. I chuckled. "All right, Ace. Draw me like one of your amphibians."

"Clasp your hands behind your head. One knee up. Perfect. Keep your eyes closed, like you're napping."

I followed her instructions, but of course I peeked a little. I couldn't resist. "Is it okay if I talk?"

"Sure. You can even move a little if you need to, but try not to change your position too much."

"Okay." I squinted at her. "I saw that sketch you did of Maya on the swing. It was incredible. It wasn't just that it was realistic. It was like you captured her soul."

"That's exactly what I love about drawing people. It's a challenge getting their…I don't know, their essence or soul or whatever magic it is that makes a person who they are. It's not the same with frogs and salamanders, you know. In the first place, I'm usually drawing them from a photograph someone else took. They don't really have a personality."

"Your frogs and salamanders are amazing, Janie."

"They're for Maya. I love making this book with her. I mean, how many seven-year-olds do you know who take something this seriously? But sometimes I want to draw something that's just for me. Sometimes I want to take myself seriously, too." Her self-deprecating laugh made my chest hurt. "I know that's silly. It's just a hobby."

I let my eyelid flutter open enough to watch the pencil flick over the paper in feather-light strokes. She was frowning, whether in concentration or at whatever bullshit she was telling herself, I wasn't sure. "Why is that silly?"

"Because it *is*." Her pencil moved faster. "When you're in your twenties, it's okay to still be figuring it all out. People expect that. But I've been a mom since I was twenty-two. I'm thirty years old. The time for finding myself is over. I should be focused on finding a real job, not silly side quests."

"You have a real job," I pointed out.

She snorted. "Yeah, *now* I do. But until a week ago, I

was a bartender at—no offense to Brax, honestly I love the Painted Cat—but it's a dive bar in a one-stoplight town. That's not a career. That's a placeholder. It's what you do until your real life starts."

"If you wanted more than bartending, you should have told Brax. He would have made you manager in a heartbeat."

"Maybe that's why I didn't ask." The pencil stopped moving, and my heart damn near stopped, too.

"You don't want to be manager?" I asked carefully.

"I don't know," she confessed softly. She sighed. She picked up the pencil again. "I mean, it's so good for me and Maya, right? No more late nights, no more weekend shifts. The money is better. But..." She chewed the inside of her cheek. "It's not a placeholder position. This is my real life now. I'm a manager, and I'll probably always *be* a manager. This is it, for the rest of my life. I'm not complaining. Brax is a great boss. I should be grateful. It's what's best for Maya."

But it's not what's best for Janie.

She didn't say that. She never would. Maya came first, always.

But we both knew it was true.

Janie shimmied her shoulders like she was brushing away the clouds. "I really do like it at the Painted Cat, you know. People tell me the craziest shit when they're drunk. I love that. And my decisions are my own. No one is coercing me."

Guilt felt like a lead brick on my chest. I didn't coerce

her into taking the management position. Brax hadn't, either. But it still felt like I had done something...well, not wrong, exactly, but I was beginning to suspect she wouldn't like it.

In fact, I suspected she would fucking *hate* it.

I needed to tell her the truth. And I would. But not today.

Because today had been perfect, and I wanted it to stay that way.

And also because I was a fucking coward.

We didn't talk for a while after that. She focused all of her attention on my body and her sketchpad. I could have watched her talented fingers fly across the paper for hours. That adorable crease between her furrowed eyebrows as she concentrated. Yeah, watching her get lost in something she loved, that she was so damn good at, that did it for me.

It should have been awkward, the way her eyes narrowed on my scar or my foot or my broken nose. But it wasn't. I didn't feel vulnerable, even though I was completely exposed. I felt seen.

This time when her eyes landed on mine, there was something different in her gaze. It wasn't just an artist's interest in a subject. Heat and...was Janie blushing, or was that the sun turning her cheeks pink?

"Tell me the truth, Ace. Are you sketching my dick right now?"

She burst out laughing. "How did you know?"

"My dick can sense these things. It likes the attention.

See how it's rising to the occasion?" I gestured toward my hardening cock.

Her lips quirked. "This isn't supposed to be that kind of drawing."

"The dick wants what the dick wants, honey. It's hard to stay soft when you're doing that."

"When I'm focusing all my attention on your dick?" She snickered. "Men are such simple creatures."

"That's not it." Or maybe it was a little, because of course I liked it when Janie was looking at my dick, but it was more than that. "It's how you look while you're doing it. So intense. Focused. If I had any artistic skill at all, I'd want to draw you like this. Completely in your element. You're beautiful, Janie."

Her flush deepened. "Oh, Jack," she murmured. "I am going to suck your dick *so hard* when I'm done."

Even with the promise of a blowjob, I didn't want this moment to end. Hell, I didn't want any of this to end. I didn't want to say goodbye to Janie and Maya in September. How would that work? Fuck if I knew. With Maya in school, a full-time nanny wouldn't be necessary. I didn't need the money, but I knew myself well enough to know I wouldn't be happy sitting around all day, either.

I didn't have a plan.

But for the first time, I was okay with that.

30

JANIE

ESSIE

I'm still waiting.

JANIE

For what?

ESSIE

An explanation. Where did you and Jack disappear to and why did you show up late for fireworks with hay in your hair?

JANIE

We decided to go for a run and ended up in a hay field, that's all.

ESSIE

Why do I feel like there's more to the story?

JANIE

Trust me, babe. There are some things sisters don't need to know about their brothers.

ESSIE

Ew.

"ARE YOU SURE YOU WANT TO DO THIS?" JACK HESITATED IN my doorway, chest and feet bare, gray sweatpants hung low on his hips.

Gray. Sweatpants. I set my hairbrush on the dresser and turned away from his reflection in the mirror to look at the real thing. Hell, yes, I ogled him. I ogled the *shit* out of him. I owed teenaged Janie that much.

"It depends on what you mean by *this*. If *this* is sleeping next to you all night and waking up with you still beside me, then yes. If *this* is an all-night sex marathon, then also yes."

He ducked his head, trying not to laugh. But when he looked at me again, all amusement was gone. "Janie," he said, eyes serious. "If I try to strangle you in your sleep, don't flick me in the forehead. Palm strike to the nose, honey. You understand? Here, I'll show you how."

"Jack!" I swatted him away, laughing. "Don't teach me how to hurt you."

He wasn't laughing at all. "I'm teaching you how to defend yourself if *I* hurt *you*. I'm not fucking around here, Ace. You're too important to me. I need to know you're safe.

There is nothing I want more than to spend all night with you in my arms, but that's not going to happen if I'm worried about you."

I tried to stay patient, but I hated that he thought he might actually hurt me. "Flicking you in the forehead proved to be pretty effective," I reminded him. "When was the last time you had a nightmare, anyway?"

"Three months ago, but that's not the point. It only takes once. Curl your fingers but keep them relaxed and loose. Palm open." He guided my hand as he talked, putting me in the right position. "And then push at an angle. You want to hit with the heel of your palm. Right here." He tapped a centimeter above my wrist. "Imagine you're sending my nose into my brain. That's how hard you need to hit, okay? Don't hold back. If you can't get to my nose go for my throat or solar plexus."

"All right, all right. Ruin your pretty face and possibly your frontal lobe. Got it."

"Good." He crossed his arms over his chest and quirked an eyebrow. "Now get your ass on the bed and show me your perfect tits."

A thrill shot through me. I loved it when Jack got all bossy with me. "Yes, sir."

With a little smirk of my own tossed over my shoulder, I sauntered to the bed, hips swaying. When I hit the foot of the bed, I crawled forward, my ass pointed directly at him, the angle making my tiny sleep shorts ride up like a bikini. It occurred to me too late that maybe I didn't want to do that. Maybe I should have turned off the lights before I gave him an unfettered view of the dimples and jiggles back there. But his sharp inhalation behind me reminded me that he had already seen every inch of me extremely up close and personal and that hadn't stopped him from coming back for more.

I spun around to face him at the center of the mattress and sat on my heels. He cocked his head, his gaze dipping pointedly to my T-shirt. I knew he could see the outlines of my peaked nipples and metal studs through the thin cotton, but he leaned back against the dresser, arms crossed like he was totally unaffected.

But gray sweatpants told no lies, and right now his were telling me that he was very much affected.

"I'm waiting, Janie," he growled impatiently.

I held his gaze as I grasped the hem of my T-shirt and pulled it up and over, then tossed it aside. And then I couldn't look him in the eyes because his were glued to my chest.

"Good girl. Now play with your nipples. Show me how you like them touched. Talk me through it."

It was one thing to put my body on display for him. Using actual words was something else entirely. The extent of my dirty talk was *yes, like that* or *harder*. I'd never done anything like this.

But then, I'd never been chased through a parade and fucked against a haystack, either.

I'd never given a blowjob in my parents' foyer where anyone could have walked in.

Most of all, I'd never had anyone look at me the way

Jack did, his gaze burning my skin like hot coals. Like he could look at me for an eternity and never want anything else. Like I was the moon, the stars, and the whole fucking sky.

That look gave me courage.

"I'm sensitive here, so I like it to start gently." I circled my nipples with a feather-light touch and his eyes tracked the movement. Round and round I went, watching him watch me. Fuck, that was hot. "I like that. When I start to feel warm and restless, I squeeze. Just a little."

He swallowed hard when I pinched my nipples lightly. "Like that," I breathed.

"Does it feel good?" he husked out.

"Mmm," I hummed, my eyes half-mast. "*So* good."

My fingers twisted my nipples, making my breath quicken. Jack uncrossed his arms and wrapped his hands around the beveled edge of the dresser, like he needed something to hold onto so he wouldn't fling himself at me. I loved watching his control deteriorate little by little. I felt so *wanted*.

My hands smoothed over the fullness of my breasts, plumping them up. I thumbed the little metal studs and my head tipped back on a moan.

The dresser creaked under Jack's white-knuckled grip. His jaw popped under the strain of holding himself tethered. "Tell me about the piercings. When did you get them done?"

"These?" I flicked them again.

"Unless you have something else hidden away. But I think I would have noticed that."

"No other piercings. Not yet, anyway." I flashed a grin. "I got pierced a couple months before Maya's third birthday." Suddenly shy, I peeked up at him. "Maybe we should talk about this later. Over strip poker or something. I don't want to ruin the mood and...I get if the whole mom thing is kind of a turnoff."

Jack's forehead furrowed and his head tilted like it took him a moment to understand the words coming out of my mouth. "Janie, nothing about you is a turnoff. Certainly not you being a mom. There's literally nothing you can say right now that could make me want you less. I'm so hard right now I fucking *ache* for you. So keep playing with your nipples, honey, and tell me about the piercings. I want to know everything about you."

His words set off a shimmer of warmth through me. How could he be so sweet and dirty at the same time? I couldn't get enough.

"I've always had sensitive breasts—in a good way. I loved having them touched and played with. I could get off on nipple play alone. Probably, anyway. I've never put that to the test."

The way his gaze dipped hungrily to my fingers strumming my nipples, I had the feeling he planned to rectify that someday. "Is that a fact?" he said casually, and I shivered at the promise there.

I squeezed my thighs together. "Mmhmm. But when I

got pregnant, suddenly I lost all that. My body wasn't my own anymore. It was Maya's. It grew her for nine months and then it fed her for twelve more. And that did *not* feel good. It took months before I could even tolerate wearing a bra without coating my nipples in lanolin first. After I weaned her, I thought I would never want anyone to touch me there again."

"But you like it now." His eyes flared as I tugged my nipples.

"It took over a year for it to feel good again. I kind of discovered it by accident. Just playing with myself." I bit back a smile at his whimper. "So I decided, I wanted something to make me feel good. Just me. I wanted my breasts to feel like mine again after belonging to someone else for so long. The piercings might be fun for you to look at and play with, but the physical pleasure of them is all mine."

Did I sound gleeful? Smug and self-satisfied? I didn't fucking care.

Jack didn't seem to care either, because he pushed away from the dresser and stalked toward me. I kept playing with piercings, my gaze locked on his, as he met me on the bed.

His hands covered mine, cupping my breasts, shaping them with his hands. "Fuck, your tits are magnificent."

The words were profane, but they sounded reverent on his lips. I didn't feel objectified; I felt worshipped.

His thumbs rolled the studs and then his mouth was there, hot and wet, his tongue sliding lewdly between our fingers to find my peaked nipples. I cried out and arched into his mouth. Pleasure coursed through me, heat rushing through every limb.

"Janie." His lips were shiny and wet when he lifted his head. "Someday I'm going to make you come using only my fingers and mouth on your nipples. And then I'm going to fuck your tits until *I* come. But I'm not going to do that now because I need you to understand something."

My brain had short circuited at the image of him fucking my breasts, so all I could do was stare at him blankly and ask, "What's that?"

"Your tits belong to you, but your pussy is *mine*."

Before I could say a word, he flipped me onto my back and yanked my shorts and underwear down my legs. He pushed away from me to peel off his sweatpants and then settled between my thighs.

I canted my hips, desperate to have him inside me, but he only dragged his dick from my opening to my clit. "Jack," I begged.

His voice was smooth and thick as honey. "You need something, baby?"

"You know what I need." I growled in frustration as he teased me with his cock, getting my hopes up as he nudged against my entrance only to take it away again, ghosting my clit in a way that was too light for satisfaction and only made me want him more.

"Then tell me what I want to hear. Who does this pussy belong to, Janie?"

Even if I had wanted to lie, my soaked pussy gave me away. "You. It belongs to you."

Jack thrust into me so hard I curled into him, clinging to his shoulders for dear life. He held himself there and looked down at me with an intensity that made my eyes water. "Good." He dragged his nose along mine, his voice nothing more than a ragged whisper, all his smirking bravado gone. "Because there's not a single part of me that doesn't belong to you, Janie."

All the air whooshed out of my lungs. I gaped at him, trying to get my bearings.

And then he slid out slowly, pushed back in inch by delicious thick inch, and I gave up. Who needed bearings anyway. Not a girl getting fucked by Jack Price, that's for sure.

We moved together in slow, deliberate thrusts, our eyes locked on each other. And then he hit a spot deep inside me that hurt so good I gasped. His eyes widened and then went half-hooded. Nothing was slow now, nothing was deliberate. We slammed against each other, hands groping, bodies grappling.

"God, you're close," he panted in my ear, his words thick and drugged. "I can feel my pussy tightening. Let me have it, honey. I need it."

I couldn't have stopped it even if I wanted to—which I very much didn't. Pleasure surged through me and I came crying his name. He pumped into me hard, his hand fisted in my hair, filling me up while my orgasm was still pulsing.

He collapsed over me, rolling to his side to keep from

crushing me, and we lay there, completely spent, until our breathing returned to normal. After cleaning up, we got right back in bed.

We fell asleep in each other's arms and didn't wake up until nearly nine.

I didn't even have to palm strike his nose.

31

JANIE

CLAIRE

Just turned off the interstate. Should be there in 20 minutes. Hope you got all your bad out, my love.

JANIE

As a matter of fact, I've decided to keep my bad around a little longer.

CLAIRE

I hope you know what you're doing.

JANIE

Not a fucking clue. :)

CLAIRE

I love you, big sis.

"Mom!" Maya sprang from the car and ran up the driveway.

Suppressing a laugh, I jogged down the steps to meet her. Maya's run reminded me of a newborn giraffe. A little awkward, a little clumsy, but super fucking adorable. She didn't hug me but she burrowed into my body for a no-armed snuggle.

I smoothed down her braid. "How was the cabin?"

"It was great. We saw so many frogs."

I met Claire's gaze over Maya's head and she grinned. *Told you so*, she mouthed.

"There were no fireworks, but we did sparklers." Maya looked up at me with her pretty mismatched eyes. "Did you get to see the fireworks, Mom?"

"I sure did." *Boy, did I see fireworks*. My cheeks flushed.

"Good. I know you like fireworks, but I don't," she stated matter-of-factly.

I brushed over her hair again, wanting to kiss her but knowing she wouldn't like it. "You don't have to feel bad about that. I love watching *Hamilton* with you."

Maya blinked at me. "I don't feel bad."

Kids. Always the center of their own universe. I laughed. "Well, good. I had a great time this year at the parade, and I'm so glad you had fun with your aunts."

Nisha lifted Maya's suitcase from the trunk. "We're happy to have her anytime. We had a blast."

"Jack!" Maya yelled right in my face. I turned and saw him round the back of the house at a jog. She pushed away from me and made a beeline for him.

"Hey, scamp." His face split in a wide grin. "I thought I heard a car pull up."

She hurled herself forward and then stopped short right at his toes, looking up at him uncertainly. "Do you want a hug?"

The soft look on his face made my chest crack open. "Absolutely, I do."

Her arms went around his waist and his went loosely around her shoulders. He hunched down and whispered something in her ear that made her whole face light up.

"Oh, Janie." Chloe's sympathetic squeeze on my arm made me jolt. I had been so wrapped up in the two of them that her existence had faded away.

But she hadn't missed a damn thing.

"You're in so much trouble, my love."

Didn't I know it.

32

JACK

JEREMIAH

You got an onboard date yet?

JACK

About that. I really appreciate the offer, but I'm staying put in Aspen Springs.

JEREMIAH

Making the manny position permanent? Still don't know how to wrap my mind around that.

JACK

Nah, she goes back to school in September, so she won't need a full-time babysitter past summer.

JEREMIAH

So what's your next move, then?

JACK

No fucking clue.

JEREMIAH

> Jack Price doesn't have a plan? Now you're scaring me.

IT TOOK MAYA EXACTLY THREE MINUTES TO ABANDON US FOR her tadpoles. The second she disappeared from view my hands were on Janie like we had been separated for weeks instead of maybe an hour.

"My mom invited us to dinner. Not tonight, with Maya just getting home, but maybe next weekend?" I breathed the words in between little kisses, my hands shaping her waist.

"Us?" Janie reared back. She grabbed me by the face and stared at me with wide, panicked eyes. "*Us?*"

"As in you, Maya, and me."

"Why?" Her voice edged toward shrill.

I would have laughed if it hadn't felt like a direct hit to my solar plexus. "Relax, Ace." I rubbed at the tension I found in her shoulders. "I haven't told her anything. She likes you and Maya, and she thought it would be fun. That's all. I suspect she wants me to get to know her new boyfriend, and she thinks I'll be on my best behavior if you're there as witnesses."

She leaned into my touch, her head lolling to the side

to give me more access. "I'll agree to anything if you keep doing that. Oh, my god, Jack." She moaned softly.

My dick twitched awake. "Don't," I warned. "Any second now Maya is going to get tired of staring at her tadpoles and she's going to come out here wondering what we're doing. So don't make sounds that will get my dick up."

She laughed. "Don't be silly. Maya never gets tired of tadpoles. Especially now that their little leg nubbins are coming in."

Nubbins. My body shuddered involuntarily. "Don't say that word."

"What word? Nubbins?"

I shuddered again. "Ugh."

She tipped her head back on an incredulous look. "Nubbins? Seriously?"

Full body cringe. I couldn't help it. "Stop saying that word!"

"That's your weakness? The word nubbins?" She snort-laughed. "Does the enemy know about this? Mr. Special Forces can hold up to waterboarding but taps out if you say—ackk!"

She shrieked as she found herself airborne and tossed over my shoulder. I brushed my palm over her ass teasingly. "Say it again, Janie. I dare you."

"Nubbins!" she hollered because my girl could never resist letting her bad out.

I gave her cheek a quick, sharp smack, making her giggle.

A loud gasp—definitely not Janie—had me spinning around.

"What—what's going on?" Maya's eyes jumped from me to her mom's butt and back again.

Janie twisted to look at her daughter over my shoulder. "It's okay, ladybug. We're just joking around."

Maya looked at me uncertainly.

"Your mom said a bad word," I explained.

Maya's eyes widened. "Was it fuck?" she whispered.

Janie's body shook with suppressed laughter. I squeezed her thigh. "No, scamp. Not fuck. I like that word, as long as you don't say it in school. She said a word I don't like."

"What word?" Maya asked, intrigued.

"Nubbins!" Janie yelled.

I spanked her again—softly.

Maya's mouth popped open. "What happens if I say it? I don't want to get spanked." But there was a look on her face. She might not want to get spanked, but she wanted in on the fun somehow.

"My mom told me kids don't get spankings. Only adults. So I can't spank you, Maya," I said gravely. Janie wheezed. "But if you say that word, I'm going to have to throw you over my shoulder like your mom and spin you until you're dizzy."

Maya's gaze shifted sideways. "Nubbins," she said slyly.

"Now you've done it!" I roared. With Janie still over one shoulder, I scooped Maya over my other.

"Hold my hand, ladybug," Janie stage whispered. "One...two...three..."

"Nubbins!" they both shouted.

I spun them around and around as they shrieked with laughter.

It was the most beautiful sound in the whole world.

I HAD a mug of tea waiting for Janie when she returned from putting Maya to bed. She padded into the kitchen in thick wool socks and those tiny ass shorts, her hair mussed from snuggling with Maya and her eyes suspiciously wide and bright.

"That took longer than I expected. Your tea might need warming up. Did Maya want extra books to make up for the weekend?"

Janie smiled as she dropped into the chair across from me. "She did talk me into an extra book, but I actually fell asleep for a couple minutes. She was super snuggly and the bed was warm. So now I'm wide awake."

"Up for a game of strip poker?" I suggested. "You win a hand, you might finally find out why I call you Ace."

She snorted. "I only win when you let me. And I only have one secret left." She circled the rim of her mug with her index finger, contemplating me. "I could just tell you."

"About Maya's dad?" My pulse quickened. I wanted to know. "Do you want to tell me?"

She rolled her lips, forehead furrowed. "You know what? I do. I'm tired of carrying it around with me. The weight of it is so fucking heavy, sometimes I feel like I can't breathe through it."

"So tell me. If I can take some of that weight from you, I'll do it. Like you did for me." I brushed my thumb over her knuckles.

"Okay." She bobbed her head like she was psyching herself up. "Okay."

I waited.

She took a deep sip of tea.

I waited some more and tried not to get antsy about it.

"Okay," she said again. "I was twenty-one. Fresh out of college. I had a low level job at Senator Rupert Warren's office in Denver. He's a state senator. Not national," she explained but it wasn't necessary. I knew who he was. He was a powerful name in the ranching community. "Anyway, mostly I answered phone calls from constituents. I attended every meeting and took notes. I was the youngest and the greenest, so even with a Georgetown degree, I had to prove myself and move up the ranks like anyone else, and I was determined to do that. Rupert took me under his wing, probably because the name Belmont carries a lot of weight."

My neck prickled with foreboding. There were plenty of good men in the world. Men who would see a smart, talented young woman with a fancy degree and mentor her because it was the right thing to do. But I had a feeling that Senator Warren was not one of those men, because if he were, Janie's lips wouldn't tighten every time she said his name.

"I thought he was…" Her gaze went sideways as she searched for the word. "Exceptional. I thought he was exceptional. He was so smart and he knew how to get things done that other people said were impossible. Good things, things I was proud to be a part of. I was in awe of him, honestly."

She took a sip of tea and licked her lips. "Not just in awe of him. I was in love with him. And I thought he was in love with me, too. I know I was dumb." She held up her hands. "You don't have to say it."

"I wasn't going to." It was hard to speak over the rage.

"Well, I'll say it. I was really fucking dumb, Jack." Her laugh was all hard edges and self-loathing. It made me want to tear something apart with my bare hands. Preferably a certain state senator. "He was twenty years older than me and married. *Married.*" She laughed again. "I knew that. Everyone knew that. But he told me that they were separated. His wife was in England teaching a summer program at Cambridge. He said it was a cover. It was harder to fake a happy marriage when they had to be in the same room together, so they put an ocean between them. Constituents like their politicians married, so they planned to quietly divorce when it wasn't an election year. That was what he said. And I was stupid enough to believe him."

Fuck that. "No." The word sliced out of me. I wanted to be gentle, but fucking hell. I was pissed. "You weren't stupid. You're a good person, and you expect other people to be good, too. That's not something to be embarrassed about. He's the one who should be embarrassed."

She didn't respond to that. That was fine. I'd tell her every day until she believed me.

"His wife came home in August. Caught us in bed together." Janie looked away, swallowing hard. "I had no idea what was going on. I couldn't understand that he had lied to me. He wouldn't return my calls and suddenly I was out of a job. I was a mess. I would go for these long drives so I could cry where no one could see me. And then one night a bear ran in front of my car. I woke up in the hospital. That was how I found out I was pregnant."

"Jesus," I whispered.

"I don't remember much from being in the hospital. But Rupert was there and my parents were there and everyone had a lawyer. I signed everything they told me to sign."

She sighed. "There's some verbiage about denial of parentage and keeping Maya out of the public." Her mouth twisted in a grimace. "Heterochromia—Maya's eyes are exactly like Rupert's. If people saw her, they'd know. But it's not like I have to lock her in a dungeon. She hates my parents' parties, anyway. But as she gets older, she has more questions about who her dad is. I hate that I can't tell her."

"That can't be legal," I said. "There's no fucking way

anything you signed in that hospital would hold up in court."

"It only has to hold up in court if I take them to court, and I won't be doing that. It's fine. My parents made sure Maya and I were taken care of. Rupert set up two trust funds, one for each of us. Maya gets full access to hers when she turns twenty-five."

A trust fund. Suddenly things were starting to make sense. "This house?"

Janie nodded, her gaze sweeping around the kitchen. "My account is set up so that I got one large initial payment, and then smaller annual distributions until Maya's twenty-fifth birthday. I used the first payment to buy this place free and clear. My parents weren't thrilled, but I was desperate to be on my own." She wrinkled her nose. "The smaller payments aren't enough to live off of, but with my job at the Painted Cat, we get by. I can request additional distributions, but my mom is the trustee. Asking her for money—even money that's technically mine—is just...it's the fucking worst, you know? She never says yes without demanding something in return. I'm so tired of people controlling my life."

Oh, hell. It wasn't the same. What I had done, that was completely different. But somehow, I didn't think she'd see it that way.

Janie pulled her mug of tea closer but she didn't drink it. It had to be cold by now. She pushed it away again. "So that's my secret. That's everything."

"Janie. Shit." I scrubbed a hand over my face, feeling sick. "I have to tell you something, honey."

33

JANIE

"What do you mean, you told Brax to make me a manager?" I pushed to my feet so fast my chair tipped over and landed with a loud clatter against the tile floor. I left it where it lay, my eyes never leaving Jack's face.

His beautiful, lying, rat bastard face.

"Janie."

I watched his lips shape my name, but all I could hear was the blood rushing in my ears from the pounding of my heart. "You're Brax's investment partner. This whole time?"

"We went in on it together, but I wasn't interested in being hands-on. I was never in town more than a few days at a time. I get a cut of the profits, but it's his bar. He handles all the business, makes all the decisions. I stay out of all that."

"But you made an exception for me." My laugh sounded brittle to my ears. "Gee, thanks. I'm flattered."

He rounded the table and I instinctively backed up.

The thought of him touching me right now made me panic. I wasn't strong enough for that. My feet tangled in the chair legs and I tumbled backward, arms flailing. He caught me—he always fucking caught me—and I half bellowed, half sobbed in his face, "No! Don't fucking touch me! Just let me fall!"

"I can't do that, Janie." His face was granite except for the muscle popping in his jaw. "Please don't ask me to."

He held me as tightly as if I were Maya having a meltdown. "I hate you," I said into the crook of his neck. It was a lie, but I wished it were true.

His body jerked like I'd hit him but he didn't let go. "I'm so in love with you I'm willing to look past that."

My stupid, stupid heart gave a pitiful leap of hope. Jack fixed things. That was what he did. Was it too much to ask that he fixed us, too? I crumpled against him. Even when he was the one hurting me, he was still the one I turned to for comfort. "No. Don't say that to me. I'm so fucking mad at you right now. It's not fair."

"I know, honey." He smoothed my hair back from my damp forehead. "I understand."

"Do you?" I pulled back to search his face. "Because I thought we were a team. We were in this together. We made a plan *together*. Yes, I needed you, but I thought—" My throat constricted around the words, choking me. "Didn't you need me, too?"

"*Yes*." He cupped my face in his large, capable palms. "Fuck, yes, I needed you. I still need you. You weren't wrong about any of that. We *are* a team."

My vision blurred with tears. "Then why did you go behind my back to Brax? Do you have any idea how that feels? Why didn't you come to me first? I told you how things were with my parents and why I was bartending. You knew how I felt about people interfering in my life but you did it anyway."

His shoulders slumped, his eyes lowering, but not before I saw the self-recrimination there. "I don't have a good answer for that. I wish I did. I saw a problem, I wanted to fix it, and I acted on that immediately. I wasn't sure what Brax's response would be, so I figured I'd talk it through with him first and see if moving you to management was a possibility. You were so tired. I thought it would be good for you. You have to believe me."

"I do believe you. That's the problem." I smiled sadly as a tear spilled over my lash line. I dashed it away impatiently. "People have been making decisions for me my whole life. Always for my own good, like I can't be trusted to do it myself. I fucking hate it, Jack. That job...it's the only thing that was completely under my control. Or so I thought. But you took that from me."

His lips pressed together and he shook his head. "I didn't take it from you. You gave it to me."

I jerked back. "What?"

"You have every right to be mad at me. I shouldn't have gone behind your back. We should have talked it out together. But you didn't have to take the management position. You could have told Brax no. Why didn't you?"

I blinked rapidly. Why hadn't I? I ran it back through

my mind. It hadn't felt like I'd had a choice in the moment, but that wasn't really true, was it? Of course I had a choice. "I did what was best for Maya."

"If you really believed that, you would have done it a lot sooner." He shook his head. "You use Maya as an excuse. You say you're making decisions based on Maya, but the truth is, you're not making any decisions at all. You're frozen, just letting things happen to you instead of *making* them happen. And now I know why. You're terrified because eight years ago, you trusted someone who didn't deserve it. You never let go of that. Never stopped beating yourself up over a mistake you made eight fucking years ago. And now the person you don't trust is yourself."

My chest heaved. "Fuck. You."

We stared at each other.

"Janie." His thumbs traced gentle circles on the side of my neck.

Because he was still holding me. Because he had been holding me this whole time. Through all that. Every harsh word, every painful truth. He'd held on. That was who he was.

But I couldn't.

I pushed him back. "I can't fight with you right now. Maya needs you here and I can't risk it. I need to think so I don't say something I can't take back."

"I'm not going anywhere, Janie. I wouldn't do that to you or Maya."

"I know." Did I? Maybe. Fuck, I was so confused. "But

this thing between us? It feels broken, and I don't think you can fix it, Jack."

He studied me seriously, his blue eyes moving over my face like he was trying to memorize every freckle, and then one side of his mouth lifted slightly. "Then I guess it's up to you, Ace."

I STARED at the ceiling long past when I should have been asleep. Tomorrow was going to be rough.

All the tomorrows were going to be rough.

How was I supposed to live with him and not touch him? How was I supposed to watch him be so wonderful with Maya and not melt? How could I have been so stupid?

I had known getting involved with Jack while he was Maya's manny was a terrible idea. Even Claire had warned me—she owed me an *I told you so*, which she would never say out loud because Claire was perfect and never petty. But I would hear it in my mind every time she looked at me.

A mistake. That's what this was. Another fucking mistake.

Not like Rupert. I knew that. Jack was good and honorable. He hadn't deceived me for his own selfish purposes. He'd done it for my own good.

And that felt...

Like absolute garbage.

I didn't need Jack to make my decisions for me. I could do that myself.

So why hadn't I?

He wasn't wrong, as painful as it was to admit. I had been in limbo for years, too terrified to make a move that would prove once and for all that I was a bad mother. Everything I did was a reaction to a mistake I had made years ago. Jack was right. I was still punishing myself. And for what? Someone else's lie? How was that my fault?

Fuck that.

Rupert, my parents—they had stolen my choices. But I had allowed it.

If I didn't want someone pulling my strings, then those strings would have to be cut.

"W HAT DO YOU THINK?" I asked.

Brax was leaning back in his fancy leather chair, elbows pressed to the armrests, fingers steepled over his flat abdomen, contemplating the ceiling.

My skin felt hot. I hated airing my dirty laundry to someone I respected. He was my best friend's husband *and* my boss. But Brax was the only lawyer in Aspen Springs—

and possibly the only lawyer in eastern Colorado who wasn't beholden to my parents in one way or another. There was no one else I could trust with this.

He had finished reading the contract five minutes ago and had been staring at the ceiling ever since. His silence felt like judgment. I cleared my throat.

Brax blinked. "Sorry. I started counting to ten but then I got distracted imagining all the ways I was going to ruin this man's life."

Relief whooshed out of me in an audible breath. "Really?"

"Janie." His head tilted on an almost offended stare. "Of course, really. It won't even be hard. This contract is bullshit. In the first place, a trustee is supposed to be a neutral third party, not your mother. In the second place, the annual disbursement you receive is nowhere near enough to support a child with special needs. And third, I just saw his smug motherfucking face on an ad talking about the sanctity of family. If he cared so much about marriage, then he shouldn't have had an affair with a twenty-one-year-old and abandoned his daughter." His jaw twitched. "I take that personally."

I buried my face in my hands. "I'm so embarrassed."

"Look at me, Janie." Brax's stern voice brooked no opposition. I lowered my hands. "The only thing you should be embarrassed about is waiting so long to come to me for help. Don't let it happen again."

Goodness. Essie's husband was...something. "All right."

"Good." His slow smile reminded me of a supervillain who was too smart for his own good. "This is going to be fun."

34

JACK

Yesterday morning, Janie had looked like shit. Blotchy skin, puffy eyes with purple halfmoons, a tired droop to her shoulders. I'd hated seeing her like that, knowing I was the source of her sleepless night. Not that I'd had it any easier. I hadn't slept a wink, tossing and turning as I replayed every word of our argument in my head. I'd looked like shit, too.

But this morning Janie did not look like shit. Her pale skin was as creamy as ever, and while the shadows remained, the puffiness around her eyes was gone. Her copper hair was up in a ponytail and she was dressed for work in ass-hugging jeans and a pretty army-green, scoop-neck blouse that seemed purposefully created to torture me. She looked like she'd actually slept, even if she hadn't managed a full eight hours.

I still looked like shit.

"Here you go, Maya." I slid the plate of eggs, bacon, and toast in front of her like I wasn't drooling over her mother. "Do you want some juice?"

"Yes, please."

"I'll get it." Janie pulled a glass from the cabinet and pivoted to the fridge, red ponytail arcing behind her. I followed it like she had me on a leash. She raised an eyebrow without looking at me as she poured the orange juice. "Do you want some?"

I didn't, but there was literally no other reason for me to be hovering over her like this. I felt like a pimply teenager talking to the homecoming queen. "Yes, please."

She handed over the carton and slipped past me. Our arms brushed. I put the juice back in the fridge without using it.

"I can make you a plate," I offered. "There's plenty more food."

"Oh." Her gaze darted around the kitchen. Everywhere but at me. "Sure, that would be great."

I really wanted her to look at me. But she was still mad, and I didn't blame her.

I fixed plates for both of us and met her at the table.

"Thank you," she said quietly.

When she finally looked at me, I wished she hadn't. There was so much heartbreak in her big brown eyes. Heartbreak I had put there. If I could turn back time, I would have smacked myself upside the head. Why the hell hadn't I simply told her I was a part-owner of the bar, and offered to make her a manager? Because she wouldn't want that dynamic between us. She would have said no, and I thought I knew what was best for her.

Shit.

Something shifted in her eyes as we stared at each other. She chewed the inside of her cheek in that way she had when she was working through something in her mind. I badly wanted to know what it was.

"Mother," Maya said. "Speaking of bacon, you're not eating yours."

Janie blinked down at her untouched food. A wry smile curved her lips. I watched her slip into mom mode like she was donning armor. When she turned to her daughter, there was no trace of sadness anywhere. "I'm getting to it, ladybug. If you want more bacon, you have to finish your eggs first."

Maya sighed. "I'm not really hungry anymore. I just like the crunch."

Janie laughed. "It's the best part." She took a bite of eggs. Good. She spent mornings in the office, but she was on her feet all afternoon once the bar opened. She needed the fuel. "So, what wonderful things do you have planned for today?"

"I want to go to the zoo."

Janie lifted an eyebrow at me. "What do you think, Jack?"

I think I'm so in love with you it hurts. I matched her cheerful tone. "Sounds fun."

"Great. I'll buy tickets."

Maya shot up from her chair. "I'll go get ready."

"We're not leaving for another hour, at least," I called as she darted down the hallway. Rush hour traffic heading into Denver was something I preferred to avoid at all costs.

"Jack."

Janie's soft voice had me snapping to attention. "Yeah?"

"You weren't wrong." She picked up her fork, set it down again. "All those things you said. You weren't wrong." She pursed her lips. "I wasn't either, for the record. That was a shitty thing you did. But..." She sighed. "For anyone else, maybe it would have been a nice gesture. I know you meant well."

"I was out of line," I said bluntly.

She pointed her fork at me. "You absolutely were. But you weren't wrong."

My heart thumped hard. I couldn't breathe for hoping. "So what now?"

She chewed her cheek like she was weighing her next words carefully. "I spoke to Brax yesterday about the trust and the contract I signed. We're meeting with Rupert, my parents, and their lawyers on Friday."

Janie sure did have a knack for surprising me. I had so many questions, but with things the way they were between us, it wasn't my place to ask. I wished I knew what was going on inside that brain of hers. What she was feeling. What she was thinking.

"What can I do to help?" I asked.

Apparently that was the wrong question because her lips flattened. "Stay out of it. I need to do this on my own."

She paused. "Well, I need to do this with Brax, but still on my own, if that makes sense."

"It does." I still hated it. If she would just let me—

"Jack," she warned because the woman was a damn mind reader.

Shit. "I won't interfere. I'll handcuff myself if I have to."

She eyed me suspiciously. "You know how to get out of handcuffs, don't you."

"Well...yeah," I admitted.

She swallowed a laugh. "*Anyway*. We don't have anyone to cover my usual shift at the bar, so the Painted Cat will be closed for the morning. It will be fine. The bar doesn't get busy until after five anyway. I might be home early. Brax doesn't expect the meeting to go past one or two."

"I'll handle it," I said before I could stop myself.

"*Jack*."

"Janie, it's a scheduling issue at my bar. The Painted Cat *is* my business." And so was Janie, whether she admitted it or not. "One way or another, your shift and Maya will both be covered. Maybe you haven't noticed, but you have a whole pack of friends who would do anything for you. Me, included. So let us help with this one little thing. Let me handle it."

Her expression softened as she considered. "All right," she said at last. "Thank you."

I pushed from my chair. "Wait a minute. I have something for you." I grabbed the deck of cards from the drawer and flipped through them until I found the cards I needed. "Here. For luck."

She looked at the cards and then back to me. "Four aces? How is that lucky?"

"Because when you're holding all the aces, you can't lose."

35

JACK

JACK

Everyone clear on the schedule?

ESSIE

James and I have Maya at ten. We're giving her a barrel racing lesson. Don't tell Janie.

JAMES

She's kidding. Janie already knows.

CHLOE

I'll pick Maya up for lunch and then bring her to the library.

HANNAH

Maya is going to be my intern for the afternoon. I can't wait!

My original plan was to have one of Janie's friends cover her bar shift, but Brax had nixed that in the bud with words like "employment fraud" and "liability." Which meant that I was now standing in Janie's usual spot behind the bar, despite the fact that the only drink I knew how to make was a whiskey neat.

Eh. That was fine. The only people here on a Friday afternoon weren't the type to order fancy mixed drinks. Most of them drank their beer straight from the can.

And then Steven McAllister sidled in with a blue baby carrier strapped to his chest, chubby baby thighs dangling at his abdomen.

"You have a baby. In a bar," I deadpanned. If he didn't recognize the line from one of the best movies ever made, we could never be friends.

But Steven laughed as he bellied—or babied—up to the bar. "You know, I heard it in my head right before you said it out loud. He scanned the tap handles. "I'll take the pilsner."

"Got it." I grabbed a pint glass and filled it up. "Why do you have a baby in a bar?"

"Chloe's at lunch with Maya and then she has clients all afternoon. I only had one horse to shoe, so I get to spend the day with Grayson. I figured, with all the girls showing up for Janie, someone ought to show up for you. So here we are."

I didn't know what to say to that. Steven and I weren't exactly friends. But he was with Chloe, and Chloe was part of Janie's circle, so maybe I should rectify that. "Thanks."

"It was Chloe's idea," he admitted. He played with Grayson's sock as he talked. "I know you're close to the Hales. I'm not trying to get between that."

I remembered what he'd said back in November. "They still have a problem with you?"

He considered. "It's a work in progress." I slid his beer across the bar. His lips quirked as he took in the foam. "That's a lot of head. You need some help back there?"

I braced my palms on the bar. "I need you to not complain."

"Sure. I can do that." His head turned at the sound of the door opening.

Adam and Zack strolled in.

"What are you two doing here?" I asked. "Don't you have cows to chase?"

Zack grinned. "And miss a chance to fuck with you? Come on, now."

Adam stiffened, but he tipped his chin in greeting. "Steven."

Steven didn't look any more comfortable than Adam. "Adam."

I sighed as I split a stern look between them. "No fights in Janie's bar."

Zack laughed. "Believe it or not, this is actually an

improvement. Chloe's threatening to sign them up for couples' counseling."

Adam and Steven side-eyed each other and promptly looked away again. I shook my head. "What can I get you to drink?"

The evil glint in Adam's eyes told me he had planned his answer in advance. "A lemon drop martini."

Zack smirked. "And I'll have a whiskey sour."

"Assholes," I muttered. I pulled out my phone to find a recipe. "Dammit, Zack, that has foamed egg whites. I'm not doing that. You both get beers. Whiskey, if you ask nicely."

Adam laughed. The sound still startled me. There had been years where he only spoke in grunts and growls. "Beer is fine." His gaze slid to Steven's glass, which was fully half foam. "You know what, I'll get it myself."

"Fine." I pointed at him. "But you still have to tip."

Adam rolled his eyes as he rounded the bar. "You want one while I'm back here, Zack?"

"Yeah, thanks." Zack turned to me, his expression serious for once. "You heard from Janie yet?"

"Not yet."

And fuck, was that eating at me. I was going out of my mind wondering what the hell was going on. I knew they were meeting at Brax's office—Senator Dipshit didn't want to risk anyone recognizing Janie at his office in Denver, so he magnanimously offered to make the drive to Aspen Springs—but that was at nine this morning. Shouldn't they be done now?

"It's going to be okay," Zack assured me. "Brax has this."

"I know."

More importantly, I knew Janie had this. Maybe she didn't trust herself, but I didn't have that problem. I trusted her completely. She would fix this.

And then maybe, just maybe, we could work on fixing us.

36

JANIE

"READY?" BRAX ASKED ME.

"No," I said.

He smiled. "Yes, you are."

We were in his conference room. Behind the closed door, I could hear his secretary, Sharon, greeting someone. I gulped. They were here.

My parents entered first. They shook hands with Brax before Dad squeezed my shoulder. Mom nodded, her voice as crisp and cool as ever when she said, "Hello, dear. It would have been nice if you had returned my calls. I'd like to take Maya shopping for back-to-school clothes."

My mouth flapped open. *That* was what she had to say to me? I stared at her, speechless, as she took a seat next to me at the conference table. When Dad sat next to her, I finally found my voice. "I think you're supposed to sit on the other side."

Mom's head whipped toward me, her eyes wide with shock. "Next to Rupert? Over my dead body."

The venom in her voice made me blink.

"We are always on your side, Janie. If you don't know that then…" She trailed off, her brow furrowed.

I squinted. Was Mom *apologizing*? I tried to remember if I had ever heard the words I'm sorry out of her mouth. Nope, never. "Then what?"

She folded her hands primly in her lap. "Then there has been a misunderstanding."

My eyes rolled to the back of my head. Classic.

And then Rupert strode in.

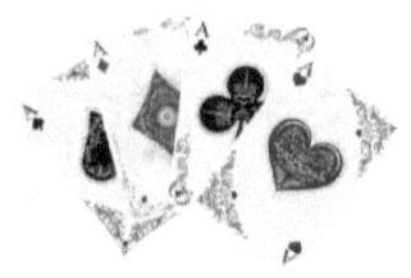

"My client will not be signing this farce of a contract." Rupert's lawyer tossed the stapled pages aside.

Brax smiled pleasantly. "You seem to be under the mistaken notion that this is a negotiation. It's not. Senator Warren will sign before we leave here today, or we will settle this in court. A very *public* court."

Rupert flinched at the word. "Don't do this, Janie. It's not the money. I can triple what you're asking for, if that's what you want. But the clause regarding Maya must be reinstated. So much is at stake here. You understand that. You've always understood that, Janie." His tone was gentle and kind. A perfectly reasonable man appealing to my better nature.

God, he was insufferable.

The contract I signed in the hospital was basically a gag order. It required me to keep Maya out of public photographs until ten years after her father's death, whenever that date might be, including yearbooks. She couldn't be within five hundred feet of him at any time. Attending the parties and fundraisers my parents threw was obviously out of the question.

The new contract guaranteed that I would never publicly name Rupert as her father and left it at that. Whatever people discovered on their own was not my problem. I had no desire to ruin his life or lay claim to his name in any way, but I was done keeping Maya hidden like she was a dirty little secret. She was the best thing that had ever happened to me, and I would never let her feel otherwise.

"Do not address my client." Brax's voice was sharp enough to cut steel. "Do not even look at her."

"You should be ashamed of yourself," Rupert spat.

I laid a quelling hand on Brax's arm for the sole purpose of keeping him out of jail and looked Rupert dead in the eye.

"Why should I be ashamed? Did I seduce an impressionable intern twenty years younger than me, lie about being separated from my spouse, and hide the resulting baby while holding myself up as a paragon of virtue to the world? No, wait, that was you." I tilted my head. "I'd say *you* should be ashamed of yourself, but why waste my breath? You can't feel shame without having a moral compass, and the only thing inside you is a rotted soul."

If glares could incinerate people, I'd be nothing but a pile of ash. If he thought he could intimidate me, he was mistaken. I wasn't twenty-one anymore. Whatever pull he'd had on me then, it was long gone now. Jack's voice was in my head, cheering me on. *Attagirl, Ace. Let your bad out.*

"I've made myself silent to keep your secrets safe. I've made my life small so that yours could be big. I have been so damn *good*. And I. Am. *Done*." I tapped the table with each word. "Sign the papers, Rupert. Because if you don't, the next thing I'm going to make myself is a whole ass problem."

Mom gasped. Dad coughed. Brax snorted.

Rupert signed the papers.

I STOOD outside the Painted Cat, staring through the window at Jack so hard that he felt the weight of it and whipped in my direction. Adam, Zack, and Steven turned a second later, but Jack had already vaulted over the bar. *God.* My heart hammered against my ribs as he barreled out the door, nearly taking it off its hinges.

He stopped inches from me, chest heaving. For a

moment I thought he might grab me, but then he put his hands on his hips. "Hey."

I burst into tears.

"Shit," he muttered. His arms ghosted around me and when I didn't protest, he pulled me tightly against his chest and kissed my temple. "It's okay, honey. I know how to make death look like an accident."

I laughed in spite of myself. "You don't have to do that. Everything is good. It's adrenaline, that's all."

"Jack." I wiped my face on the sleeve of my fancy wool blazer. "I love you."

His irises flared and then narrowed. "Why does that sound like there's a *but* coming?"

"But if you want to be with me so you can fix me, this is never going to work." No matter how hot the whole bar-vaulting thing was. "I can't be your mission."

He pulled back, his forehead furrowed. "What?"

"I know you've been feeling lost since you left the military, Jack. I get it. But trying to fix my life isn't the answer. I don't want you to save me and I..." My voice cracked on a sob. "I can't save anyone. I'm still trying to figure out my own shit."

"Huh." He mulled that for a moment. "Wait here, okay?"

Before I could ask why, he jogged inside. A moment later he was back with something in his hand.

"For you." The plastic paper crinkled as he slapped it into my hand.

I looked down and my stomach flipped. "Jack," I said slowly. "Why are you giving me M&Ms?"

"I know you don't remember this, but twenty years ago we met by the river. My dad had bailed, Essie was upset, and I didn't know how to fix any of it. You gave me your candy for Essie. You didn't even know me, but you helped me anyway."

"I remember. I thought you didn't remember." My whole world was tilting upside down.

He laughed. "I told you, Janie. I never lose track of anyone, but especially not you. We've always been a team. Fucking *always*. Even at ten years old, you were someone I could count on. I've never forgotten that. I trust you, Janie. I trust you with your life and I trust you with mine."

I blinked rapidly, my lips parting.

"Both of us are a little disoriented right now, but so what? We'll work it out together. I've learned my lesson, I promise. I'm not going to fix anything for you. I'll fix it *with* you. You do that for me, too."

I sniffled. "Really?"

The look he gave me was so Jack. Exasperation and tenderness in equal measure. "Don't you get it? You're my ace. As long as I have you, I can't lose."

My heart. My *heart*. It was full to bursting.

"I don't have my life where I want it to be. I don't have a plan, and yeah, I'm never going to be comfortable with that. But I'll get through it." He cupped my face in his palms, his eyes boring into mine with so much love that it stole my breath. "I'm not lost, Janie. I know the direction home. I'm looking right at her."

My eyes swam with happy tears. "I love you, Jack," I choked out.

"I love you, too."

He kissed me. Muffled whoops from inside the bar made us break apart, laughing.

"I have to go back in before they rob me blind," he said. "Are you heading to the library to pick up Maya?"

I nodded. "See you at home, soldier."

37

JACK

"This party gets bigger every year," Ted Hale mused. He had a can of Coke in one hand and a spatula in the other. He didn't drink alcohol since he'd taken to it a little too well after his wife passed away from cancer several years ago.

It was the fourth annual end-of-summer bash at Lodestar Ranch. Adam's son, Ben, had started it right around the time James had started working at the ranch and it had been a tradition ever since. There was always good friends and good food—and an excessive amount of watermelon, courtesy of Ben's garden.

Right now, Ted and I were on grill duty. Ted had the burgers and I had the brats. Ben was showing Maya his garden. James had her eye on them while she chopped watermelon, but Ben was a teenager now and probably one of the most responsible kids I'd ever met. He'd keep Maya safe. Steven had Grayson strapped to his chest again and was setting up a game of cornhole with Adam. Janie, Essie, Chloe, and Brax were making watermelon margaritas, and Zack was pushing Hannah on the old rope swing.

"We keep adding new people to the family." Ted pointed his Coke at the yard. "This year, that's you. Seems strange that this is your first time. You've always been family, Jack. You and Cat and Essie. But I suppose you were off being a hero. Anyway, we're glad you're here now. There was a time when some of us worried that maybe you wouldn't ever be." He said it lightly enough, but I heard the real emotion in the words.

"I sometimes worried about that myself," I confessed.

Not that I had ever really thought much about dying. With the work I did, death was an ever-present threat. At some point, I tuned it out and stopped worrying about it.

But being *here*. Love and laughter and *fucking feelings* right on the surface where I didn't have to go digging for them? I hadn't thought it was possible. I'd had to shut all that off to do my job because worrying about all the hearts you'd break if you died was a surefire way to cause second-guessing, and second-guessing led to mistakes, and mistakes led to death, which led to the broken hearts you were trying to avoid in the first place.

I remembered the day I met Maya, how it seemed like I might never feel again. Like I was a mountain, and people were nothing more than ants. I wasn't a mountain anymore. I had finally zoomed back in.

I felt it all now. The good, the bad. All of it. And I was fucking grateful.

Ted lifted a burger slightly to check its char, then flipped it over completely. "I'm always a little sad when summer ends and Ben goes back to school. I suppose you'll be going through that yourself with Maya. What's next for you?"

That question would have made me spiral six months ago. Now I shrugged. "I'm looking at a few options. I want to keep the first few weeks of school flexible for whatever Maya needs. Janie tells me those weeks can be pretty hectic. After that…" My gaze went to the mountains. "I have a job offer with a search and rescue team. I volunteered on a rescue a couple weeks ago and I think it could be the right fit for me."

Ted hooted. "Back on your hero shit, eh?" He clapped my shoulder, and then his large, gnarled hand lingered there in a paternal squeeze. "I'm proud of you, son. I know Cat is, too. Hell, we all are."

I shifted from one foot to the other. That kind of talk still made me want to crawl into a hole and hide. Some things never changed, I guessed. "Thanks," I said gruffly, sipping my beer to hide my red face.

"Yep." Ted nodded briskly. "Hard to believe how much things have changed around here in the past four years. Two of my boys married, and Zack is engaged. I have the feeling Chloe is giving the whole lot of them baby fever."

Grayson was being passed around the embroidery club now. Ted and I fell silent as we watched them coo over his chubby cheeks and little hands. Janie took Grayson from

Hannah and lifted him in the air to tickle his belly with her nose, making him giggle with delight.

My breath caught. My chest ached.

Aw, fuck.

Ted snickered next to me. "One thing at a time, son. One thing at a time."

"WILL you push me on the tire swing, Jack?" Maya's hand caught mine as I was about to climb the porch steps.

"Sure. Let me put the food in the fridge and then I'll be right back, okay?"

We had been the first to leave the party—even beating Chloe and Steven. The second Maya had started showing signs of overstimulation, we had said our goodbyes. Ted had sent us home with a heap of leftovers.

"I can take that in." Janie reached for the container. "You go ahead. Swinging seems to help Maya's brain calm down. Love you." She rolled up on her toes and kissed me before disappearing inside.

I watched her go, feeling lucky, and then turned back to Maya. "Okay, scamp. Let's swing."

AFTER MAYA WENT BACK INSIDE, I stayed on the porch to watch the stars come out. It didn't take long for Janie to poke her head out to check on me.

"Hey. You want company?"

She asked because sometimes I didn't, and she was fine with that. Janie was good at letting people be exactly who they were, never trying to mold them into something more palatable. Me, Maya, customers at the Painted Cat, it didn't matter. I loved that about her.

I loved a lot of things about her.

"I want *your* company," I said and she came all the way onto the porch. She settled next to me on the swing.

"I was thinking," she began. "About September."

"I've been thinking about that, too."

"We've only been dating for two months. That's way too soon to move in together, right?"

I tensed. We still had our separate rooms, but I spent most nights in her bed. "I suppose it depends on the couple."

"Well, obviously we're talking about you and me." She didn't say *doofus* but I heard it in her voice.

I smiled. "Obviously."

"So you think it's too soon?" she pressed.

"I think if you ask me to leave so we can follow a proper relationship timeline, I'm going to remind you that technically, our relationship started back in November. But if you insist, of course I'll go. You should expect an angry phone call from my mother, though."

Janie rolled her eyes. "You're such a mama's boy." She wrinkled her nose. "In a good way, I guess. If there is such a thing."

"There is absolutely such a thing." I threaded our hands together. "Please don't ask me to go."

Her breath hitched. "It seems silly for you to move out if you're going to move back in again someday."

"Very silly."

"But you won't be Maya's manny September. I won't be paying you."

I cocked an eyebrow at her quizzically. "What are you getting at, Ace? Figure out what I'll owe you for rent and household expenses, and I'll pay it."

"That's not what I meant." She huffed. "I mean, I think you should move into my room. When you being here is not a financial transaction."

I snorted a laugh. "So I don't get confused about what you're paying me for? Don't worry, honey. I'll always let you give me blowjobs for free."

"Jack!"

She tried to whack me with her free hand but I captured that one, too, and hauled her, laughing, onto my lap.

I gripped her chin and brought her in for a kiss. "I love you, Janie, and I can't wait to move in with you."

Her dark eyes sparkled back at me. Forehead to mine, she whispered, "Welcome home, Jack."

And I smiled. The words finally felt right.

EPILOGUE
JANIE

Three years later

My hand cramped and I dropped the pencil to massage the ache. In an instant, Jack took over, his strong fingers working the knotted muscle at the base of my thumb more effectively than I ever could.

"Take a break, Ace. You've been at this for hours."

"I want to get through these commissions before the baby comes." The baby—a boy—wasn't due for another month, but I had a mountain of work and planned to take a solid four months of maternity leave after his arrival. I bit my lip, squirming as he dug his thumb into a sore spot. "Fuck, that hurts so good. Don't stop."

Jack ignored my writhing and hunched forward to get a better look at the sketch I was working on. A couple's first date at a cozy little coffee shop. The man and woman sat across from each other, smiling. They didn't know it yet, but it was the last first date for both of them.

Reference photographs were scattered across the table. The coffee shop from various angles, particularly the table where they sat and the view out the window. Lots of the couple, alone and together, also from every angle imaginable.

The man had commissioned the drawing of their first date as a gift for his wife on their fifth wedding anniversary. At the time, they hadn't known it would be anything other than another disappointment, so of course they hadn't taken photos. That was where I came in. Recreating real events with real people at real places was my specialty. With enough photographs, I could learn their personalities and facial expressions well enough to make a drawing feel like I had pulled the memory straight from their brains.

People were incredibly sentimental, it turned out. I had a six-month waitlist and so much work that I'd cut my hours at the Painted Cat to two days a week. I would have quit altogether, but Brax begged me on his knees not to make him do paperwork, and anyway, I actually liked working the bar.

"You captured them perfectly," Jack said, his gaze moving from the photographs to my drawing and back again. "It's incredible how you do that."

"I'm pretty proud of this one." I grinned.

Maya wandered into the kitchen in search of a snack, book in hand. She grabbed a yogurt from the fridge, pulled the aluminum top off, and licked it clean while staring at us.

"I've come to a decision," she announced.

I rolled my lips together. *I've come to a decision* was Maya's new phrase. It had a tendency to make even the most mundane sentences sound deeply profound. I had the feeling she knew that. Maya was growing into a flair for the dramatic.

"Let's hear it," Jack said, not letting up on my hand. Bless him.

"I've decided to call you Dad."

I stopped breathing. My free hand went to my round belly. She hadn't been interested in calling him Dad when we got married two years ago, and Jack hadn't pushed her on it. But a week ago, it suddenly occurred to Maya that her new baby brother would call him Dad and maybe she should, too. But when Jack had told her he'd love that, she'd shrugged and, in typical Maya fashion, said she'd think it over.

Apparently, she was done thinking.

"Oh?" Jack sounded perfectly casual, but I knew he wasn't because he was no longer massaging my hand. He was squeezing it for dear life. "Great."

We stared at Maya. Maya stared back.

"Do you..." Jack cleared his throat. "Do you want to try it now? See how it feels?"

"Okay, Dad." She tilted her head.

Jack's hand spasmed around mine and I squeaked. Immediately the pressure eased.

"So, what do you think?" Jack asked.

She shrugged. "It's fine, Dad. I like it."

He swallowed hard. "Good. I like it, too."

The look on his face. God, this man. The way he loved my daughter made my chest crack open, like my heart couldn't contain it all.

His phone buzzed and he blinked. He pulled it out, read the text, and pushed to his feet. "Lost hiker. Are you going to be okay here?"

I snorted. "Unless you plan on being out there for a whole month, then yes. Maya and I are fine. The baby's staying put. I love you. Now go be a hero, soldier."

"Not a soldier." He gripped my chin, angling my face toward his for a kiss. "I love you, Janie."

I grinned. *Don't I know it.*

ABOUT THE AUTHOR

Elizabeth Bright is a USA Today best-selling author of small town romance with heart, humor, and heat. When she's not dreaming up new stories, she can be found hiking or rock climbing. She lives in Washington, D.C. with her two daughters and very needy dog.

Sign up for Elizabeth's newsletter at elizabethbrightauthor.com

ALSO BY ELIZABETH BRIGHT

<u>Lodestar Ranch</u>

A Cowboy in the Streets

Just Say When

Wild, Wild Cowboy

Call Me Yours

Carry Me Home

<u>Hart's Ridge</u>

Make Me Love You

Don't Call Me Sweetheart

Trust Me

Christmas at Hart's Ridge